*to Catherine—
It's the voice on
the line that of a killer?*

HOTLINE TO MURDER

By

Alan Cook

*Alan Cook
30 May 2005*

1663 LIBERTY DRIVE, SUITE 200
BLOOMINGTON, INDIANA 47403
(800) 839-8640
WWW.AUTHORHOUSE.COM

This book is a work of fiction. People, places, events, and situations are the product of the author's imagination. Any resemblance to actual persons, living or dead, or historical events, is purely coincidental.

© 2005 Alan L. Cook. All Rights Reserved.

No part of this book may be reproduced, stored in a retrieval system, or transmitted by any means without the written permission of the author.

First published by AuthorHouse 03/25/05

ISBN: 1-4208-3825-3 (sc)

Library of Congress Control Number: 2005902069

Printed in the United States of America
Bloomington, Indiana

This book is printed on acid-free paper.

BOOKS BY ALAN COOK

Lillian Morgan mysteries:
Catch a Falling Knife
Thirteen Diamonds
Nonfiction:
Walking the World: Memories and Adventures
Other fiction:
Walking to Denver
History:
Freedom's Light: Quotations from History's Champions of Freedom
Poetry:
The Saga of Bill the Hermit

ACKNOWLEDGMENTS

Many thanks to Dawn Dowdle and my wife, Bonny, for helping to make this book readable.

DEDICATION

To all the Hotline listeners, young and old, who put their own psyches on the telephone line, in order to help others.

CHAPTER 1

The three-story building looked like any of a thousand small office buildings in a hundred cities, with its gray stucco exterior and its glass doors. It blended in so well with the retail shops that most of the customers of the strip mall in Bonita Beach didn't even realize it was there. And that made it a perfect location.

Tony had never been inside this building. All of the training sessions had been held in a local church. The students hadn't been told the location of the Hotline office until they graduated. It was confidential.

He rode the elevator to the third floor and found room 327. There was no name on the door. He took a deep breath and put a half smile on his face. He hesitated. This was much harder than going on a routine sales call. Finally, he tried the door handle. The door was unlocked.

He opened the door and walked into the office. Nobody was in sight. Minor relief. It gave him a moment to get his bearings. The best word for the place was utilitarian. About what you'd expect for the office of a struggling nonprofit organization. Tony assumed it was struggling. Didn't all nonprofits struggle?

A girl emerged from one of three doorways and immediately smiled.

"Hi, I bet you're Tony."

"Hi." Tony remembered to put a smile on his own face. She must be his mentor for this shift.

"I'm Shahla. Glad you're on time. The guys on the four to seven shift just left, and it's a little creepy here alone at night."

"Tony." She already knew that. Why was he so flustered? "Uh, how do you spell your name?" he asked, trying to hide it.

"S-h-a-h-l-a. Excuse the food. I haven't eaten dinner. Are you hungry? There're snacks in there."

She pointed her head back over her shoulder. She carried a paper plate full of chips and a coke. That was dinner? Maybe for a teenager. Tony tried to remember his eating habits when he was younger. He shook his head to signify that he wasn't hungry.

Shahla walked into a room with a sign that said "Listening Room" over the door, and set the food on one of the three tables. Tony followed her.

She turned back to him and said, "I understand that you let the class use your condo for one of the Saturday sessions and that you have a really neat pool. That was a nice thing to do." She gave him a thumbs-up sign.

"How did you hear about that?" Tony asked, caught off guard.

"Joy is my friend. She was one of the facilitators for the class. She swam in your pool."

"I remember Joy." That was an understatement. He was not likely to forget the blonde Joy, especially how she looked in a bikini.

"I'm supposed to show you around," Shahla said, after a sip of coke. "This is the listening room. We write the names of repeat callers on the board each day so that if they call a second time, we can tell them they've already called."

"Repeat callers get only fifteen minutes a day," Tony said, quoting from the class, where facilitators had done comical imitations of some of the chronic Hotline haunters. There were several names on the white board from earlier shifts, including Prince Pervert, Lovelorn Lucy, and Masturbating Fool. "Don't you hang up on the bad calls?"

"Yeah, if they start talking about sex in an explicit way or if we think they're masturbating, we tell them it's an inappropriate call and hang up."

She spoke in a casual voice, but Tony felt uncomfortable. He wasn't used to talking about masturbation with a teenage girl. He said, "And the books are for referrals?"

"Right. We have a couple of different telephone directories, including a local one, and these other books contain numbers we can give to callers, depending on their problem. They have names of counselors, drug and alcohol programs, shelters, that sort of thing." She pointed out the books on one of the tables. "And this is the Green Book which tells about the repeat callers."

Tony made a mental note to look through the books.

"I'll show you how to sign in and also the rest of the office." Shahla led the way out of the listening room.

She had long, dark hair and dark eyes—eyes that he knew he had no business gazing into. She wore jeans cut low across her hips and a midriff-bearing top with spaghetti straps. Two other straps peeked out from beneath the outside ones. No navel ring, however. In fact, the only piercings he saw on her were one in each ear containing a stud. He couldn't guess her nationality, offhand, but assumed her parents were from somewhere in the war-torn Middle East. He wasn't surprised. The class had been composed of predominantly teenagers, belonging to a rainbow of races. But she spoke better English than he did.

"I guess most of the listeners are young," Tony said as he signed in twice: on the daily time sheet and also the permanent record of hours worked by each listener.

"Yeah, we have to get our community service hours to graduate from high school."

"A lot of the kids in the class were sixteen."

"I'm seventeen."

She said it with enough emphasis so he knew the difference was important. "Are you a senior at Bonita Beach High?"

"Yes. I've been on the Hotline for a year and a half."

Shahla took him into what must be a supply room. Except that in additional to metal cabinets, it also contained a sink and some bags of chips and pretzels.

"Food," she said, pointing. "There's drinks and stuff in the refrigerator. And there's water."

A five-gallon Sparkletts bottle sat upside down on its metal stand. She led him out of that room and through the one remaining doorway. The room they entered was the largest one yet. It contained three desks, with all the appropriate office paraphernalia on top of them.

"These desks belong to Gail and Patty."

Tony had met them at the class sessions. Patty was the Administrative Assistant and Gail was the Volunteer Coordinator.

"What about the third desk?"

"Several people have left. Patty's only been here for three months. Here's Nancy's office."

Shahla went through a doorway to an interior office containing just one desk. Nancy was the Executive Director. Tony had met her, too. She appeared to him to be very competent. He glanced at a couple of framed certificates and some photographs of the local beach on the walls of her office, and then they walked back to the listening room.

"Can you help me with something until the phone rings?" Shahla asked. She pulled a sheet of paper out of a folder she had brought with her. "I'm trying to put together a resume so I can get a part-time job. Can you take a look at it for me?"

"Do you really need a resume to work at McDonald's?" Tony asked. "Or do you aspire to something grander?"

"I'm not really qualified for anything grander yet. I figured a resume would give me an advantage over the competition."

Tony was impressed, not only by the resume, but by Shahla's thinking. With a shock, it occurred to him that perhaps she *was* qualified to do more than work at McDonald's. She had done two things when she met him that would do credit to a top salesperson. She had complimented him and asked for his advice, which had immediately endeared her to him. This was no airheaded teenager.

The telephone rang. Shahla said, "Okay, you're on the air."

Tony's nervousness returned. He took a breath to calm himself and picked up the phone. "Central Hotline. This is Tony."

There was an audible click at the other end of the line and then silence.

Shahla, who had pushed the speaker button, smiled. "You've just had your first hang up." She walked over to a sheet of paper pinned to one of the bulletin boards and put a mark beside August 16.

"Do you think it was one of the obscene callers?"

Shahla shrugged. "Who knows? We all get hang ups."

For some reason Tony felt marginally better about taking the calls. There were some people who didn't want to talk to him even more than he didn't want to talk to them.

Five minutes later the phone rang again. He answered it with slightly more confidence.

"Tony?" a female voice said in response to his greeting. "Have I talked to you before?"

"I don't know," Tony said. "Who's this?"

"This is Julie."

"Hi, Julie."

Shahla placed the call on the speaker. There was no echo so callers didn't know they were on a speaker. She reached for the Green Book and riffled through its pages. She set the book in front of Tony so he could read about Julie. Meanwhile, Julie, who had apparently figured out that Tony didn't know her story, had taken off like a windup toy, talking about her ex-husband who had run away with his secretary, and a number of other men with whom she had apparently had affairs, but who had screwed her in one way or another. This wasn't just a bad joke; she was crying on the line.

Tony barely had an opportunity to get in an occasional verbal nod, consisting of "Uh huh," and no opportunity to practice other skills he had learned in the class. He belatedly wrote the time down on a call-report form and scanned the written information about Julie. She had been calling for several years. She complained about men and almost everything else, and her nickname was Motormouth. About all the listener could do was to give an occasional verbal nod and hang on for fifteen minutes.

After a while, Tony realized that some of the incidents Julie was talking about had happened years earlier. He felt like telling her to get over it and get a life. Perhaps it was a good thing he couldn't get a word in edgewise.

At the end of fifteen minutes, Shahla swept her hand across her throat in the classic "cut" gesture. However, that was easier said than done. Tony tried to interrupt Julie several times; she talked right over him. Finally, she stopped for a moment to take a breath, the first time Tony remembered her doing so, and he told her he had to answer other calls.

"Oh," Julie said, and then, "If you hang up just like that, I'll be depressed for the rest of the day. Can I just tell you one more thing?"

"Okay," Tony said, feeling helpless. He avoided Shahla's eyes.

She told him about a time a man had sent her flowers.

"That must have made you feel special," Tony said, congratulating himself on introducing feelings into the conversation.

"Very special. But what I wanted to say was I got some of that same feeling just now because you listened to me, and you didn't judge me."

When he was at last able to end the call, he figured he had been on the line for twenty minutes. "Can you get fired for giving a repeat caller more than fifteen minutes?" he asked.

Shahla smiled and said, "Julie is one of the hardest ones to get rid of. Don't feel bad. I have trouble with her too. And you ended the call on an upbeat note, which is a miracle for her."

The phone rang again. Tony, who was still thinking about the previous call, tried to mentally brace himself. He answered the phone. Nobody spoke, but he was quite sure the line was open. He said, "Hello," as he pressed the button to place the call on the speaker.

A male voice said, "I don't want to go on."

Startled, Tony looked at Shahla. She mouthed the word, "Suicide." He thought, my God, this is a real call. I'm not playing a role in a class, anymore.

CHAPTER 2

"You don't want to go on," Tony repeated, using a subdued tone of voice to match the caller's. He realized he had just used reflection, another listening skill.

The silence that followed was as deafening as a rock band. He wanted to say something more, but he didn't know what to say. Shahla was listening intently to the speaker, but she didn't give any helpful hints.

"I'm going to end it," the sad voice finally said.

"What's your name?" Tony asked. He needed to establish rapport with the caller.

After a pause the caller said, "Frank."

"Hi, Frank. Do you think you're going to hurt yourself?" He couldn't bring himself to use the word "kill."

"Yes."

"How are you going to do it?"

"I have a gun."

The guy was serious. "Where is it?"

"In my hand."

"Is it loaded?"

"Yes. It's pointed at my head."

Tony looked at Shahla in panic. She pressed the mute button and said, "Try to get him to put the gun in another room."

"Frank," Tony said, "I'll make a deal with you. I'll talk to you, but I can't do it when you have a gun in your hand. I'm afraid there might be an accident. Will you do something for me? Unload the gun and place it in another room."

Silence. Then Frank said, "I won't unload it."

"All right, but please put it in another room, out of sight."

They went back and forth for several minutes. Finally, Frank agreed to take the gun to another room. While he was off the line, Tony said to Shahla, "I'm sweating."

"Stay with him," Shahla said, "You're doing fine."

Frank came back on the line and, without being asked, assured Tony that the gun was gone. That was a good sign. Tony said, "There are people who care about what happens to you."

"Nobody cares."

"I care. I care very much." And Tony found that he did care.

Slowly, Frank's story came out. He had a degenerative disease that was making his muscles useless. He was disabled and his physical condition was deteriorating. At some point he would be completely helpless. Tony wracked his brain, but he couldn't think of a way to put a positive spin on that. He tried to keep Frank talking. There were long periods of silence, during which Shahla's support helped Tony remain calm. The phone rang a number of times, but she ignored it.

An hour into the call, Frank said, "This isn't going anywhere. I'm going to hang up now."

"Don't hang up," Tony blurted. "I have something more to say."

Silence.

Tony talked desperately, repeating things he had said, previously, while expecting to hear the click of a hang up at any moment. He had to get some agreement from Frank. Frank had said several times that he didn't have any relatives or close friends, but he had mentioned that he did have a cat. Tony decided to focus on the cat.

"What kind of a cat do you have?" Tony asked.

"Alley cat. He kept hanging around the neighborhood. The neighbors fed him. I never did. But he came in the house one day when I left the screen door open. I couldn't boot him out."

"How long have you had him?"

"Five years."

"What would he do without you?"

"Go back to being an alley cat."

"But he obviously likes you, Frank. You can't desert him."

It was a thin thread, one that might break at any moment. Tony kept Frank talking about his cat. Little by little, Frank agreed that he should stay alive because of his cat. Or did he? Part of the time he seemed to be ready to disavow any agreement.

Before he hung up, Tony said, "Please call us tomorrow and tell us how you're doing," knowing that Frank might never make the call.

As he put down the receiver, Tony realized that his shirt was soaked. He glanced at the clock. It was almost ten. He had been on the call for two hours. He said, "I'm not sure I convinced him."

"You did the best you could," Shahla said. "That's all you can do."

"To be honest, if I were in his shoes, I would probably want to end it too."

"That's the hardest call you'll ever get on the Hotline. The suicide calls I've had are like, 'I'm going to kill myself on the anniversary of my father's death.' 'Oh, when is that?' 'Next February.' Okay, that's six months away. So I figure I'm safe."

They chuckled, which reduced the tension that had been present in the room for so long, like a compressed spring.

"I have to go to the restroom—badly," Tony said. "I've had to go for an hour."

"That's one thing I forgot to tell you," Shahla said. "Down the hall to the right. The key is hanging by the door. While you're gone, I'll fill out your evaluation form."

"Evaluation form?" He should have known there would be an evaluation form. "I hope I passed."

"Oh you did. With flying colors."

***

Tony parked his car in one of the two carport stalls allotted to his townhouse and noted that Josh's car occupied the other one.

He had hoped Josh would be out. It was too much to hope for that Josh would be asleep at this hour. He didn't feel like talking to his roommate—housemate—he had to quit thinking like a college boy. After all, he had been out of college for almost ten years.

He opened the wooden gate leading to his small brick patio. The sliding glass door to the house was open. He slid open the screen door. As he entered the house, he saw light emanating from the living room and heard the sound of the television set. Blaring. Explosive. Bang bang bang. Not a good sign. On the other hand, if Josh was fully involved in one of the ultra-violent movies he loved, maybe Tony could whoosh past him and race up the stairs without being detained.

"Hey, Noodles. Where you going so fast? I want to hear about your evening."

Caught. And "Noodles." How Tony hated that nickname. But this wasn't the time to lecture Josh for the thousandth time about it. Josh lay fully reclined on the reclining chair, facing the big-screen TV, which was the only thing in the living room that belonged to him. He held a can of beer in his hand. A cooler sat beside the chair to prevent him from, heaven forbid, actually having to walk into the kitchen to get more beer. Empty cans littered Tony's carpet, undoubtedly dripping beer into it.

"I can't talk with that thing on," Tony shouted, over more explosions. He headed for the stairs.

Josh picked up the remote, aimed it at the TV like a gun, and muted the sound. "There. I don't want to hurt your sensitive ears. Here, have a brewski."

He picked a can out of the cooler and tossed it to Tony, oblivious to the fact that it was wet from melted ice. As Tony caught it, cold water spattered his face, arms, T-shirt, and jeans.

"So, how did things go during your first night on the Hotstuff Line?"

That wasn't a question Tony could even begin to answer, given his current state of mind. He was still thinking about the suicide call. He popped open the can and took a long swallow. The cold bite of the liquid felt good sliding down his throat. Maybe this was what he needed.

"What's the matter? Some pussy got your tongue? Talk to Uncle Josh. Okay, let's start at the beginning. I believe, back in the days when you were actually speaking to me, you said you would find out where the Hotline office is for the first time tonight. So, where is it? And sit down, for God's sake. Don't look like you're about to fly off and execute some noble deed."

Josh flipped back his too long, but already thinning, red hair and folded his hands on his ample belly, while precariously balancing his beer can on said belly.

Tony sat down on the sofa underneath the living room windows. He took another long swallow. He had to talk to Josh sooner or later because Josh never let go. But it hadn't occurred to him that he was going to have trouble with this question. "The location is confidential."

"The location is confidential." Josh mimicked him, but with a voice of exaggerated piety. "So this is how you treat your uncle Josh, after all the years we've known each other, after all we've been through together. After all the times I saved your worthless ass in college when you were about to flunk a course. After all the girls I fixed you up with. This is how it ends. 'The location is confidential.'"

"Can the damned dramatics, Josh. I'm not going to tell you, okay? I signed a statement, and I'm not going to risk getting fired. I'll tell you anything else."

"I didn't know you could get fired from a volunteer job. But Josh has a big heart, and I'll let it pass. Even though it's breaking. And let me risk another question, even if it means another bruise on my ego. You told me you were going to have a mentor tonight. Tell me about your mentor."

Tony said, "Yes, I did have a mentor. She was very good."

"Jesus, you sound like a first-grade reader. What was her name?"

"Uh, Sally," Tony said, using Shahla's Hotline alias. Among his other faults, Josh was a bigot.

"And is this Sally a babe?"

The last thing Tony was going to do was to admit to Josh that she was a babe. He said, "She's a teenager. She's seventeen."

"So, is there a statute of limitations on babedom? Today's teenyboppers are hot. I'll bet she was wearing low-cut jeans and a top that was barely there. And a thong. Did you happen to notice when she bent over? Or does your new-found sanctity prevent you from peeking?"

Josh was uncomfortably close to the truth. To head him off, Tony said, "I took several calls. One was from a guy who was talking about blowing his brains out."

"Holy shit." Josh's blue eyes widened, and he looked at Tony with what might be respect. "Did he have a piece?"

"He said he did."

"What kind?"

"Our discussion didn't go into that kind of detail. I got him to take it into another room."

"So, did you convince him that life was worth living?"

Tony hesitated. That was the question he had been asking himself all the way home. "I...I'm not sure."

"You mean, at this very moment he might be lying on the floor with his fucking brains scattered all over the room?"

A gruesome picture flashed into Tony's head. He said, slowly, "At this very moment he might be lying on the floor with his fucking brains scattered all over the room." He couldn't look at Josh. He knew Josh was staring at him, with the freckles covering his face changing color, as they did when he felt emotion.

"Noodles, you need another beer."

Josh tossed this one across his body, and it spattered Tony and the sofa with cold water. Beer was Josh's answer to all the world's problems. Maybe Josh was right. By the time he went to bed, Tony had drunk at least a six-pack.

CHAPTER 3

It was Friday evening, August 30, two weeks after his first mentoring session. Tony walked into the building where the Hotline was located. Once again he smelled the odor he had come to associate with it. Perhaps it was some sort of cleaning compound. Instead of riding the elevator, he went up the stairs, taking them two at a time, all the way to the third floor. He was glad there was nobody at the top to see him puffing—to see how out of shape he was.

He had also taken the stairs at his second and third Hotline sessions with a mentor, eschewing the elevator. Why? He could barely admit it to himself, but the reason apparently had to do with the fact that he wanted to get into better shape, lose those extra pounds that pushed his belt out. Why? It was ridiculous to think that he would do something he had never done in his life, at least for a woman—any woman, let alone for a seventeen-year-old. Someone who was legally jailbait.

He had not seen Shahla since the first session. His mentors for the other two sessions had also been teenagers, a boy and a girl, and they had been good, but they had made no lasting impression on him. Now he was on his own, an experienced listener. As he walked to the office, he wondered whether there would be anyone else on the lines tonight, or whether he would be alone. He barely dared hope that Shahla would be here, and he knew the odds were long against it. She had not been signed up on the calendar the last time he had looked, several days before.

Tony tried the handle of the brown door. It was locked. He looked at his watch. Ten minutes to seven. Perhaps there was no listener on the four-to-seven shift. Sometimes that happened with a volunteer organization. Fortunately, he had learned the combination to the lockbox on the door. He entered it and pulled off the cover, looking for the key inside. Except that the key wasn't there. What was going on?

He was at a loss, a feeling he was unfamiliar with. What should he do? Could there be somebody in the office behind the locked door? He had already stored the office phone numbers in his cell phone. He took out the phone and called the administrative office number. No answer. He tried the Hotline number. No answer.

Maybe this was his way out. He had made a good-faith effort to work his shift. If the Hotline was so disorganized that he couldn't even get in, it wasn't his fault. Looking back over the last few weeks, he had done everything he set out to do. He had taken the Hotline training class and passed. He had survived three mentoring sessions and received good marks. He had shown empathy. In fact, he had learned all the skills that Mona, his boss at his real job, had wanted him to learn, when she had suggested that he volunteer for the Hotline. And although he had agreed to work at least three shifts a month for a year, if the Hotline staff members didn't keep their part of the bargain, why was he obligated to keep his?

But back to the present. There was a slight chance a listener was inside, on another call. If so, she—or he, would presumably be coming out in a few minutes—unless she was on a long call. Decision time. Tony decided to wait until five minutes after seven.

He nervously paced up and down the corridor, wondering when a guard might come by and ask him what he was doing here. None did. At three minutes after seven, he tried the Hotline number on his cell phone again. No answer. He left.

***

Tony went into the third bedroom on the second floor of his townhouse, the one he used as a home office, and fired up his computer. He slept in one of the other bedrooms. Josh occupied the second. Tony decided to check his e-mail. He had an e-mail address at work, of course, but he reserved his home e-mail for his personal life. He could also surf the Internet a little, find out what the stock market did today, visit an adult chat room. After all, he had no girlfriend at the moment.

His spam filter captured a lot of the junk, but some still got through. There was the usual pleading letter from a high-ranking nobody in Nigeria offering him millions of dollars if he would just share his bank account number. He deleted the letter without reading it. After the first few dozen, they all sounded the same.

An e-mail message from the Hotline caught his eye. He clicked on it immediately, partly because he was feeling guilty for skipping his shift, even though it wasn't his fault. It was from Nancy, the Executive Director, addressed to all listeners. He scanned the note in mounting horror and then went back and read it carefully.

It said, in part, "As you probably know by now, one of our listeners, Joy Wiggins, was murdered last night behind the building in which the Hotline office is located, after she worked the 7 to 10 p.m. shift." It went on to express the deep shock and sorrow of the Hotline staff and to say that the Hotline would be closed until further notice.

Tony violently shoved his rollered chair away from the computer with his feet, as if the mouse had burned his hand. He stared at the screen from four feet away, hoping the words would read differently from there, but they didn't. Joy had been a facilitator for the Saturday class that was held in his townhouse. She was one of the girls and boys who had swum in his pool—and the one he remembered most distinctly.

He continued to stare at the computer screen, fighting the idea that a beautiful girl like Joy was dead. It must be a mistake. He remembered seeing her laugh, he remembered her bikini-clad body, and he remembered her critiquing one of the role-play calls he had made during that class, with wisdom beyond her years. She had given him a good suggestion about using silence during calls.

She had been killed almost twenty-four hours ago. Why hadn't he heard about it before now? Tony went back over his day. He had rushed out of the house that morning, barely taking time to drink a glass of orange juice and eat a piece of toast. He had driven seventy-five miles to a little burg east of Los Angeles and had spoken at a meeting of a women's club. On the way there, he had listened to a CD on salesmanship—another one of Mona's ideas. He hadn't listened to the news on his car radio.

He had spoken to the women about what his company, Bodyalternatives.net, could offer them. Bodyalternatives.net was a new type of company—one that was based on the Internet. Its website, which was getting over a million hits a month, with the number rapidly increasing, featured help for people who had some sort of problem with their bodies—or who were just plain dissatisfied with them. Most of the company's income came from plastic surgeons and other healthcare professionals who advertised on the site.

Tony's job, as Manager of Marketing, was to make healthcare contacts, sell advertising space on the site, and also to reach out to potential clients. That is what he had been doing by giving a speech to the women's club. He had used his newfound listening skills to good advantage, had not judged his audience, and had shown empathy when answering questions. For example, he had not laughed when a woman complained about the crow's-feet beside her eyes that nobody else could see. Mona, who was president of Bodyalternatives.net, would be pleased. He intended to emphasize the good things he had done in his call report.

Tony had made several other calls during the day, but he had always listened to the tapes when he was in his car. He had grabbed a quick dinner in a fast-food restaurant and gone directly to the Hotline, without going to the office or coming home. That's why he had been out of the loop.

He rolled his chair back to the computer to look for news reports. They weren't difficult to find. The story had a sensational aspect, and it had been picked up by all the news services. The first thing he read was that Joy's body had been discovered in a pocket park behind the mall, cut and bruised, almost naked. Some items of her clothing had been lying nearby.

When Joy hadn't returned home last night, her parents had driven to the mall. They had found her car parked in the lot behind it. Listeners on the seven-to-ten shift were supposed to call the guard when they left and could request an escort out of the building. They exited by the back door because the front door was locked at night. On the three evenings Tony had worked, he had acted as the escort. Actually, the time he had worked with the boy, they had escorted each other.

Joy's parents had called the police when they found the car, but not Joy. A search had turned up her body within an hour. Tony tried to picture how devastated Joy's parents must be. He couldn't do it. He couldn't put himself in their place. And he didn't want to. He would never have children.

There was more information. The police had talked to the building guard. The guard claimed he had escorted Joy out to her car and seen her get into it. But he had not seen her drive away. She was an honor student and a member of the Bonita Beach High School volleyball team, one of the best high school teams in the country. Among other volunteer activities, she worked at the Central Hotline, the news reports said.

Who would do such a thing? There were a lot of weirdoes out there—stalkers, rapists. The murderer must have been lying in wait for Joy. Someone who knew where the Hotline was located? Listeners were supposed to keep its location secret, but there were so many of them. Word must leak out—to family, friends. And from there, to whom?

A noise downstairs told Tony that Josh had arrived home from his job. He worked in the television industry, which allowed him to start late in the morning. Of course, he got home late, also, but that was fine with him because he didn't like to go to bed. Tony could follow Josh's progress in his head. First he would open the refrigerator and take out a can of beer. Then he would scan his mail, neatly separated for him by Tony. After that, he would come upstairs to change his clothes. A clump clump clump told Tony that Josh was right on schedule.

Tony was prepared when Josh poked his head into the doorway and said, "Tony, baby, I'm awfully sorry about the girl. I found out about it when I got to the station. We had a ton of people covering it. I meant to call you on your cell phone, but I got tied up."

"That's okay," Tony said. Josh was always meaning to do things he never got around to doing. Actually, Tony was glad he hadn't heard about Joy until tonight. It would have completely ruined his day. "I suppose there isn't anything new that's not on here." He motioned toward the computer screen.

"Not much. Autopsy pending. My guess is that she was raped."

"Is that confirmed?"

"Not yet, but why the hell would a guy drag her into the bushes and tear her clothes off if he wasn't going to rape her?"

"I don't know."

"Did you know her? She was a real babe. We got a picture of her from her parents."

"I knew her slightly." Tony wasn't going to tell Josh that she had been here at the townhouse, swimming in the pool. Josh would complain that Tony had excluded him. That's exactly what Tony had done, of course, making sure that Josh was out of town on the weekend he had volunteered to hold the class here.

"Do you know what she was wearing?" Josh asked, as if he were revealing a scandal. "Short shorts, skimpy top. No underwear. If a girl's dressed like that, she's asking for it."

"It was a warm night. And maybe the killer took her underwear with him. Maybe he has an underwear fetish." Tony was heating up. "Where do you get off, anyway, saying that she was asking for it? That's antediluvian thinking, Josh."

Josh backed away in mock surprise. "Sorry, Noodles. I forgot that you're a born-again feminist. Working for women. Working with girls. Listening to their problems. You're pussy-whipped, that's what you are. You're not the Tony I used to know who could pick up a girl on the street just by smiling at her and then would dump her with a frown. Now I bet you tell them you feel their pain."

Usually, Tony would have had a fast comeback for Josh, but he was in no mood tonight. He stood up and said, "You have exactly three seconds to get out of this room before I throw you downstairs."

It was doubtful that he could throw the larger Josh anywhere, but Josh knew his temper and was smart enough not to aggravate him further. Josh backed out of the room with his arms up in a gesture of surrender and went down the hall to his own room.

CHAPTER 4

Tony was driving to an appointment when his cell phone rang. He pressed a button and said, "Tony speaking."

"Hi, Tony," a female voice said. And after a pause, "It's Carol."

Carol? Why was his ex-girlfriend calling him? He felt the same thrill she had evoked in him when they were dating and he saw her or heard her voice. Then he became wary. "Hello, Carol."

"Can you talk? You sound distracted."

"I'm driving on the 405. I don't like to talk on the phone when I'm driving."

"Is there a better time when I can call you back?"

No, there wasn't a better time. If she had something to say, he wanted to hear it now. He went into defensive mode. "I'm late for an appointment, but I can talk to you for a minute."

"That's big of you. All right, I guess I deserve that. Anyway, Josh called me. He's worried about you."

Josh called Carol? That got Tony's attention. Josh and Carol got along like cobras and mongooses. Or was it mongeese?

"Josh is worried about me?" That was reflection. He was using his listening skills in ordinary conversation. Perhaps, if he had mastered these skills when Carol was his girlfriend, she wouldn't have dumped him.

"He says you've changed. He says...well, he didn't explain it very well, but he doesn't think you're the same person you were."

"Maybe that's an improvement. As I recall, you didn't like the old Tony."

"You know better than that. It's just that…"

She hesitated. The old Tony would have interrupted at this point. The new Tony used silence as a tactic, waiting her out.

"It's just that you didn't seem to respect my feelings."

Feelings. Now he knew a lot more about feelings than he had. Maybe that's what Josh didn't like about the new Tony. Josh was not known for his empathy. But calling Carol was potentially a mistake on Josh's part. If Tony and Carol had stayed together, Carol would have moved into the townhouse and replaced Josh. Although Tony hadn't gotten around to telling Josh that.

Where was this conversation going? What did Carol want? Should he get his hopes up?

"Tony?"

He changed lanes to pass a slower car. "I'm still here."

"You were quiet for so long I wasn't sure. What I was wondering is, would you like to…uh, well, get together and talk some more?"

He was tempted to say, talk about what? Haven't we talked about it all, ad nauseam? Or at least he had listened while she talked. Well, sometimes he had argued. Sometimes he had let his mind wander. He didn't want to be the bad guy now. He also didn't want to get hurt anymore. He said, "When would you like to get together?"

"What are you doing this evening?"

"I have to go to a meeting."

"Oh. I'm going out of town on business tomorrow. I won't be back for several days. I hoped we could see each other today. What time is your meeting?"

"Seven."

"When will it be over?"

She was starting to act as if she owned him. Again. "I'm not sure."

"May I ask what kind of a meeting this is?"

He didn't want to get into that. It would require too much explanation, which he didn't owe her. Maybe if he said it fast. "I-I joined a Hotline. The meeting tonight is for all the listeners."

"Josh told me about your foray into the Hotline. He also said the Hotline closed down. Because the girl who was murdered worked there."

"I think it's going to start up again."

"Josh said you listen to people talk about their problems. But if you can listen to other people's problems, why couldn't you listen to my problems?"

Josh was talking too much. And Tony didn't have an answer for Carol. He looked at his watch and said, "Carol, I've gotta run. I'll talk to you later. Bye."

He broke the connection before Carol could say anything more.

CHAPTER 5

Tony filed into the Bonita Beach High School auditorium along with the other Central Hotline listeners. He recognized some of them because they had been in his training class. Patty, the Hotline administrative assistant, sat at a table just inside the door, checking listeners' names on a list as they entered.

Tony said hello to her, and she smiled at him. She knew his name because she had been at several of the training classes and, being one of the few adults, he stuck out. Patty was a young and pretty brunette with an oval face, large eyes, and a boyfriend. She was also taking college courses at night, so if she had a class scheduled for this evening, she was cutting it.

He found a seat near the front of the auditorium, over on the side, so he wouldn't block the view of any of the shorter listeners behind him. The room had a flat floor, not inclined, and the metal folding chairs weren't fixed in place. In spite of these drawbacks, it was nice of the school district to allow the Hotline to use the auditorium of the high school for this meeting. All the listeners would not have fit into the Hotline office. Joy had been a student here, and Tony was sure the school district was cooperating in everything to do with the investigation of her murder.

The mood of the listeners was subdued as everybody found a seat. There wasn't the usual banter and laughter that one would expect from a young crowd. Tony estimated that close to a hundred people had showed up, a high percentage of the active listeners.

The stage contained a lectern with a microphone. Three chairs sat beside the lectern. A few minutes after seven, two women and a man climbed several steps to the stage from the auditorium floor and sat in the chairs. The women were Nancy, the Executive Director of the Hotline, and Gail, the Volunteer Coordinator. Tony didn't recognize the man.

After a whispered discussion among the three, Nancy stood up and came to the lectern. A middle-aged woman, she had her hair cut short and curly. It was a brownish color that made Tony suspect it might be dyed. She wore a smart shirt and pair of slacks and had a look of authority. Even before she said a word, Tony admired her aura of composure in a difficult situation.

The audience became quiet without being asked. Nancy tapped the microphone to see if it was turned on and then started speaking. "Thank you for coming tonight. This is a hard time for all of us. As those of you who attended Joy's funeral and listened to her friends and family talk about her know, Joy was a very special person."

Tony hadn't attended her funeral. His rationalization was that he had barely known her and couldn't afford to take time off from work, but in a rare self-analytic moment, he had admitted to himself that he had a fear of funerals. Now he had to contend with a certain level of guilt.

Nancy looked around the auditorium and continued, "But all of you are very special people. As listeners on the Hotline, you have made a commitment that few people can make. You have committed yourselves to help others—not just go through the motions of helping others, with surface gestures such as donating money or old toys. You have agreed to enter their worlds, to listen to their problems, to walk a mile in their shoes, to feel what it's like to be disabled or abused or bi-polar or even suicidal. You have invested not just your time, but your emotions, as well. And that is what is difficult to do. That's what sets you apart and makes you special. That's what puts you in a class by yourselves and gives you a bond with other Hotline listeners that nobody who hasn't been a listener can share. And all of you have a permanent bond with Joy."

The woman was an orator. As Tony listened to her, he felt his usual cynicism slipping away. He looked at the listeners around him with new eyes. He even looked at himself with new eyes. He had been planning to quit the Hotline, using Joy's murder somehow as an excuse, but how could he do that now? He felt tears rolling down his cheeks, which he tried to hide by brushing them away with his sleeve, but when he dared to look around the room again he noticed that there were not many dry eyes in the place.

Nancy was saying, "We are going to reopen the Hotline, starting tomorrow. Joy would want us to keep it open. Our callers need us and want us to keep it open. We will be making changes to increase our security. However, to those of you who feel they can't continue as listeners, we understand. But we would like as many of you as possible to stay. In a few minutes we'll tell you about some of the changes we are implementing. But first, I want to introduce Detective Croyden to you. Detective Croyden is with the Bonita Beach Police Department. He will bring you up to date on the investigation and answer any questions you may have."

Nancy sat down, and Detective Croyden walked to the lectern. He was an athletic man, wearing a dark business suit with pinstripes, but primarily some shade of brown. His hair was trimmed so short that it was barely there. He looked overdressed for the modern casual world, but Tony realized that he had at least one gun hidden beneath his jacket. He would have been handsome if his nose hadn't tilted to one side. It probably hadn't always been like that.

Detective Croyden took a few seconds to survey the room. He had a penetrating gaze that prevented his audience from fidgeting or talking. When he started speaking, he had everybody's attention.

"I want to add my thanks to you for coming tonight. This is a difficult time for you. I am going to level with you as far as what we know. I won't hold back just because many of you are young. Nancy and Gail told me that as listeners, you are used to hearing strong language."

He paused again for a moment which, Tony realized, had the effect, planned or not, of riveting the attention of the audience on him even more. "First, let me tell you what we know and what we don't know about the murder, itself. Joy walked out to her car after her shift ended at ten o'clock, escorted by the building guard. The guard remembers it as being approximately five minutes past ten. She got into her car. The guard walked back into the building. As of the time he entered the building, Joy had not started her car, but he didn't see anybody in the parking lot. The only other vehicle belonged to him. So he figured she would be okay.

"What happened after that is speculation because we don't have any witnesses. The murderer—I will use the word 'suspect' and the masculine pronoun, although we are not ruling out the possibility of a female at this point—may have gained access to the car, previously. He may have been hiding in the backseat. Another possibility is that he was hiding behind a nearby bush in the park that borders the parking lot. Whatever the case, he was able to gain control over Joy and get her into the park."

Nobody moved in the auditorium as the listeners waited for Detective Croyden to continue.

"Once in the park, he was able to get her clothes off, except for one sandal. The other sandal was found nearby. Also found was a tank top and a pair of shorts. Both were ripped, as if they had been removed with considerable force. She had bruises on her face and other parts of her body and several small cuts, as well, which could have been inflicted with a knife. However, the cause of death was strangulation."

There was an audible gasp from the audience, even though everybody must have already known this. It had been in the papers, on TV, and on the Internet.

We think the suspect must be a physically strong person. Joy was a big girl, and she was an athlete. It would have taken somebody quite strong to control her. However, there is no evidence that she was raped."

This was new information. That's why the police hadn't ruled out the possibility of a female suspect. But it would have to be a strong female.

Detective Croyden continued, "In fact, we have nothing from the suspect that would contain DNA—no skin, no body fluids. The suspect was lucky in that respect. But that doesn't mean we won't get him. And you can help. I have talked to a few of you—those who were especially close to Joy. I don't have time to talk to all of you, but if any of you knows anything that might help us, please come forward at the end of the meeting. I will give a business card to everybody who wants one and leave some with Nancy. If you remember anything, if you come across any piece of information, please call me immediately. Even if you think it's inconsequential, tell me. Don't pass judgment yourself. And now, are there any questions?"

Some people in the audience looked around, but nobody raised a hand for a few seconds. Then a girl timidly put up her hand. Detective Croyden pointed to her and said, "Yes?"

"What about underwear?" the girl asked. Nobody laughed. "None of the reports have mentioned underwear being found."

"We have reason to believe that Joy was wearing underwear," Detective Croyden said, with a straight face. "We think the suspect took it with him. He may have a fetish of some sort. That could help us in our investigation."

Detective Croyden had used the word fetish, just as Tony had. He was glad to have official support for his conjecture. When nobody else raised a hand, he got up his nerve and raised his own hand.

When Detective Croyden recognized him, Tony stood up and said, "What about the guard as a suspect? By his own admission he was the last person to see Joy alive, other than the suspect. Couldn't he be a suspect?" He had mangled the question, but he thought it was a valid one.

The detective said, "We haven't ruled anybody out. We are investigating anybody and everybody at this point. We have talked to the guard several times. We have no reason to believe that the guard was involved in the murder."

It was a carefully worded answer, calculated to relieve their minds, since they worked in the building. It had the intended effect.

Then a boy raised his hand and asked whether the Hotline phones would be tapped.

Detective Croyden appeared to consider his answer before he gave it. Then he said, "The Hotline phones will not be tapped. Typically, phone tapping is done to allow the police to overhear conversations and to attempt to determine the location of the caller. Nancy has pointed out that if the phones are tapped, the Hotline could no longer claim that your conversations are confidential, and you would have to shut down for good. Although I believe that there would be some value from tapping the phones, we are not going to do it at this time. We will depend on you, the listeners, to file full reports for any calls that you consider to be suspicious." He looked as if he might be going to say something more, but then he asked for the next question.

A few more people raised their hands and asked questions, but that didn't produce any new information.

When the questioning stopped, Detective Croyden turned the microphone back over to Nancy, who said that Gail would explain how they would get the Hotline restarted. Gail was older than Nancy and a longtime Hotline employee. She had taken the job, which was part-time, as a sort of second career after her children had left home. She was beloved by all the listeners. And because she was in good shape, she looked younger than her years as she approached the lectern.

First, Gail said a few words about Joy. Then she said, "The security of the Hotline has been compromised to some extent by the news reports. It is possible to piece together from the reports which building we are located in. Not everybody will make the connection but, unfortunately, the people most likely to make it are the ones we least want to. The good news is that our office number hasn't been publicized. And of course, we aren't listed on the building's list of tenants.

"But still, you should be careful when you come to work. If anybody suspicious is loitering near the building, report them to the guard. The guard will call Detective Croyden. We don't want people following any of us up to our office. Fortunately, a lot of young people frequent the mall, so it is fairly easy for you teens to get lost in the crowd.

"As for the new rules, we haven't completely finalized them yet, but the emphasis is on security. Therefore, at least two people must work the four-to-seven and the seven-to-ten p.m. shifts. On the late shift, at least one of the listeners must be male. If we can't get the required listeners for these shifts, we will cancel the shifts. The listeners will walk to their cars together. On the seven-to-ten shift, the male will make sure any female listeners have safely left the area before he leaves. That means staying with someone who is waiting for a ride until that person's driver arrives. And you will still use the guard as an additional escort after the seven-to-ten shift."

Gail talked a little about the procedure for signing up to work, and then she said, "I would like all the male listeners to meet with me on the stage right now."

Because he was sitting in an end seat, Tony was the first one to mount the steps to the stage. Over the next few minutes, between twenty-five and thirty other men and boys came up on the stage. Most of the female listeners clustered in front of the stage to sign up for shifts and talk to Nancy and Detective Croyden. Almost nobody left.

Gail ushered the males over to a corner of the stage, away from the chatter of the others. As they clustered around her, she said, "I realize we're putting a lot of pressure on you guys. In a way, we're implying that you're not in any danger, which you realize is not completely true. So, if any of you have doubts about this or want to talk about it, now's your chance."

Tony looked around at the others. He estimated that four of them were adults. At least two were older than he was.

One of the older men said, "I have a license to carry a gun. I could bring it with me to the Hotline."

Gail shook her head. "No, Dick, no guns in the Hotline office. We don't want an armed camp. Or the risk of a shootout. Although there's no evidence that the suspect used a gun."

But there was also no evidence that he hadn't used a gun. He certainly had a persuasive method of getting Joy into the park. Tony didn't necessarily agree with the no gun policy, but as the new kid on the block, he figured he'd better keep quiet. But he had another question. "I assume different guards work the evening shift on different days. Have the police taken a look at all of them?"

"Nancy and I have talked at length to Detective Croyden about the guard situation," Gail said. "And also to the building management. We would not have reopened the Hotline if we hadn't been convinced that the guards were completely trustworthy."

Gail had a positive way of talking that made you believe her. And Nancy did too. If they thought that the guards were reliable, Tony would take their word for it. There was some further discussion about safety procedures, which Tony used as an opportunity to glance around at the other men and boys. Most of them looked as if they could handle themselves in a fight. One of the boys was quite small, but he had a determined look in his eye. None of them talked about quitting the Hotline.

When they finished talking, they went back to the front of the stage where the signup sheets were located. Tony noticed that the teens filled most of the weekend slots quickly, since they didn't have school those days. At first he thought he'd sign up for the seven-to-ten shift once a week, but after some hesitation, he ended up putting his name down for Mondays and Fridays for the rest of September.

CHAPTER 6

Tony kept a wary eye out for any suspicious people as he entered the building to work his first shift since Joy's murder. There were the usual customers entering the shops in the mall, but nobody seemed to have any interest in him. Inside, he took the stairs two at a time to the third floor and was pleasantly surprised to find that he was not panting quite as hard as he had in the past. The workouts at the health club he had joined must be paying off.

The door to the Hotline office was locked, but it was now standard procedure to keep it locked after the office staff left for the day. He entered the combination to the lockbox and extracted the key. Upon entering the office, he saw two people, one male and one female, in the listening room, both on the phone. By the time he signed in, the man had ended his call.

The man walked out of the listening room and said, "We had some callers asking about Joy. Whether she worked for the Hotline. That's how some people get their kicks. We told them we couldn't give out any information."

"Thanks for the warning," Tony said. "I'm Tony."

"Nathan."

They shook hands. Tony noticed that Nathan didn't look him in the eye. He remembered that Nathan had been at the Friday meeting. He guessed that the man was a few years older than he was, with sandy hair. Nathan was taller, but Tony was stockier. Nathan was wearing jeans and a sweatshirt, in spite of the summer warmth.

"How long have you been on the Hotline?" Tony asked. It was a standard question.

"Six months."

"This is my first shift without a mentor. I guess I'm about to lose my vir...."

Tony stopped in mid-word and Nathan laughed, a strange laugh that sounded like the cackle of a hen after laying an egg. "It's okay; you can say it."

The girl came out of the listening room, and when Tony gave his name, she introduced herself as Cecile. They shook hands. Most girls shook hands these days. Upon being assured that Nathan was walking out with Cecile, Tony went into the listening room and appropriated the table he liked best—the one facing the window.

He came back out to check the calendar. They were supposed to be working in pairs. But if nobody else had signed up, he would work alone. He wasn't afraid. However, the calendar showed that S. Lawton was scheduled to work this shift. The name didn't register with Tony.

He had just settled down in his chair when he heard the outside door open behind him. When he swiveled the chair around, he saw Shahla entering the office. She waved at him. His heart gave an involuntary leap before he got it under control. What was she doing here? Perhaps she had just come in to sign up for future shifts. If so, she should have come in earlier. Now he would be obligated to walk her out, because of the new rules.

Tony came out of the listening room, realizing that he looked forward to walking her out of the building. But instead of looking at the calendar, she was signing in on the daily time sheet.

"Hi," he said. "I-I didn't know you were working tonight."

"Maybe if you'd looked at the calendar, you'd know," Shahla said with a slight smile, as she also entered her hours in the logbook.

"But the per..." Tony stopped, realizing that he was about to make a complete ass of himself. S. Lawton. Of course. Shahla Lawton. He had pictured Shahla as having an unpronounceable last name. "One of my new year's resolutions was to learn to read. I guess I'm going to have to get going on that."

"You are," Shahla said, leading the way into the listening room and setting a book she had brought with her on one of the tables.

Tony followed her and went back to his table. Shahla was wearing a skirt tonight. It wasn't short—it came to her knees—but he was glad to see any kind of a skirt on a girl. It made her look feminine. Skirts seemed to be few and far between these days. Mona always wore slacks to work at the Bodyalternatives.net office, as did the other women. And most of the girls in his Hotline class had worn jeans or shorts.

He sat down trying to think of something sensible to say. "Uh, I didn't see you at the meeting."

"I came in late and sat in the back." Shahla wasn't looking at him. "I almost didn't come at all."

"You were close to Joy, weren't you? This must be very difficult for you." He wouldn't have said that before he took the Hotline class.

"Joy was my best friend. We double-dated to the prom last year."

Shahla still wasn't looking at him. She was suffering. Tony could picture it. He remembered the rule about showing empathy but not sympathy. He said, "You didn't have to come back."

"I came back because I want to make sure that the guy who killed Joy gets caught."

"Detective Croyden seems to be competent. I'm sure he'll find whoever it was."

"I'm not so sure. At least as long as we have a confidentiality policy about our callers."

"Well, he was given a copy of the Green Book." The policy had been bent to that extent. That fact had come out at the meeting. "Do you think one of our callers is the…suspect?"

The phone rang before Shahla could answer. She said quickly, "I'll get it," and picked up the receiver. "Central Hotline. This is Sally."

She listened for a few seconds and then put the call on the speaker. Tony heard a male voice say, "…found Joy's murderer yet?"

"Who's this?" Shahla demanded rather than asked.

"Let's just say I'm a friend." The caller talked softly, with pauses between sentences. "But you're looking in the wrong places."

"Where should we look?"

"If I told you that, it would make it too easy for you. But you don't think she'll be the last one, do you?" There was a click.

Shahla hung up the phone and said, excitedly, "I know who that is. That's the Chameleon. I can tell by the way he talks. He made scary calls before Joy was killed, too. He would call at night and say he could see us. That would freak us out, even though if you look out our window there's nothing but the parking lot and the park. How could he see us?"

"Try calling him back with star sixty-nine," Tony said.

"We can't call out from these lines."

And the phone system didn't capture the number that was calling. Tony had never spoken to the Chameleon. He suspected the Chameleon hung up whenever a man answered the phone. He had read his profile in the Green Book, however. The Chameleon was a longtime caller. True to his name, he used many aliases. He had a gadget that disguised his voice. Sometimes he impersonated females. He had a different story for every call, but it usually involved sex at some point. Sometimes he made veiled threats. The Green Book instructed listeners to hang up on him when he was recognized since he abused the Hotline.

"Let's do this," Tony said. "Mark the call report to Detective Croyden's attention, like Gail wants us to do. The Chameleon is a logical suspect, just because he calls so often. Although that sounded like a crank call to me. He probably just didn't want to be overshadowed by Joy."

"He's a really creepy guy. I think Croyden should talk to him. But how can he? We don't have his telephone number, and we don't know where he lives or anything."

Tony was looking at the Chameleon's profile in the Green Book. "Maybe Croyden can find him. He told somebody he lives in El Segundo. He's in his late twenties. He has a job as a security guard."

"That really sets him apart, doesn't it? I'm sure the police will be able to walk right to his door."

Tony could understand Shahla's frustration. He wanted to help her. He said, "Okay, let's do this. We'll start a file of our own on likely suspects. We'll make copies of the call reports of suspicious callers. We might spot something that the police don't."

"We're not supposed to take information on callers out of the office. And we're not supposed to use the copy machine…"

"This is a state of emergency." Tony wanted to assuage Shahla's fears about violating the Hotline rules. "Besides, there's nobody here to see us. I'll do the copying and keep the copies so you won't get into trouble."

Shahla reluctantly relented. It was obvious that her parents had instilled a moral code in her. He was glad to know that. He had met enough young people who had no apparent values. He, himself, was perhaps one of them. But he was changing, he kept telling himself. However, as he had said, this was a state of emergency.

He took the call reports out of the box where the listeners had placed them. They dated back two days to Saturday, the day the Hotline had reopened. Fortunately, Gail didn't collect them every day. But that also meant Croyden hadn't looked at them yet. He must have plenty to keep him busy, however. Tony and Shahla pulled out the reports marked to Detective Croyden's attention and also several identified as calls from the Chameleon. He often called more than once a day, in defiance of the rules.

In between taking routine calls, Tony made copies of these reports on the Xerox copier. Then he sorted the original call reports back into chronological order and replaced them in the box, while Shahla was on a call. He did group three calls from the Chameleon about Joy together so that they would get the special attention of Gail, and hopefully Croyden.

After Shahla had hung up and completed her call report, she said, "I have the feeling that we're not covering all the possibilities."

"We don't have to," Tony said. "That's the job of the police."

"But the police aren't, either. Have they asked you for an alibi for the night Joy was killed?"

"Huh?" Tony looked at Shahla, wondering if she was kidding.

"Well, what were you doing that night?"

"Uh..." Tony was flabbergasted. "Do you think I'm the murderer?"

"What I think doesn't matter. You've seen the cop shows on TV. They question everybody, including their friends."

"Well, it's a relief that you count me as a friend," Tony said, trying to lighten the atmosphere, which had suddenly become very heavy. "Let's see, what was I doing?" He hadn't thought about it before. He hadn't thought of himself as a suspect before. He drew a blank. He tried to work backward from the time he had heard about Joy's murder. He had been busy all that day. And the night before? He had done some preparation for his talk to the women's club. He had been lonely and restless. Josh was out somewhere. Carol was out of his life permanently.

"I went to a movie."

"What movie?"

"Uh...*Lost in Translation*, with Bill Murray. It's about this American actor who goes to Japan to make a Suntory commercial..."

"Whom did you go with?"

For some reason he didn't want to admit that he had gone by himself. "I...uh, couldn't find anybody to go with."

"So you went alone. Can anybody vouch for you?"

"No." He would be just another faceless patron to the ticket taker. And he hadn't seen anybody he knew.

"So you don't have an alibi." Shahla looked at Tony with an unfathomable look in her eyes.

"Ticket stub. I save ticket stubs. I throw them into a bowl. It shows the date and time of the show. It didn't get over until about 10:30."

"A ticket stub, eh?" Shahla said, imitating a prosecuting attorney. "That was clever of you. You purchased a ticket, but didn't actually see the movie. Or you left in the middle..."

"You don't really believe I killed Joy," Tony said getting hot despite his attempt to stay cool. He felt sweat forming in his armpits.

"What I think is that Detective Croyden should be asking these questions," Shahla said. "But since he isn't, maybe you and I should."

"Does that mean I'm exonerated?"

"For the time being. But only because you don't appear to have a motive. However, in this kind of case, when the murderer is finally caught, the neighbors always say, 'But he was such a nice boy. He couldn't have done it.' So we have to look for hidden motives."

Tony was able to chuckle. "I think you've got a career all mapped out in the district attorney's office."

"Actually, I'm going to be a writer. But I may write true crime. And I may have my…" Shahla became choked up and couldn't continue for a moment, "…first story."

"You have to be careful about doing your own investigating. What if you asked the real killer for an alibi? What do you think he'd do to you?"

Tears welled up in Shahla's eyes and started running down her cheeks. Tony had an urge to comfort her, to touch her, to hold her. He knew that was the wrong thing to do. Empathy, not sympathy. He said, "This must be very diff.…" He'd already said that. He gave her a tissue from a box on one of the tables.

Shahla wiped her eyes and said, "When I heard about Joy, I didn't believe it. It still doesn't seem real. She can't be gone."

The phone rang. Tony reached for it, but Shahla said, "I'll get it," and answered before Tony could. She immediately placed the call on the speaker. She pressed the mute button and said, "It's him."

The caller was saying, "…advice on how to prevent what happened to Joy from happening to you."

"What's your advice?" Shahla asked.

"You girls need to wear more clothes. When you walk around strutting your stuff, showing off your body, wearing tight short skirts up to your butt, with no underwear, you're asking for it."

It was an inappropriate call. The Hotline rules said to hang up at this point. But it was obvious that Shahla had no intention of hanging up.

She had the Chameleon's page from the Green Book open in front of her. She said, "Is this Fred?" using one of several names the Chameleon had previously given Hotline listeners.

There was silence at the other end of the line. Shahla said, "I need to call you something. Is it okay if I call you Fred?"

More silence. Then the caller said, "All right. Tell me, Sally, are you wearing underwear?"

"Are you on a cell phone, Fred?" There was a pause, and Shahla said, "Fred, talk to me."

"How did you know?"

"I'm clairvoyant. Are you at work?"

Tony was reading the Green Book over Shahla's shoulder. Did he really work as a security guard?

"What makes you think that?"

"Just a guess. Where do you work?"

"That's none of your business."

"You sound like an interesting person. I was hoping we could get together."

Tony was disturbed by what Shahla was doing, but he knew if he cut off the call, she would hate him forever.

There was silence on the line. Tony and Shahla looked at each other. Tony found himself holding his breath.

"Are you on the level?" The voice was almost plaintive.

"What do you think, Fred?"

Shahla's answer was brilliant. Let him draw his own conclusion. The imaginations of the callers didn't work like those of "normal" people. He might convince himself that she was interested in him.

"Well, I don't know."

Tony suspected that Fred, or whatever his name was, had problems relating to women in real life.

"What time do you get off work?" Shahla asked.

"Midnight."

"And what's your cell phone number?"

After a hesitation, Fred reeled off an area code and seven-digit number. Tony quickly wrote it down and mouthed to Shahla to have him repeat it. She asked him again, and he gave the same number a second time.

Then Shahla said, "Where shall we meet?"

Another hesitation. Then he gave an intersection. Tony wrote down the names of the streets while Shahla verified them with Fred.

"Shall we say 12:15?" Shahla asked.

"All right. Listen, I gotta go."

The line went dead. Shahla looked jubilant. "We got him," she almost sang. She danced around the room.

"Not so fast, young lady." Tony was alarmed at Shahla's reaction. "First of all, we don't know whether the information he gave us is correct. But in any case, we have to pass it along to Detective Croyden." He pulled the detective's card out of his wallet.

"No. Croyden is at home with his wife and kids. We can't blow this."

"Somebody will be on duty. I'll call them."

Tony lifted a telephone receiver, but Shahla grabbed it at the same time. They froze, with Tony sitting and Shahla standing. Each had one hand on the receiver. Their hands partially overlapped.

Tony's first inclination was to jerk the receiver or yell at Shahla, but with an effort, he brought himself under control. Then he became conscious of the touch of her hand on his. He couldn't let that affect him, either. He said, "What do you think we should do?"

"Meet him."

"Us? Together?"

"Sure. If they're two of us, we'll be safe."

"It isn't going to happen. First of all, you're not going anywhere except home. You've got school tomorrow. And how would I explain to your parents that I was running around the back streets of El Segundo at midnight with their underage daughter? Second, we're going to turn this over to the police."

Shahla kept her grip on the receiver and Tony's hand. She said, "Tony, the police will screw this up."

"What makes you say that?"

"Because…because. It was…it's too long a story, but you can believe me when I say that I don't trust the police."

He finally heard himself saying, much against his better judgment, "All right, this is what I'll do." He looked at his watch, which was on his left or unengaged hand, to gain time. It was almost ten o'clock. "We'll close up shop, and you'll go home. I will meet Fred, the Chameleon, at the designated time and place."

"I'm going with you."

"No, Shahla, you're not."

"You'll get hurt going all alone."

"My roommate has a gun. I'll take it with me."

They stared at each other, neither one moving. If this is a test of wills, Tony thought, I've got to persevere. I'm responsible for her safety.

Shahla said, "So you aren't going to call the police?"

"No."

Shahla relaxed her grip on the receiver and his hand. Slowly she pulled her hand away. Slowly he hung up the receiver.

Shahla scribbled on a piece of paper and handed it to him. "This is my cell phone number. Promise you'll call me when you get back."

"Who knows what time that will be? You'll be asleep. And I'll wake up your parents."

"No you won't. I have my own room. And I won't be asleep. I'll be waiting."

"That's a really bad idea. What if I forget to call?"

"I'll go crazy. So promise you'll call, okay? Even though we've just met, I don't want to lose another…friend. I'll worry until you call."

Tony felt trapped. "All right, I'll call you."

Shahla gave him a hug so quick he wasn't sure it had really happened.

CHAPTER 7

Beams from a streetlight filtered through tree leaves to where Tony sat in his car, like water seeping through a membrane, providing just enough light so that it wasn't pitch black inside the car. He had picked this spot for its darkness. The car would just be an innocuous shadow to a person standing at the intersection, fifty feet away, and he would be invisible to that person. The intersection itself was much better lit, with streetlights on two corners.

Tony was nervous. He caught himself lifting his chin in a basketball head-fake movement. Except that he had never been very good at basketball, because of his lack of height. The head-fake, which appeared when he was under stress, was modeled after that of one of the all-time greats, Elgin Baylor, who he had seen play only in videos, never in real life. Elgin was now an executive with the Los Angeles Clippers, a hapless professional basketball team that was not to be confused with the many-times NBA champion Los Angeles Lakers that Elgin had once played for.

He looked at his watch. He could just barely see the hands. Ten minutes past twelve. Five minutes to the meeting time with Fred the Chameleon. But Fred expected a juicy teenage girl, not a slightly overweight male marketing manager. What was he going to do if Fred actually showed? He only had a vague plan.

What was he doing here, anyway? Why had he given in to Shahla? At least he had done one thing right; he had not let her come with him. That would have been a disaster. It wasn't that he was afraid. Well, not very afraid, anyway. El Segundo just wasn't a very scary place. It wasn't an upscale community like Bonita Beach, but the few people he had seen on the street didn't look like hoods or gangbangers.

He had Josh's gun, a nine-millimeter. And it was loaded. He had fired it only one time when he had gone with Josh to a firing range. But Josh had given him a quick review, and he felt fairly confident about using it. He patted the hard bulk stuck in his belt, underneath the sport coat he had donned, and wondered for the tenth time whether the safety was really on so that he wouldn't accidentally shoot himself in the balls.

Josh had been surprisingly good about not asking too many questions. Tony had told him he had a midnight meeting, about which he was somewhat apprehensive because of the location, but he hadn't mentioned that it was in connection with Joy's murder. Josh would have volunteered to come along, and knowing him, Tony was afraid he might cause trouble. Josh pictured himself as a vigilante.

Tony heard footsteps as somebody approached from behind and walked past his car on the sidewalk. He froze, wondering whether he was really invisible. At least he was on the other side of the car from the pedestrian. And it was difficult to see into a Porsche without the convertible top down. As the person came into his field of vision, Tony saw that he was a man wearing jeans and a light jacket, possibly leather, against the Los Angeles night chill. He was also wearing a baseball cap. He walked rapidly, his body slouched, his hands in his pockets.

Did he look like somebody who was expecting to meet a girl he didn't know? Not really. He looked furtive, like a person who was afraid of human contact. Tony watched to see if he turned the corner or crossed the street when he got to the intersection, but he didn't. He stopped under the streetlight and glanced quickly around. He reminded Tony of a small animal watching for enemies.

Was this the infamous Chameleon? He did look weird, but not dangerous. He was thin and his slouch made him look short. Tony couldn't see his hair because of the cap. He was too far away, and it was too dark for Tony to get a look at his face.

It was time for Tony to execute his plan, what plan he had. He pulled out his cell phone. The dial lit up, in response to his touch, and he entered the number Fred had given to Shahla. He pressed the Send button. The phone rang in his ear. The man on the corner gave no indication that his cell phone was ringing, and Tony couldn't hear another ring, if there was one, even though his window was cracked open.

After several rings, an answering service came on the line. A male voice said, "This is…" and gave the telephone number Tony had attempted to enter. "You know what to do," the voice continued. Then there was a beep.

Tony pressed the button to end the call. The man on the corner hadn't moved. Either he had ignored the call or he didn't have his cell phone with him. The third alternative, of course, was that Fred had given Shahla a bogus number. Was the voice on the phone Fred's voice? Possibly. But Tony wasn't certain. It didn't sound quite the same as the voice he had heard at the Hotline. And not only did Fred have many different voices, according to the Green Book, but the reception on this phone and the office phones also had some built-in distortion.

Tony had done all he could. It was time for him to leave. But he didn't want to start his engine with the man standing there. The man would know that Tony had been watching him and might be startled into doing—what? Now the man was smoking a cigarette. Tony looked at his watch and thought he read the time as 12:20.

His anxiety level grew. He couldn't wait here forever. And he had the uncomfortable feeling that he should be doing more, with the man still in sight. He made a decision. He quietly opened his car door, just as another car went through the intersection and masked the noise. He stepped out as his heartbeat accelerated. He left the door ajar so that the sound of it closing wouldn't alert the man.

However, Tony also didn't want to sneak up on him. He stepped up onto the sidewalk and started to approach the man, deliberately making noise with his sneakers slapping the pavement, trying to give the effect that he had been walking for some time. The man couldn't fail to hear him.

The man didn't turn around as Tony approached, but he did raise his head. A frightened animal, listening. He dropped his cigarette on the ground and stamped on it. Then he abruptly started walking across the street. Fast. Still slouching, but his hands weren't in his pockets. As he reached the other side, he turned around and took one quick look at Tony. Then he redoubled his pace, along the street at right angles to the one on which Tony was parked. He didn't look back again.

Tony watched him, trying to picture his face. His cap brim had shielded it from the streetlight. All Tony could remember was a black void. He walked slowly back to his car, wondering how he was going to get enough sleep to stay awake at work that day.

It wasn't until he was almost home that he remembered he had told Shahla he would call her. He didn't want to wake her up, but he had promised. This time he stopped directly under a streetlight and turned on his dome light for good measure so that he could see to press the buttons.

After two rings a sleepy voice said, "Hello."

"Did I wake you?"

"Tony? No, I was awake. What happened? Are you okay?"

"Yeah, I'm fine. A guy showed up, but I couldn't get him on the cell phone. I'm not sure he's the one."

"Oh. Well, we can talk more about it tomorrow."

"I'm going to pass the information on to Detective Croyden."

"Tony. You can't!"

"I have to. It's the right thing to do. Go back to sleep. Goodnight." He quickly pressed the button to end the call so that he couldn't hear her protests.

***

Detective Croyden sat down hard on the swivel chair in his small cubicle and said, "Okay, Tony Schmidt, what have you got for me?"

Tony seated himself just outside the cubicle—there wasn't room inside—on the folding chair that Croyden had carried over and wondered how strong Croyden's chair was. Croyden was no lightweight. In fact, he had probably played football at sometime in his life—perhaps linebacker.

Tony realized that despite the fact that he had had most of the day—or at least snippets here and there between talking to clients on the phone—to think about what he was going to say, he still hadn't come up with anything good. But he had to get out of this mess before he got himself in any deeper.

He gave a head-fake and dove in. "One of the callers to the Hotline has been talking about Joy in such a way that we think it's possible he might be Joy's killer."

Croyden picked up a spiral notebook and started writing with what Tony thought was a Mont Blanc pen. He said, "Who's we?"

"Shahla Lawton, one of the other listeners, and me." He wondered how Croyden could afford a Mont Blanc pen.

When Tony hesitated, in order to let Croyden ask more questions, the detective said, "Go on. Tell me the story." He leaned back in his chair and crossed one ankle over his knee. A thick and hairy leg showed above a white sock. The chair creaked. He had his jacket off, and Tony could see the gun in a holster on his left side. Tony pictured Croyden drawing the gun. He must be right-handed.

And Tony did tell him the story. In fact, he told Croyden more than he intended to. Croyden didn't need a class in active listening. He was so good at using silence and occasional probing questions that Tony knew he was talking himself into trouble. About the only thing he didn't tell about was the gun he had borrowed from Josh. And he made it sound as if going to meet the Chameleon was his idea, not Shahla's.

When Croyden was apparently satisfied that Tony had nothing more to tell, he planted both feet firmly on the ground. He leaned forward and looked Tony in the eye, the way a linebacker looks at a quarterback he is about to sack. The broken nose in the middle of his tanned face enhanced the image. He spoke, his words coming slowly. "Have you been trained as a police officer, Tony?"

"No...sir." The 'sir' came out involuntarily.

"Were you in the Marine Corps, by any chance?"

"No."

Croyden spoke faster. "How about the Green Berets?"

"No."

"The Navy Seals?"

"No."

"Then what the hell were you doing risking your life trying to impersonate somebody who knows what they're doing?"

"It was a stupid thing to do."

"Actually, I wouldn't care so much if you lost your life through your own stupidity. But in this case, you spooked a possible suspect. Give me one good reason why I shouldn't slap the cuffs on you for trying to play the hero?"

Tony couldn't think of any.

Croyden took his eyes off Tony's and lowered his voice. "I'm going to tell you something that I don't want to go beyond this room. We subpoenaed the records of the Hotline's incoming calls from the phone company for the last month. We found the numbers for all the obscene callers by comparing the times of the calls to the times listed on the call reports. We are in the process of checking out each of these perverts. I'm telling you this so that you know we're actually doing something and not just sitting on our butts."

"What about confidentiality?"

"That's why I don't want you to say anything. Your boss, Nancy, is afraid that if this leaks out, the Hotline will lose its status as a confidential service. Mind you, we're only checking on the callers you call masturbators, and I don't believe they deserve confidentiality."

"So you've already got a line on the Chameleon." Tony felt redundant.

Croyden still wasn't looking at Tony. "Well, we've had a problem with that guy. He calls from a cell phone. We checked it out, and the number belongs to a woman who couldn't be the Chameleon. She says she lost her phone and doesn't know who's using it. She may be stonewalling, but we haven't been able to convince her to tell us anything more."

"So the number he gave Shahla…"

"Even if he gave her the number he is using it may not do us any good." Croyden looked at Tony and said, "What were you doing the night Joy was killed?"

The change of subject was so abrupt that Tony was taken aback. He stared at Detective Croyden.

"Routine question," Croyden said. "For the record."

"I-I went to a movie. Alone. But I kept the ticket stub." That demanded an explanation. "I keep all my ticket stubs."

"What time was that?"

"About eight to 10:30."

"Don't lose the stub," Croyden said, making a note. He didn't even say anything about how Tony could have purchased the ticket to provide himself with an alibi.

CHAPTER 8

When Tony arrived at the Hotline office for his Friday evening shift, he found the door unlocked. He entered the office, wondering about this breach of the rules, and saw that there were two people in the listening room, both males. Apparently, they weren't worried about outsiders getting in.

As he entered his hours in the book, one of them came out of the listening room. He was a teenager, tall, blond and a little bit gawky, wearing a Bonita Beach High School T-shirt. At the same time, Tony heard a voice behind him say, "Hey, Kevin, we need to talk to you for a minute."

Tony turned and saw Shahla coming out of the snack room carrying a plate of chips. What was she doing here? He had been convinced that she would never speak to him again. Maybe she had worked the four-to-seven shift with these guys and was just finishing up. And who were "we"?

Shahla continued, "Kevin, this is Tony."

They said hi and shook hands.

"Kevin is a senior at Bonita Beach," Shahla said to Tony. "Tony is new here."

At least she was speaking to him.

"What we need to know," Shahla said to Kevin, "is what you were doing the night Joy was killed."

"Aren't you going to read me my rights?" Kevin asked with mock indignation.

51

"Your rights just went down the toilet," Shahla said. "Answer the question."

Tony had hoped Shahla was off this kick. At least she had waited until he showed up. But she was being awfully blunt about it.

"All right, officer," Kevin said, "I know when I'm defeated. I was at lacrosse practice."

"Sure you were," Shahla said. "At night and before school started? A likely story. What were you really doing?"

"It happens to be true," Kevin said. "We had preseason practice. And since we have to share the field with the football team and the soccer team and some of our players had summer jobs, we practiced at night. It's a good thing we got lights on the field last year. The coach and all the other players can vouch for me."

"What time did practice end?"

"It was almost ten. And then we took showers. We've got the same practice schedule tomorrow night. I'll tell you what, why don't you come into our shower room at ten tomorrow evening. We're a friendly group. Then you can see for yourself."

"No thanks."

"Watch out for these guys," Kevin said to the man who was just coming out of the listening room. "They'll try to pin Joy's murder on you."

"Maybe they're trying to cover up for themselves," the man, who Tony recognized as Nathan, said, with a half-smile.

Nathan was wearing the same sweatshirt he had worn at his last Hotline session on Monday.

"What we want to know," Shahla said, without smiling, "is what you were doing and where you were the night of Joy's murder."

Nathan said, "You don't want much, do you? But by the way, I've already told this story to Detective Croyden."

"Humor us and tell it again," Shahla said munching on a chip.

"No problem. I was at church."

"What church is that?" Tony asked, feeling that he should be helping Shahla.

"The Church of the Risen Lord."

"I've never heard of it." And the fact that Nathan didn't look either of them in the eye made the story sound suspect.

"It's northeast of the airport, about ten miles from here."

"Is that where you live?" Shahla asked.

"Near there. They have Thursday evening services that sometimes go until pretty late. Eleven or so."

"And you have someone who can vouch for you?"

"Of course. I have a lot of friends there."

"All right, you two can go," Shahla said still without smiling.

"Thank you, Your Honor," Kevin said, with a little bow. "Come on, Nathan, let's get out of here before they ask us more questions."

"Shahla is tenacious, isn't she?" Nathan said. "I like that in a girl."

They went out the door together.

Tony looked at Shahla and said, "What about you?"

"What about me?"

"Didn't you work the four-to-seven? Aren't you leaving?"

"If you'd look at the time sheet, you'd know that I'm working the seven-to-ten."

Tony hadn't signed in on the time sheet yet. He did so now and, sure enough, Shahla was signed in for the seven-to-ten shift. She went into the listening room. He followed her, noticing that she had her dark hair in a ponytail, fastened with an elastic band he had recently learned was called a scrunchy, for reasons unknown. He liked ponytails. He said, "I wasn't sure you were speaking to me."

Shahla sat down at the table by the window, the one Tony liked, and said, "I shouldn't be, but I need your help."

Tony vowed to claim his seat first in the future. He sat down at one of the other tables. "Did Detective Croyden talk to you?"

"Yes. He came to my house."

"How did you like him?"

"He's not as bad as I thought he would be. He asked some good questions and he seemed to know what he was doing."

"But you're still conducting your own investigation."

"That's why I need your help."

Tony was checking the bulletin board to see if there were any new notices. He spotted one from Gail. He read it aloud to Shahla: "When you take a call from the Chameleon, be sure to record everything he says. We particularly want information about where he lives and where he works. Don't hang up on him unless his talk gets particularly offensive. Do not under any circumstances give him any information about Joy, the Hotline or yourselves. Do not agree to meet him anywhere. Give your call report to Nancy, Patty, or me, immediately. If none of us is here, place it on my desk."

"Detective Croyden has been talking to the ladies in the office," Tony said.

"Duh. I'm surprised you didn't get fired."

"How can you get fired from a volunteer job?"

"You know what I mean."

"And yet you were willing to go with me. Nay, you insisted on going."

"But I wasn't planning to tell Croyden about it."

"Okay, truce." Tony liked this high-spirited girl too much to want to be at odds with her. "What do you plan to do now?"

The phone rang before she could say anything. Tony answered it. "Central Hotline. This is Tony."

"I've got a problem," a female voice said. "I need to talk to someone."

"You can talk to me," Tony said. "Who's this?"

"Gertrude."

He would bet a week's pay that her name wasn't really Gertrude, but she could be anonymous if she wanted to be. When she didn't immediately say anything more, he said, "What's your problem, Gertrude?"

"I like sex."

He was tempted to say, "That's a problem?" but she sounded quite young, so he waited her out. He put the call on the speaker so that Shahla could hear it.

After a pause she said, "I'm sixteen, but I like to have sex. What do you think I should do?"

The Hotline rule was to not give advice because the listeners were not trained counselors. Tony asked, "What would you like to do?"

"Should I stop having sex?"

"Do you want to stop?"

"No. I like sex. I'm always horny. But other kids are saying bad things about me."

"So you're getting a bad reputation? How do you feel about that?"

"How do you think I feel? I feel awful. So what do you think I should do? Should I go on fucking every boy I go out with or should I stop?"

This was turning into an obscene phone call, but it was also somewhat titillating. Tony had never heard of a call like this coming from a girl. He looked at Shahla. She had a look of surprise on her face. Then she walked out of the listening room. Tony took the call off the speaker, figuring that Shahla didn't want to listen.

"I can give you the number of a sex hotline," Tony said to the caller.

"Don't brush me off," the girl said. "Tell me what to do."

"Have you talked to your parents about this?"

"Are you crazy? Of course not. I'm talking to you. So what should I do?"

"What would you like to do?" Tony repeated. He felt trapped. He wondered whether he should tell her this was an inappropriate call and hang up.

"You're no help. You're just like all the others."

There was a click. She had hung up before he could. Tony stared at the receiver and said, "Whew."

"Welcome to the club," Shahla said. She had returned to the listening room with more chips. "You're not a virgin anymore."

"I guess not." He wondered whether she was a female masturbator. Or perhaps it was a crank call. He finished filling out the call report and said, "Where were we?"

"We were talking about motives the other day. I was trying to think of someone who might have a motive to kill Joy."

"And did you come up with anyone?"

"I've got a possibility. Her name is Martha, and she's a listener on the Hotline."

"You think the killer might be a female?"

"Detective Croyden said that was a possibility. And Martha is big enough and strong enough to do it."

"Tell me about Martha."

"She's a senior at Bonita Beach, and she's on the volleyball team."

"Joy was on the volleyball team."

"Joy was the star of the volleyball team. Because of her and several others, the team was expected to win the league championship."

"How has the team been doing without her?"

"They've only played two games so far. They've split."

"Sounds like they miss Joy."

"Definitely."

The phone rang, and Shahla answered it. Tony could tell from what she said that the caller was a harmless repeat who called almost every day. She would be tied up with him for fifteen minutes. Tony wondered why she thought that this girl Martha might have killed Joy. Maybe Shahla didn't like Martha. Was she so anxious to find a killer that she was guilty of wishful thinking? Tony had to admit that she was right about the Chameleon being a potential suspect. But Croyden was handling him now. It wouldn't do any harm to listen to Shahla. But if Martha really was a suspect, they would contact Detective Croyden, regardless of how Shahla felt about it.

Tony wandered into the snack room and made himself some popcorn in the microwave. It didn't have butter on it, so it couldn't be fattening—could it? He carried the bag back into the outer room. He noticed that an envelope was lying on the carpet, partially underneath the outside door. It hadn't been there when he came in. Somebody must have slid it under the door. Tony had locked the door after Kevin and Nathan left. He was going to observe the locked-door rule, especially when Shahla was with him. Now he was glad he had.

CHAPTER 9

The envelope was white, business-size; there was nothing odd about it. Tony picked it up and immediately wondered whether he should have done that. What about fingerprints? He held it gingerly between his thumb and forefinger and looked at it from different angles. There was no writing on the outside. And it wasn't sealed. The flap was just tucked in, and it would be easy to open. But should he open it? He held it up toward the overhead light. There was definitely a piece of paper inside. He set the envelope on the white table and stared at it.

Turn all evidence over to Detective Croyden. And Tony would. But first he was going to look at it. He took a handkerchief out of his pants pocket and picked up the envelope again, this time through a layer of cloth. He wasn't going to get any more fingerprints on it. He covered his other hand with another piece of the handkerchief and worked the flap open. Then he carefully extracted the paper from the envelope, using the handkerchief to keep his fingers from touching the paper.

It was a regular piece of white paper, folded in thirds. Very neatly. Tony shook it to unfold it and placed it on the table.

"What's going on?"

Tony jumped, startled by Shahla's voice just behind him. He had been concentrating so hard that he had almost forgotten about her. "Do you always sneak up on people?" he asked to cover his loss of composure.

"Next time I'll wear a bell so you'll know I'm coming. I saw you out here looking as though you were practicing a magic trick. What are you trying to do, make the envelope disappear?"

"Somebody slid it under the door."

"Do you think it was the murderer?" She looked apprehensively toward the door.

"I don't know, but the door is locked. Don't touch anything. We don't want to leave fingerprints. Let's see what it says on the paper."

Tony and Shahla bent over the table. The writing on the paper was printed in black ink, by a computer printer.

"It's a poem," Shahla said.

"Read it," Tony said. She was the writer. He had never read poetry, other than the few poems required in English classes, and didn't want to embarrass himself by reading it badly, even if it was a bad poem, which it probably was.

"It's called 'Spaghetti Straps,'" Shahla said. She read,
> "She wears a summer dress, spaghetti straps
> to hold it up, or is this so? Perhaps
> it's gravity, the gravity of con-
> sequences should it fall. If she should don
> her dress one day but then forget to pull
> them up, those flimsy wisps of hope so full
> of her ripe beauty, do you think the weight
> of promises within, or hand of fate,
> would slide it down, revealing priceless treasures?
> If so, would she invoke heroic measures
> to hide the truth, for fear this modest lapse
> would air the secret of spaghetti straps?"

"What do you think?" Tony asked. He didn't feel qualified to comment on it as a poem and he wasn't about to be the first to comment on its contents.

"It's actually a pretty good poem."

"You're not offended by it?"

"Are you kidding? After some of the stuff I've heard, this is a nursery rhyme. If our grosser callers like the Chameleon talked like this instead of the way they do, I wouldn't hang up on them so fast."

"So you don't think the Chameleon is capable of writing this?"

"Not from what I know about him. Unless he's hiding his talent under the bed with his dirty magazines."

"Can you think of any callers who might be able to write like this?"

Shahla contemplated the question for a period of time. Finally, she said, "When I first started on the Hotline, there was this guy who called a lot who said he wrote poetry. But he wasn't from around here. In fact, he said he lived in Las Vegas."

"So he was calling long distance."

"For a while after 9/11 our 800 number was nationwide so that people suffering from—what's it called?—post traumatic stress disorder could call us. But as I understand it, the number cost too much to keep so now our 800 number is just for California. Anyway, since that change, he doesn't call as often as he did."

Shahla went and got a copy of the Green Book and pointed out a page to Tony. The Hotline handle for him was "Paul the Poet." His story was that he had been abused by his parents as a child.

The telephone rang. It was Tony's turn to answer it. A woman with a cultured voice was on the line, with a slight New York accent. She was definitely a cut above the usual Hotline caller. Tony immediately pegged her as living in West Los Angeles, perhaps Beverly Hills. He would try to get that information before the end of the call.

The call went on and on. She was middle-aged, married and divorced, and trying to decide what to do about her boyfriend. He had his pluses and minuses. In fact, she recited them so readily that Tony wondered whether she had already taken a sheet of paper, drawn a line down the middle, and written the pluses on one side and the minuses on the other.

While they talked, Shahla took a number of calls. At the end of two hours Tony figured that he and his caller had solved most of the world's problems. Or at least the problem of her boyfriend. She had a plan of action and thanked him for helping her arrive at it.

After Tony hung up, Shahla said, "I thought you were going to marry her."

"She's too old for me," Tony said laughing, "but it sounds like she has some money. Maybe it's not a bad idea." He looked at the clock on the wall of the listening room. It was almost ten. He said, "Time flies when you're straightening out the world. I want to make a copy of that poem before we get out of here."

"On the copier?"

"No. Flattening it on the copier might destroy any fingerprints. I'll enter it on one of the office computers and then print it out." Tony went to the administration room, turned on Patty's computer and typed in the poem, using Microsoft Word. He had honed his typing prowess writing papers in college and made short work of it. Then he printed it. Shahla asked him to print a copy for her. When he was through, he deleted the poem from the computer.

"No sense leaving evidence," Tony said. "Now, we'll replace the original poem in the envelope and place that in a larger envelope to preserve whatever there is to preserve." He used his handkerchief to handle the documents, determined to keep them as clean as possible. "Then I'll take the evidence to the police station."

"Tonight?"

"Yes, tonight. No time like the present. And I need to explain to them how my fingerprints got on the envelope."

"I'll go with you."

"We've been through this, Shahla."

"This is different than the other night. First, it's Friday night. There's no school tomorrow. And it's only a few blocks to the police station. I'll call my mother and tell her exactly where I'm going so she won't worry." Tony's look must have been disbelieving because she said, "Yes, some teenagers do actually communicate with their parents. Besides, I never got a chance to tell you why I think Martha may be a suspect."

Shahla whipped out her cell phone before Tony could mount a solid defense and got her mother on the line. Her side of the conversation went something like this: "Hi, Mom, it's me. I won't be home for a little while…I have to go to the police station…Just to give them some evidence…Don't worry, I'm going with Tony. He's a lot older, but he's pretty strong. He'll keep us safe…I'll see you later…Bye."

"Do I have to show her my muscles and my AARP card?" Tony asked.

"It's okay. I may have exaggerated a little, but she trusts me."

CHAPTER 10

The guard who walked out with them was a middle-aged nonentity. Tony wondered whether he had been the one on duty the night Joy was killed but decided not to ask him because he didn't want to get trapped into a long discussion about what had happened to her.

There was one slight deviation to the plan. Tony had Shahla drive her car home, and he followed her. It was a couple of miles out of their way, but he didn't want to have to return her to the mall in the middle of the night. She ran inside her house and told her mom she was riding to the police station in his car.

"What kind of a car is this?" Shahla asked as she returned and settled into the passenger's seat.

"It's a Porsche Boxter." Tony was proud of his car, the one outward sign that he had accomplished something in his life. Well, there was the townhouse, which he had shoehorned himself into, but he still needed to have Josh live there as a tenant to come up with the payments. He had leased the Porsche—a manageable down payment, and reasonable monthly payments made him look respectable. Of course, when the lease ran out, he would be left with nothing. But he would cross that bridge…

"It's small. And it sounds as if the engine is behind us."

"It's behind our seats. Located for maximum stability."

Shahla looked nervously over her shoulder. "I hope it stays there."

Those were not the comments of a car buff. Shahla wasn't impressed. Maybe he should have settled for a Honda. He made it all the way up to third gear on Pacific Coast Highway and felt a little better as he listened to the purr of the engine. He needed to take a trip to the desert so he could let it run for a while, like a racehorse. It was not built for the stop-and-go driving of a city.

They arrived at the police station within five minutes. Bonita Beach was a compact city. Joy's murder had reverberated through it like a fire siren and left the residents feeling betrayed and anxious. The full impact to the city and to the Hotline had grown on Tony as his shock had worn off, and now he wanted to find the murderer as much as Shahla did.

They walked into the station together and approached the counter, behind which sat a young female officer doing something with a computer. After a few seconds, she looked up and said, "Can I help you?"

Tony explained that they had some possible evidence for the murder investigation. He expected her to just take the envelope and their names, but she said, "Detective Croyden's here. I'll get him. Have a seat in there."

She pointed to a doorway that led into a conference room. Tony and Shahla went into the room containing a worn wooden table and worn wooden chairs. On the wall were posters relating to drugs, alcohol, and other temptations of the flesh. The posters exhorted the reader against yielding to these temptations.

Shahla said, "'Can I help you?' means, 'Am I able to help you?' I was tempted to say, 'I don't know. Can you?'"

"So what should she have said?" Tony asked. He had never paid much attention in English class.

"'May I help you?' That asks for permission."

"Thank you for the lesson."

"No charge."

"Well, if it isn't two of my favorite people. I might have known I'd see you on Friday the thirteenth."

Detective Croyden had entered the room while they had their backs to the door, looking at posters. Tony turned around and said, "Working late, aren't you?" He knew why Croyden might be sarcastic with him, but not Shahla, unless she had let some of her dislike of the police show when he talked to her.

"Crime never sleeps," Croyden said. "What have you got for me?"

He didn't ask them to sit down, and he didn't take a seat himself, so the three of them remained standing. Tony thought he looked tired. There were bags under his eyes, and his facial wrinkles were pronounced, as was his broken nose. Tony pointed to the brown envelope he had set on the table and told Croyden what was inside. He related how he had found and handled the white envelope, mentioning that several of his own fingerprints might be on it.

"But at least you came to your senses before you covered it with your prints," Croyden said, with what might be faint praise. "Do you know what's inside it?"

Tony missed a beat while he reconsidered his first answer and then said, "No." He hoped Croyden hadn't noticed his involuntary head-fake.

"All right, we'll take a look at it. You said the Hotline office door was locked. That's good. Did anybody knock or did you hear any sounds outside the door?"

He directed this question to both of them. They shook their heads.

"All right. Tony, do you have any objection to the desk officer taking your fingerprints so that we can eliminate the ones on the envelope?"

He could probably refuse, at least temporarily, but what would be the point. "No objection." It appeared that Croyden was dismissing them.

Shahla said, "Detective Croyden, since the person who left the envelope knows where the Hotline is, doesn't that sound to you as if the…killer might work for the Hotline?"

Croyden looked at her for a while, and Tony began to wonder whether he was ogling her breasts instead of contemplating his answer. He finally said, "Sha…" and stumbled.

"Shahla."

"Shahla, first of all, we don't know whether the envelope was left by the killer. Assuming it was, there is a possibility that he—or she—works for the Hotline. But other people know where it is, too."

"You mean, like ex-listeners. But we just moved to this building six months ago, so that eliminates most of them."

"A smart caller could find out. One of your listeners could have slipped and given away your location to a caller. Like the Chameleon. I told Nancy she had a security leak big enough to drive a Hummer through."

Tony said, "It's my observation that the listeners are very security conscious. I don't know how the Chameleon might have found out."

"But you know and I know that some of these guys can sweet-talk the teenyboppers on the phone, and they'll lose their heads. Look at all these young girls who are seduced on the Internet."

"We're not like them," Shahla said hotly. "We've been through the training and, anyway, we're a lot smarter than the dippy girls who look for love online."

"What have you found out about the Chameleon?" Tony asked to try to defuse the situation.

"Still working on it," Croyden said stiffly. "Did you get any calls from him today?"

"No." If there had been calls from him during the previous shifts, his name would have been on the board.

"He hasn't called since you went after him. Looks like you scared him away. And made our job harder."

Tony was tempted to make a retort about the police not being able to find him, even with subpoenaed call records, but Shahla didn't know about those.

Croyden said, "Listen, I'd love to chat with you, but I've got work to do. Tony, come over to the counter, and we'll get your prints."

"What if there are prints on the envelope that aren't on file somewhere?" Shahla asked.

"We'll try to match them against any suspects' prints. Why, did you touch the envelope? Do we need to take your prints?"

"No," Shahla said hastily. "I...don't want to get my fingers dirty."

***

"I'll have a piece of cherry pie with a big scoop of vanilla ice cream on top," Shahla said to the waitress at the Beach House, the local all-night diner.

"Uh…coffee—decaf," Tony said when she looked at him. He didn't want to stay awake the rest of the night.

"Well, at least you're not anorexic," Tony said to Shahla. "But we can't eliminate the possibility that you're a binge eater." It had been Shahla's idea to stop here.

"I'm not a binge eater unless you call eating all the time bingeing."

It was true. She was always munching on something at the Hotline. "So how do you maintain your girlish figure?"

"I'm on the cross-country team."

"You didn't tell me that."

"A girl doesn't tell all her secrets."

"I thought you were going to get a job."

"With all that's been happening, I haven't had time to look for a job. But what about you? I don't know anything about you except that you own a condo…"

"Town house."

"…you own a town house and drive a noisy car."

"I'm one of those poor people who have to work for a living."

"What do you do?"

"I'm marketing manager for an Internet company that gives people who are dissatisfied with their weight or the appearance of their bodies alternatives as to what to do."

"You mean like plastic surgery?"

"Yeah, and having their stomachs stapled."

"Ugh, gross. Who would want to do any of that?"

"Lots of people. When you're young and have a perfect body, you don't realize that not everybody else does. Do you know how many teenagers want nose jobs or even boob jobs?"

"I don't have a perfect body."

"Okay, the violins are playing, but I don't want to hear about it and 99.9% of the rest of the world doesn't want to, either."

Shahla smiled. "Tony, you're funny. So what do you do when you aren't working or driving your noisy car?"

Or going out with women. But his love life was in a tailspin, and he wasn't about to discuss it. "I like to hike." Although he hadn't been hiking for a long time. And his gut showed it.

"Where do you like to hike?"

"Have you ever been up the Palm Springs Tramway?"

"No."

"Well, from the top of the tram you can hike up Mt. San Jacinto. It's beautiful up there."

"I'd like to do that sometime."

The waitress brought their food, and Shahla dove into her pie and ice cream. Tony sipped on his decaf. After he had allowed her to take several bites, he said, "Tell me about why you think Martha might be a suspect."

"Jealousy. Joy was the star of the volleyball team, and Martha was riding the bench, mostly. Now she's replaced Joy in the lineup as an outside hitter. But she's not as good as Joy and never will be." Shahla emphasized the last sentence.

"That doesn't mean she killed Joy. Jealousy? There must be more to it than that."

"How about insane jealousy? They've known each other all their lives, and Joy has always been better at everything. School. Sports. Attracting boys."

"How do you fit into this?"

"What do you mean?"

"You said that they've known each other all their lives. But Joy was your best friend. Couldn't you be feeling a little jealousy because of their closeness?"

Shahla glowered at him and took a big bite of pie.

"Well, look who's here."

Tony knew who it was even before he raised his eyes. He would know his ex-girlfriend's voice anywhere. And Carol was with a man—not a bad looking man, a prosperous-looking man. Tony felt a twinge of something inside. And she was looking good, with a skirt and sweater that didn't hide her curves. Her short brown hair with red highlights set off a smiling and perfectly proportioned face. No need for a nose job there. And she looked happy.

"Hi, Carol," he said belatedly. "Uh, this is Shahla. Shahla works on the Hotline with me."

"Working the late shift, eh?" Carol said, pointedly looking at her watch. Tony realized it was almost midnight. "Hi, Shahla. I'm so glad to meet you. This is Horace."

Tony awkwardly stood up from the booth and shook hands with Horace. He didn't see a ring through his nose, but maybe it was invisible.

"Well, we won't keep you," Carol said. "It must be way past Shahla's bedtime. But it was great to see you both." She tucked her hand into Horace's arm and guided him to a table in the corner.

"Who was that?" Shahla asked, her eyes wide.

"That was my ex-girlfriend," Tony said, following Carol with his own eyes and wondering how she still had such control over his emotions.

"She's very pretty. But..."

"Pushy? Sarcastic?"

"I didn't want to say anything bad about her."

"You don't have to. I know all her faults by heart."

***

"I love your house."

Tony had driven Shahla home, and they were sitting in his car in the driveway of a roomy and modern two-story house—the kind Tony would like to be able to afford someday. A house without attached neighbors.

"Fortunately, my father had lots of life insurance. And my mom works."

"Your father? Your father is...?"

"My father is dead."

"I'm sorry. I didn't know that." Tony couldn't imagine what it was like to lose a parent. Both of his parents were still alive.

Alan Cook

"He was murdered."

"Ohmygod."

"It's been long enough so that I can talk about it. Five years. But the pain never goes away."

"It must be very hard for you." Before taking the class he wouldn't have known what to say. But that didn't seem strong enough, somehow.

Shahla was silent. And Tony didn't know what else to say. Should he ask for details? It was time for her to go into the house, but he didn't want to push her to get out of the car. That would seem heartless. He saw a light on in an upstairs window. Perhaps her mother had heard them drive in. As Shahla had said, his wasn't the quietest car in the world. At least Mom would know her daughter was safe.

"My father was coming home from a meeting at night," Shahla said softly. She seemed to be speaking to herself. "He stopped at a place like a 7-Eleven to get a loaf of bread or something. A man came into the store and pulled a gun on the clerk. I don't think he even saw my father. The clerk gave him the money, and the robber was going to take him to the back of the store, probably to shoot him. My father intervened, and the bastard shot him."

"Oh." When Shahla remained silent, Tony said, "And the clerk?"

"The robber lost his cool at that point. He shot at the clerk and then took off. The clerk was wounded, but he survived. That's how we know what happened."

"And they didn't get him?"

"No, they did. But the police screwed it up. They didn't read him his rights, or something. The man made a confession, but the court threw it out. It was a big mess. He never went to jail."

"No wonder you don't like the police."

Tony had been looking straight ahead out the car window at the house, but Shahla was silent so long that he stole a look at her. In the moonlight he could see tears running down her cheeks. He felt very awkward. He should do something to comfort her, but what?

She laid her head on his shoulder. He didn't dare move. He felt tense and uncomfortable. He had never felt that way with a girl before. After what seemed like an eternity, but was probably no more than five minutes, she lifted her head and said, "I have to go."

She gave him a quick kiss on the cheek and got out of the car. After she entered the house and closed the door, Tony sat for a minute, with conflicting emotions. Then he started the car, revved the engine, and backed out of the driveway.

CHAPTER 11

Nobody stopped Tony as he walked through the door into the gymnasium. He knew that a visitor entering the high school campus was supposed to report to the administration office first, but school was over for the day and, anyway, the gymnasium was next to the parking lot, somewhat removed from the classrooms.

The inside of the building immediately brought back memories of every gymnasium he had ever been in, with its wooden pull-out bleachers and the basketball nets at either end. And perhaps a faint odor of sweat, or was that his imagination? Tony could remember his own days on his high school basketball team, vividly, although his memories consisted mostly of him riding the bench while the taller, quicker and more talented players received the playing time.

A volleyball net dominated the center of the floor. A couple of dozen fans were scattered throughout the bleachers, some students, some parents. A few may have been grandparents. He was too old to be a student and too young to be a parent. Where did he fit in? Feeling self-conscious, Tony picked a seat near the door of the gym and put his cell phone on vibrate. If he received a call, he would run outside and take the call there. He didn't want to have the background noise of a sporting event if Mona, his boss, called. And since it was 3:30 in the afternoon, that was a real possibility.

Tony hadn't responded positively to Shahla's feeling that Martha might be Joy's killer, thinking that it sounded more like jealousy on Shahla's part. Martha and Joy had enjoyed a certain amount of intimacy over the years, in spite of the supposed differences in their ability. He had decided, however, that if he was going to actively assist in the investigation, every lead was worth following up, to determine if it should be reported to Detective Croyden. But he didn't want Shahla present to color his judgment.

The teams were huddling around their coaches; the match was about to start. The Bonita Beach players wore white home uniforms with red numbers on the shirts. The other team was dressed in green. The players on either side placed their hands together in the center of their circle and shouted bonding words, intended to psych them up for the battle to come. Then the six starters of each team trotted onto the court.

Tony had no trouble picking out Martha from Shahla's description. She was tall and lanky and looked a bit awkward, in a body that had grown faster than her coordination. Acne spoiled her otherwise pretty face, indelibly marking her as a teenager, even though with her size she could have been a lot older.

The female referee, who sat on a platform at courtside, blew her whistle and gestured with her arm. A Bonita Beach player served the ball and the game began. Tony was immediately impressed by the quality of the play. Of course, here in the beach volleyball capital of the world, outstanding players were the rule, but Tony, who had grown up in western New York, was always fascinated with them.

Each player knew her role. One of the back players would dig out a smash so hard that Tony barely saw it and bump it to the setter. The Bonita Beach setter moved like a ballet dancer. She handled good balls and bad balls alike, making perfect sets, low, high, and sometimes backwards over her head in response to secret signals that Tony didn't understand.

Unfortunately, the Bonita Beach hitters didn't do as well. They scored some kills, but they also hit balls out of bounds or into the net. And too often two of the opposing players would leap at the same time as the hitter and block the ball back into the Bonita Beach court, often for a point or a side out.

In the middle of the first game, Tony felt his cell phone vibrate. He got up from his seat and walked quickly through the door of the gym, extracting the phone from his shirt pocket as he went. Outside he pressed the Talk button and said, "This is Tony."

Hotline to Murder

"Tony, Mona."

"Hi." Several students were talking loudly nearby. He walked away from them, hoping their voices wouldn't carry over the phone.

"How is that presentation coming for the lunch tomorrow?"

He was presenting the company program to a group of doctors. Mona, who didn't usually accompany him for these presentations, was going with him. Everything had to be perfect.

"It's almost ready. I've got one more call to make, and then I'm coming back to the office to work on it. I should be there by six." It was the correct thing to do. Mona was a workaholic, and he knew she'd still be there. He looked at his electronic organizer. "Oh, I forgot. I'm supposed to work at the Hotline tonight. Well, maybe I can skip that."

"Do you have any calls scheduled for tomorrow morning?"

"Well, no."

"Can't you finish the presentation then? I don't want you to miss the Hotline. I've noticed a change in you since you started there. You're more sensitive to people."

"Thanks. Yeah, I guess I can finish it in the morning." That's what he had been planning to do before Mona called. And now it was her idea, which was good. And his working on the Hotline had also been her idea. Whatever it took to keep her happy. Within limits.

They said goodbye, and Tony walked back inside. As he took his seat, Martha spiked the ball into the net. She hit the ball hard, but not always where she wanted it to go. Occasionally she scored with a blistering shot, and the handful of spectators would yell their approval. When she learned to control her shots, she would be a standout. Tony guessed that would happen within two years. She did better on defense. Using her height and jumping ability to advantage, she blocked several shots.

Tony hadn't seen Joy play volleyball, but he suspected that she had looked a lot like Martha on the court—with better coordination. Shahla said she had been a league all-star. Bonita Beach could have used her today. The opponents lacked an outstanding player, but their teamwork eventually paid off in a close victory. Their players were ecstatic. They probably hadn't beaten Bonita Beach for a long time.

After the game, the Bonita Beach players congratulated the players of the other team, an act of good sportsmanship Tony appreciated. As the sweat-soaked players headed toward the locker room, he stepped in front of Martha and said, "Nice game, Martha."

She glanced at him with a who-is-this-guy look, made a rueful face and said, "Thanks."

"I'm Tony, from the Hotline," he said, falling into step beside her. She was taller than he was.

"Oh." She stopped walking and faced him. "I've heard about you. What are you doing here?"

Who had talked to her about him? "I've been reading good things about your team, and I wanted to see it in action."

"Yeah, right. It was good before Joy…" her voice broke, "when Joy was on the team."

"That's what I want to talk to you about," Tony said. "May I buy you a coke at the Beach House?" It was only a few blocks away.

"I've got to shower. And I've got a lot of homework."

"I'll wait here until you shower. And I'll only take a few minutes of your time." Tony gave her his best pickup smile, the one he had used so successfully in college.

"Well, all right. I'll meet you outside in a few minutes."

Tony congratulated himself on still having the old charm, but he suspected that the reason she had accepted had more to do with the fact that they both worked on the Hotline. That created a bond between people.

***

"Joy was my best friend," Martha said, stirring the milkshake she had ordered, with a straw. "I loved her. We grew up together. We did everything together. We learned to play volleyball together."

Shahla had also said that Joy was her best friend. This tended to confirm his jealousy theory—not that Martha was jealous of Joy, but that Shahla was jealous of Martha. He said, "I suppose the other players were a little envious of the fact that Joy was an all-star."

They had driven to the Beach House in separate cars. Many of the Bonita Beach students had their own cars, or at least had ready access to cars. This amazed Tony, who hadn't had a car until he had bought one for himself after he finished college. He wondered if this affluence was good for them.

Martha shook her head. "It doesn't work that way. When you're part of a team, you want the team to win. With Joy on the team, we were winners. Without Joy, we're…well, we're kind of mediocre. And she didn't have a big head. She was a team player. We shouldn't have lost today. With Joy, we would have won easily."

She was lecturing him. Could she fake that level of intensity? Tony knew from his own experience as a teenager that they could be devious. But she sounded sincere. Seeing her up close, he realized that when she lost her acne, she would be a knockout. And when her coordination improved, she would be a good volleyball player. She didn't have to take a backseat to anybody. He sipped his black coffee and shifted tactics. "Do you have any idea who might have killed Joy?"

"Detective Croyden asked me that question. It sounds crazy, but maybe it was somebody who wants the Bonita Beach volleyball team to lose. We've been dominating the league for years. The other teams would give a lot to beat us. You saw how they celebrated today. And it's not just the kids. It's the parents. When I was playing AYSO soccer, sometimes the referees had to red-card a rowdy parent."

"Well, that narrows it down to a few hundred suspects."

Martha smiled. "It's just my idea. I don't know of anybody in particular."

"When Detective Croyden asked me what I was doing the night Joy was killed, I realized that I had nobody to vouch for me. Did you have that problem too?"

Martha noisily sucked the dregs of her milkshake through the straw and looked at Tony. She said, "I was studying at the library. When it closed at nine, I went over to visit Joy. She didn't like to work alone at night."

It took a moment for this to sink in. "You saw Joy the night she was killed?"

Martha nodded. "I was just there for a few minutes. I didn't take any calls because I wasn't working."

"What time did you leave the Hotline?"

"About 9:30."

"Did you walk out with the guard?"

"No. I left by myself."

"And then did you go home?"

Martha shook her head. "I went and walked on the beach. Alone. I sometimes do that. I didn't get home until about eleven."

"How did Detective Croyden react to you telling him this?"

"He didn't say anything; just wrote it all down. But he did ask me a lot of questions about my relationship with Joy. I think he was satisfied, especially because I volunteered that I had seen Joy. If I hadn't told him, he wouldn't have known."

"Has it occurred to you," Tony asked, "that you might have been the one to get killed?"

"Yeah. All the time." Martha had a haunted look on her face. "I feel guilty about it. That Joy got it instead of me. Or that I didn't stick around until she left. I might have been able to prevent it. I have nightmares about that night. It's strange, but as a result, I'm working harder to be a better volleyball player. And a better person."

CHAPTER 12

Tony arrived at the Hotline before Shahla. She had signed up to work every shift he worked. Although he knew she had done it only because she hoped that he could help solve Joy's murder, he felt good about it, because it meant she trusted him more than the other men and boys on the Hotline. Still, there was the possibility that he wouldn't meet her expectations. Again. He thought back to his encounter with the Chameleon.

A boy and girl were working the four-to-seven shift. Tony said hello to them but didn't bother to introduce himself. They left before Shahla arrived, so she didn't get the opportunity to quiz them about what they had been doing the night Joy was killed. Tony was glad, because he became embarrassed when she did that. He guessed he wasn't cut out to be a detective.

He signed in and took the good seat by the window. No sooner had he sat down than the phone rang. He answered it with his usual greeting: "Central Hotline. This is Tony."

"I'm fifteen, and I'm a runaway."

There was nothing like being smacked in the face by the first pitch. It was a girl's voice. Tony thought fast. He said, "Are you safe where you are right now?"

"I'm at a phone booth." She named an intersection in Santa Monica. "And I'm not going back home."

Tony decided not to ask her reasons. It wasn't his job to judge her. It was his job to make sure she was safe. Shahla had just come in through the door he had left unlocked for her. He put the call on the speaker and looked out the window. The sun was setting. He didn't want the girl to be out there alone in the dark.

"Do you have any friends or relatives who can help you?" Tony asked.

"Not here. Not nearby."

She sounded frightened. She may be having second thoughts, but whatever crisis impelled her to leave home must outweigh her fear. Tony was frantically leafing through the directory of available services in Southern California. He said, "There are shelters you can go to. Some of them will pick you up."

At that moment, his eyes focused on such a shelter with a Santa Monica address. Thank God. "I've got a number for you. Do you have money so you can call the number or do you want me to call it for you? Oh, they take collect calls."

"I've got some money."

"Do you have a pencil and paper?"

"Yes."

"Okay, write this down." He gave her the number. "Call it immediately. If they can't help you, call us back. Okay?"

"Okay. Thanks."

"And call us back to let us know that you're all right."

She promised and hung up. Tony hated to lose the connection. The chances were that she wouldn't call back.

"She'll be okay."

Tony looked up into Shahla's dark eyes.

She said, "That's a tough call because we probably won't find out what happened. But you did the best you could."

What if that wasn't good enough? Tony continued to brood about it.

"I see you grabbed the good seat."

Shahla feigned being upset and sat down at another table.

He had to shake himself out of his depression. "You snooze, you lose."

"I had to take my mom to her class. It was the only way I could get the car."

Apparently, they were a one-car family. Unusual for Bonita Beach. But with her father dead.... She had a tough road to travel with only one parent.

Shahla went to the snack room and came back with her usual plate of chips. She said, "Have you thought over what I told you about Martha?"

He had not told her he was going to talk to Martha. He was hoping that as a result of their meeting he could report that she had an ironclad alibi and couldn't possibly be a suspect. Unfortunately, it hadn't turned out that way. Martha's alibi was clad in a light mist that could be blown away by a gentle breeze. However, Detective Croyden also knew that.

Tony wanted to keep Shahla out of it. He didn't believe Martha had a motive for murdering Joy, even though Shahla might not agree. If Shahla was jealous of Martha's relationship with Joy, she might do something she would regret.

"I think Detective Croyden has already talked to her. I understand he talked to all the members of the volleyball team."

"Who told you that?"

Who told him that? "I can't remember. Maybe Croyden did."

"But he hasn't talked to all the members of the Hotline."

"There are a lot more of us. And I think he's talked to everybody who knew Joy."

"How does he know who knew Joy?"

Tony didn't like getting the third degree. He said, "Let's work on that poem. Have you thought of anybody else who might have written it?"

"No. And before we start speculating, shouldn't we find out if there were any fingerprints on it?"

"How are we going to do that? I know. I'll call our Indian buddy and see if he'll tell us."

"Our Indian buddy?"

"Crooked Nose." Tony took out his cell phone and then extracted Detective Croyden's card from his wallet. Croyden had been working late on Friday. Maybe he was working the afternoon-evening shift to give him a better opportunity to talk to people who might have knowledge of Joy's murder.

"Tony, it's Native American, not Indian."

"Sorry. When I went to school they were still Indians." Tony called the number on the card. He could picture it being answered by the officer on the desk. He asked for Detective Croyden.

"Croyden."

"Hi Detective Croyden, this is Tony Schmidt."

"Tony Schmidt. What have you got for me?"

"A question. Were there any fingerprints on that envelope Shahla and I brought in?"

"Your fingerprints were on it."

"Okay, but were there any other prints?"

"I suppose you'll bug me until I tell you. No. There were no other prints on the envelope or on the paper inside. Whoever sent it was probably wearing gloves. They shouldn't show those damn police shows on TV. They make the perps too smart."

"One more question. What was in the envelope?"

"I don't have to tell you that. You already know."

"How would I know?"

"You're going to play dumb, is that it? Okay, no games. It was a poem."

"Written by the killer?"

"Either that or it's a prank."

"May I have a copy of the poem?"

"Go flog yourself."

Croyden hung up. Shahla was on a call. As soon as she saw that Tony was free, she put the call on the speaker. The voice sounded like a woman with a cold.

"...stare at me when I go out without wearing a bra. I think they can see my nipples. It makes me very uncomfortable."

Shahla pressed the Mute button and said, "It's the Chameleon."

The Chameleon? Oh, yes, he sometimes imitated women. "How do you know?"

"Because I've heard him use this voice before."

The breathy voice was saying, "What do you think I should do?"

Tony said, "Try to find out if he wrote the poem."

Shahla cancelled the Mute and said, "So, do you wear tops with spaghetti straps?"

"Spaghetti straps. I love to wear spaghetti straps. Do you like to wear spaghetti straps?"

"Sometimes. But we have to wear bras in school. Do you know that the assistant principal has the job of bra-snapper?" Shahla winked at Tony. "It's his job to make sure all the girls are wearing bras. I don't like it when he checks from the front—and his hand slips. On purpose."

"It's so…when men have their hands all over you." The Chameleon dragged this out, making it sound as if the hands were at work on him.

"He's masturbating," Shahla mouthed.

"Hang up," Tony mouthed back.

Shahla shook her head.

"I don't like to wear a bra," the Chameleon said in a breathy monotone. "I like my tits to be free of restraint. It makes me feel so…free."

"I know a poem about spaghetti straps," Shahla said.

"Men shouldn't be allowed to make us feel uncomfortable. We should be able to wear what we want."

"She wears a summer dress, spaghetti straps to hold it up…"

"I love spaghetti straps. I could wear them every day."

"You and I have a lot in common. Let's get together. What do you think?"

There was a click.

"I think you violated just about every Hotline listening rule," Tony said. "Again." He was relieved that the Chameleon had hung up.

"Just following orders, General."

"But I didn't ask you to try to meet him again."

"Cold feet? I thought we were in this together."

"Anyway, you scared him off. It's probably just as well. And he didn't pick up on the poem."

"I guess I was a little abrupt. But I don't think he wrote the poem. He's about as poetic as a mud fence. But that doesn't mean he isn't the killer."

"Okay, but let's let Croyden handle him. Fill out a call report, and we'll leave it for Nancy to give to him. But don't mention the poem."

"Aye aye, sir." Shahla gave an imitation of a salute. "I don't know what you think of me, but I'm not really a bad person. I get good grades. I don't smoke, drink, or do drugs. And if I listen to dirty talk, it's because it's part of my job."

Tony was taken aback for a moment. She was fishing for a compliment. He was not great at giving compliments. "I-I think you're doing a super job. Just don't do anything risky."

Shahla held his eyes. "Do you care what happens to me?"

"Of course I care what happens to you."

Shahla seemed satisfied with that. She filled out the report while Tony took a call from somebody who wanted a referral to a therapist. When he hung up, Shahla was on another call. It wasn't until an hour later that they were both free at the same time. Tony still figured that their best bet to help the investigation was to try to track down the writer of the poem, especially since Croyden didn't have any leads there.

He looked up the information on Paul the Poet. The page in the Green Book said that Paul still lived at home, even though he was in his late twenties. He apparently had a job and girlfriends, so he wasn't completely stunted. That he lived at home didn't square with his claim of having been abused by his parents. But he did admit to sleeping with a teddy bear and a night-light.

"It's funny," Shahla said as they read it. "When you talk to him, he brings up this abuse issue, but then if you ask him where he lives, he says he lives at home. I asked him once who paid his phone bill. He didn't give a straight answer. And I think he has a job. It doesn't all make sense."

"I've discovered that our callers don't always make sense. How often have you talked to this guy?"

"Many times." Shahla spun her chair around to face him. "He's one of our more intelligent callers, in spite of the contradictions. We actually had some good conversations about poetry. He read a few of his poems to me."

"And were they really good?"

"They weren't bad. They showed talent."

"So you think he could have written the poem?"

Shahla hesitated and then said, "He's the best guess I have right now."

"So he just happened to be in Southern California. And he just happened to write a poem he wanted to deliver to the Hotline. And somehow, he found out the address of the Hotline."

"Sounds farfetched, doesn't it?"

"Especially if he's going to be a murder suspect. Why would he come all the way here to murder somebody? Did he ever show animosity to you on the phone?"

"No, he was one of the easiest repeat callers to talk to. He was always appreciative. He often thanked me for listening to him." Shahla kicked the floor with her feet and spun her chair around, a child at play. "I guess we can eliminate him."

Tony furrowed his brow. "Still, it would be nice to talk to him. Did he ever give any indication of where in Vegas he lives? Or where he works? There's nothing here."

"Not that I can remember."

"Wait. The book gives a last name for him. Vicksburg."

Shahla shrugged. "Who knows whether that's correct? Our callers use a lot of aliases."

"But since we don't ask for last names, he must have volunteered it. I'm going to Google him."

Tony went into the office and started up Patty's computer. It asked him to enter a password. He looked at Shahla, who had followed him.

"The password is 'm-i-g-i-b,'" Shahla said.

"How do you know that?"

"Patty told me. I helped her with some computer stuff one time."

"What does it mean?"

"She wouldn't tell me. But her boyfriend's name is Marty. So I remember it as, 'Marty is great in bed.'"

Tony didn't comment on that. He connected to the Internet and then the Google search engine. He typed in "Paul Vicksburg." On the first try he got mostly references to pages about Vicksburg, Mississippi, and the Civil War, so he modified his search with the word poet.

"He's got a website," Tony told Shahla, who had come in to see what he was doing. "And there's poetry on it."

They looked at the pages together. The poems were the kind of plaintive meanderings that had always put Tony to sleep, but he noticed that some of them did rhyme, just like the spaghetti strap poem. They showed the egotistical nature of a person who thought his problems were the most important problems in the world. Still, Tony realized, many people believed that, including some of the Hotline callers. Poets went a step further and put the thought into words.

"Is this the guy?" Tony asked Shahla, after she had read several of the poems.

She reread one of the poems and said, "He recited that poem to me on the phone. I'm sure of it. Does it say where he lives?"

It didn't, but there was a "Contact me" button. Tony clicked on it and found the poet's e-mail address. He said, "Let's say we want to arrange a meeting with him, like you're always trying to do with your beloved Chameleon. Would he respond better to an e-mail from a man or a woman?"

"A woman. He likes girls. Isn't this the point when we have to turn the evidence over to Detective Croyden?"

Tony smiled at her imitation of his voice and said, "I haven't been to Vegas for a while. I just might take a run up there. My car needs the exercise anyway. What's your e-mail address?" He added, "Keeping in mind that you're not going to be the one to meet him."

"Are you sure you want to do this? That's a long drive for probably nothing."

"You're the one who wants to follow up every lead."

"Yeah, but…"

Tony was surprised at Shahla's reluctance. It took him several minutes of talking before she agreed that this might be a good idea. But all at once her face lost its frown, and she smiled, like clouds parting to let the sun shine.

She said, "Okay, you're right. We need to check this out."

The first part of her e-mail address was "writeon," which was gender-neutral. Having the word "write" in it didn't hurt, either. Both of Tony's addresses, business and personal, had "tony" in them, so they agreed to use Shahla's. Shahla was able to log into her e-mail from Patty's computer.

Tony said, "You're the writer. Compose a note to him that he can't resist. Tell him you'd like to meet with him on Saturday afternoon. Let him name the place."

He watched as Shahla worked. She wrote fast and confidently and then made a few changes until she was satisfied: "Hi, Paul. I have read and enjoyed the poems on your website. They have spirituality that I find lacking in today's poets. As I read them, I am drawn into an ethereal world of promise. I would love to meet you. I heard from another one of your admirers that you live in Las Vegas. Is this true? It so happens that I will be in Las Vegas on Saturday. Can we get together in the afternoon? That would be fantastic. Name the time and place. Yours, Sally."

"'Spirituality' and 'ethereal world of promise'? What does all that mean?"

"Not a thing," Shahla said with a smile. "But poets love big words."

"You're too smart for your own good. Just remember, if he should happen to reply to this, I'm the one who's going to meet him, not you."

"Of course," Shahla said, her eyes wide with innocence. "I never thought anything else."

CHAPTER 13

As Tony opened the back gate to the small patio of his townhouse, he saw that all the downstairs lights appeared to be on. Then he heard explosions through the open sliding door and figured that Josh must be watching a war movie on his big-screen TV. He heard raucous laughter and knew that Josh had some of his friends over. On a Monday night.

This had happened before, and Tony thought he had put a stop to it. The rule was that Josh could have friends over on Friday or Saturday nights, but not the other nights. Tony had hinted that he would make an exception for a well-behaved woman, as long as Josh and the woman did whatever consenting adults do behind the closed door of Josh's bedroom, but Josh never seemed to have women over anymore. Was this the same Josh who had tried to date every coed at the University of Michigan?

Time for action. Tony slid open the screen door and entered the townhouse. He marched through the family room, down the short hallway, and into the living room. The scene was much as he had anticipated. Josh reclined on the reclining chair with a can of beer in his hand. Two men sat on the couch, each with his own can of beer. They were all casually dressed, in jeans and T-shirts touting athletic teams or running events that they undoubtedly hadn't participated in. If they were like Josh, their main exercise was elbow bending.

Spilled potato chips littered the carpet and were in danger of becoming a permanent part of the weave. The ubiquitous cooler sat on the floor at Josh's side. Tony glanced at the screen of the television

Alan Cook

set and recognized a scene from the movie, *Saving Private Ryan*. Nobody saw him for a few seconds. All eyes were intent on the screen. He cleared his throat, between explosions.

Josh turned his head toward Tony and said, "Noodles. You're home from the Hotstuff Line. The hero returns to collect his reward for valor."

Tony knew what was coming and stepped aside as Josh tossed a can of beer to him, so that most of the ice water flying in formation with it missed him as he reached out and deftly caught it with one hand. He had always had good hands. If he had only been taller and about twice as fast, he could have been a wide receiver. He popped open the beer and took a swig.

Josh aimed his remote at the TV and put the movie on Pause. "Noodles, I want you to meet two of my buds."

Josh named two names that didn't register in Tony's consciousness. He did shake hands with them, not bothering to apologize for having a wet and cold hand from the beer, because their hands were equally wet and cold.

"There was a time when Tony would have been here partying with us," Josh said. "But, alas, that doesn't happen anymore. Because Tony has been saved. Speaking of being saved, how went the battle tonight? Did you convince any queers with AIDS that were about to blow their brains out not to, even though that's probably a mistake? And was that underage babe working with you tonight? What's her name—Sarah?"

"Sally."

"Sally." He turned to his friends. "Tony has a tough job. He answers telephones and listens to the problems of people more fucked up than we are, all night. So you think you should feel sorry for him, right? But what you don't know is that while he's doing it, he hangs out with these teenage babes who don't wear any clothes."

"Cool," friend one said. "I wish I could get a job like that."

"The only problem," Josh said, standing up, "is that they have their bodies pierced in so many places that you can't touch them without getting stabbed."

"That's not true," Tony said, realizing how dorky he sounded.

Josh ignored him and said, "It's not just their ears, although some of them have enough metal in their ears to build a tank." He lifted his T-shirt and said, "Belly buttons." He pointed to his own belly button, which stuck out, along with the rest of his belly. "Wouldn't I look great with a navel ring?" He moved his belly in and out, using more muscles than Tony had seen him use in a while.

The friends laughed. Tony wondered how he could put a stop to this.

"Nipple rings." He pushed his T-shirt higher and grabbed one of his nipples with the same hand. The other hand still held a can of beer. "How do you suck on that with a ring in your mouth. Ugh. But worst of all is the clit ring. Does Sally have a clit ring, Tony?"

Tony had to restrain himself to keep from throwing his beer can at Josh. He said, "I want to talk to you in the other room. Now."

Josh was still playing to his friends. He shook his head and said, "When Noodles uses his school-teacher voice, I have to listen. It won't be pretty." He unpaused the movie and said, "I don't want you guys to have to hear it."

Tony led the way through a short hallway into the family room and then turned left into the kitchen, placing the maximum amount of distance between them and the living room. He turned to face Josh, who had followed him. He was seething so much he couldn't talk. Josh stood and sipped beer, an innocent look on his face.

"First of all," Tony said, finding his voice, "you're not supposed to have guys over during the week."

"Oh, yes. Dumb me." Josh struck himself on the forehead with the heel of his hand. "Dorm rules. But I figured since you weren't here, it would be okay. I planned to kick them out before you got home. Sorry. I lost track of the time. What time is it, anyway?"

"It's ten-thirty. And I don't care whether I'm home or not. You disturb the neighbors with all your noise."

"Okay, okay, I know when you're provoked. I'll tell them to leave now."

"Wait. I've got something more to say. I don't like the way you talk about the girls on the Hotline. In fact, I don't like the

Alan Cook

way you talk about all women. You know what you are? You're a misogynist."

"A what-gynist? Is that anything like a gynecologist? Tony, my boy, you have flipped. You have absolutely flipped. Do you know what that job has done to you? It has made you into a wimp, a wuss. A goddamned wuss. You are not the same Tony I knew. And I don't like the new model."

"Well then, maybe you should move out."

This stopped Josh in his tracks. He became quiet. Gone was the bluster. His face became as red as his hair. He stared at Tony. "Move out? You want me to move out?"

"If you don't like what you call the new me. If you don't like the rules around here. If you can't become a civilized member of society. Don't you think, Josh, that after all these years, it's time for us to grow up? If you can't handle that, then yes, you should move out."

"I'll be out of here in thirty days." Josh turned on his heel and stomped out of the room.

***

Tony couldn't sleep. He was having second thoughts about Josh moving out. For financial reasons. How was he going to make the payments on the townhouse without Josh? He might have to get another housemate. And as obnoxious as Josh was, at least Tony knew him and his habits.

He knew that although Josh might spill beer and potato chips on the living room rug, he wouldn't completely trash the place. He had a steady job and paid his bills. He might bring in loud friends to party with, but at least they wouldn't be drug dealers and hoods. He was a bigot, but Tony could ignore that. Most of the time. He might badmouth women, but he didn't physically abuse them. He might belittle Tony's job on the Hotline, but he wouldn't actually interfere with anything Tony did.

Maybe he should talk to Josh in the morning. Well, he probably wouldn't see him in the morning because Josh would still be in bed when he left. But tomorrow evening for sure. This thought didn't give Tony peace. There was something else. Something unresolved. He had called Josh a misogynist. A woman hater. He had never thought of Josh as hating women before. Was this true?

Tony started remembering things. Josh aggressively pursuing women in college. But did he do it because he liked them? Sometimes it had seemed to Tony as if he had a score to settle. Josh had been his hero because he could get the girls. Tony had learned from him. Learned very well from him. But in spite of the reputation he had gained of picking them up and then dumping them, Tony's relationships had lasted longer than Josh's.

Tony couldn't remember Josh ever dating the same woman for more than a month or two. When the romances fizzled, it was always the woman's fault—never Josh's. Tony had met many of them. They were personable, good-looking, smart. No, Tony didn't believe that the women were always at fault. It was something about Josh.

Tony remembered things Josh had said. "Women were put on earth for our pleasure." "A broad lying on her back with a sack over her head and her legs spread is pretty much like every other broad." Were these the statements of a man who liked women?

And Josh's nickname for him—Noodles. It dated from college. A bunch of the guys and gals had been eating sushi and drinking sake at a Japanese restaurant. At some point, one of the guys and one of the gals went outside to the guy's van. The guy came back a while later and said the girl was in the van, stripped and waiting for anyone who wanted to have her. Josh had immediately volunteered.

When he returned, he tried to get Tony to go. "She's hot to trot, Tony. Never pass up a free piece of ass."

The prospect had sickened Tony. She was probably too drunk to know what she was doing, and the idea of following Josh and another guy almost made him puke. One or two others may have gone; Tony didn't remember. But Josh had never let Tony forget that he had failed, in Josh's eyes. Thus the nickname, Noodles. Tony would rather eat a bowl of noodles than get laid.

A thought struck Tony like a bolt of lightning. Did Josh hate women so much that he would murder a girl? A girl he envisioned to be part of a plot to alienate Tony from him? Impossible. But Josh did call Carol about him and that was out of character. He knew that the Hotline closed at ten p.m. because of the hours Tony had been working. Yes, but he didn't know where it was. Or did he?

Tony turned on the lamp beside his bed and sat up, more awake than ever. He got out of bed and walked silently from his bedroom into the study across the hall. He could hear Josh snoring behind the closed door of the third bedroom. Loudly. Snore, snore, then break for a few seconds. Then snore some more. It sounded like the snort of a mad bull before he charged. Josh always seemed to snore after he had been drinking.

Tony turned on a light in the study and stood in the doorway. From here he could see his bookcase. Standing on a shelf of the bookcase, in plain sight, was his notebook for the Hotline. It contained all his notes from the class. Tony went to the bookcase, picked up the notebook, and set it on his desk. He opened it up. The first page, neatly three-hole-punched, had printed on it the address of the Hotline and a map showing how to get there.

This information had been given to the students after they graduated from the class. Tony had never thought about hiding it from Josh. As far as he knew, Josh never went into his study. But Josh had been upset when Tony wouldn't tell him where the Hotline was. After all, they were supposed to tell each other everything, like fraternity boys. Of course, Tony had stopped telling Josh everything years ago, but he had never told Josh he wasn't telling him everything.

Where was Josh on the night of the murder? Tony realized that he didn't know. He hadn't seen Josh all evening. In fact, Josh had returned home after he had. After he was in bed. And as far as Tony could remember, Josh had never said anything about that evening, which wasn't like him. Because he still told Tony everything. Or did he?

There was nothing Tony could do about it now. Reluctantly, he went back to bed. But his mind wouldn't shut up. He did manage to get a few minutes of restless sleep before the alarm went off.

CHAPTER 14

Tony was running on coffee. It had been a long day, with several intense sales calls and a lot of driving. That, coupled with his lack of sleep and the late summer heat, made him feel as if he couldn't take another step. Or even get out of his car. And getting out of a Porsche was no mean feat.

He was parked in front of the Church of the Risen Lord. He had looked up the address after Nathan had said he was a member, out of curiosity more than anything else, since he had never heard of it. And today, after his last call, he had been in the neighborhood, if you could call being within five miles the neighborhood. He had gotten here with the help of his *Thomas Guide.* "Here" was somewhere northeast of the Los Angeles Airport.

It wasn't much of a church. The small building had obviously been used for something else before the Risen Lord had occupied it. It had no steeple or visible cross. No stained-glass windows. It did have a crude sign on the small, weed-infested lawn in front, announcing its name and telling when it had services. There were Thursday evening services at 7 p.m., which tended to support Nathan's story of where he had been during Joy's murder, assuming they went on for three hours.

Since he was here, he should do more than stare at the front from his car. Tony opened the car door and laboriously lifted himself up from the seat. It was hot in the open air after the coolness of the air-conditioned car, but evening was coming and with it cooler temperatures. That was something you could always count on in

Los Angeles. He shut the door and locked the car, looking around at other cars parked on the street. None were Porsches, but some were new. There was no indication that people feared that their cars would be stolen. And it was still broad daylight.

A small gravel parking lot sat beside the church, with weeds poking through the gravel. The only car in the lot was a Chevrolet that had a few miles on it. Maybe a few hundred thousand miles. Tony walked up the cracked sidewalk to the dilapidated front door. A coat of stain would help it, just as a coat of paint would help the stucco walls of the church.

Tony tried the door; it was unlocked. He opened it and stepped into the gloomy interior. The only light came from several windows along each side wall. He could make out wooden pews and a raised platform at the other end. In addition to a lectern, the platform supported a table with candlesticks and a picture of a man, probably Jesus. It was too dark to tell for sure. Some seats at one side of the platform might be for a choir. A small organ stood near them.

Nobody was in sight. He wasn't sure he wanted to talk to anybody, anyway. He stood at the back, wondering why Nathan was attracted to this particular church. It didn't look very substantial. He was about to leave when he heard footsteps resounding from contact with a hard floor, coming from somewhere behind the platform. He hesitated, wondering whether it would look as if he were up to something if he left now.

A man came through a doorway that Tony hadn't seen before, in the wall behind the platform. He was a big man, and he walked rapidly, with a purpose that gave Tony a moment of trepidation, until he realized that the man hadn't seen him. He took a step to attract the man's attention.

The man stopped halfway down the aisle that went between the rows of pews and said, in a deep voice, "How can I help you, brother?"

Tony's first thought was to wonder whether Shahla would claim that the man should have said, "How may I help you, brother?" He hesitated for an awkward moment and then decided that truth was the best policy. He said, "I know somebody who attends services here and I was curious."

The man came up to him and stuck out a giant hand saying, "I am the Reverend Luther Hodgkins."

Tony said, "Tony Schmidt," failing to match the resonance of the Reverend's voice. His hand got lost in that of the larger man. He was dark-skinned, with graying hair, and could have played football with Detective Croyden. He was dressed in a colorful Hawaiian shirt.

"Who is this parishioner of whom you speak?" Reverend Hodgkins asked, or rather rumbled.

"His name is Nathan..." Tony tried to remember Nathan's last name.

"Nathan Watson?"

"Watson...right. He's white."

"We do not discriminate at the Church of the Risen Lord. What has Nathan told you about the church?"

"Nothing, actually. He said he had attended an evening service here on Thursday, August 29."

Reverend Hodgkins stepped past Tony and opened the outside door, letting in a slanting ray of light from the setting sun, which momentarily blinded him. The Reverend turned around and surveyed Tony, who realized he had let in the sunlight so that he could see him better.

"Are you with the police?" the Reverend asked.

"No sir," Tony said, blinking to regain his eyesight. He stepped back from the doorway so that the sun wasn't in his face. "Nathan and I, ah, work together. I was interested in finding out more about the church."

"Nathan is a faithful member of the Church. However, I'm not surprised that he has not told you anything specific about our beliefs, because we have been ridiculed by nonbelievers in the past. However, if you are serious about wanting to learn the truth, I will be glad to enlighten you. Take a seat."

Reverend Hodgkins sat down at the end of the last pew and motioned Tony to sit in the pew across the aisle from him. Tony wasn't sure he wanted to learn so much about the Church that he

Alan Cook

be required to sit down to do it, but he was under the spell of the Reverend. He sat.

"First, I must apologize for the lack of lights," the Reverend said. "The electric company lists its employees among the nonbelievers. However, we will not be needing electricity or anything else of the material for very long."

As soon as Tony sat down, his feeling of tiredness came back to him, and he slumped on the hard, wooden bench. However, the statement of Reverend Hodgkins woke him up with a jolt. The Reverend was looking past him, lost in some sort of reverie. Tony waited for him to continue.

"All churches seek the truth. Few find the whole truth. Others have tried to pinpoint the Day of Judgment. They have failed, resulting in great embarrassment and financial loss. It is only now, with the advent of powerful computers and the Internet, that I have been able to do what others failed to do."

"The Day of Judgment?" Tony had been raised in a Protestant church-going family, but it had been years since he had been inside a church, except for weddings and his grandfather's funeral.

"The day when Christ shall return to earth and clasp the faithful to his bosom. The day when the believers shall rise triumphantly into heaven. The day when we will no longer need the worldly goods that keep us fettered. The day when the chains of greed and ambition shall be cast off."

The Reverend's voice grew louder as he talked, filling the small church auditorium. He was no longer seeing or speaking to Tony. He went on in the same vein, while Tony wondered whether he was going to preach a whole sermon. He apparently came back to reality, because he stopped after a couple of minutes.

Tony said, "Reverend, when is this Day of Judgment?"

Reverend Hodgkins looked at him. When he spoke, it was back in his normal voice, which was loud enough. "It is for the believers to know when the great day will occur. Our parishioners will be ready. Ready to be swept up to glory."

"In other words, I have to join your Church in order to receive this information?"

"In one word—yes."

Tony remembered hearing stories about people who thought they had pinpointed the Day of Judgment. "So all your followers are selling or giving away all their possessions and meeting on a hilltop on this glorious day?"

Reverend Hodgkins fixed Tony with a disconcerting stare. Perhaps a suspicious stare. He stood up. Tony stood up. The Reverend walked to the entrance and said, "Brother, I have things to do, and I'm sure you do too. I hope that God goes with you on your journey."

The interview was over. Tony had enough presence of mind to shake hands with the Reverend as he went out the door and say, "Thank you for a most enlightening conversation. God be with *you*, Reverend."

The Reverend stood in the doorway and watched Tony as he climbed into his Porsche. Or perhaps he was looking at the car. There was a gleam in the Reverend's eye that Tony didn't think he had seen before in a man of the cloth.

CHAPTER 15

When Tony reached home, he wanted nothing more than to drink a beer, eat a frozen dinner heated in the microwave, collapse in front of the television set for a couple of hours, and then retire to bed for some much-needed sleep. As he pulled into his carport, he saw that Josh's car wasn't in the space next to his and that buoyed his spirits. He wasn't up to facing Josh at the moment, especially after their fight last night.

The temporary uplift was dashed when he opened the refrigerator and discovered that all the beer was gone. Josh and his buddies had drunk it all. Unless there was some left in the cooler. He fruitlessly looked for that container in the living room and finally went out onto the patio and discovered it upside down, where it had been left to drain. Beerless.

He settled for a glass of white wine from a half-empty bottle in the refrigerator. It was the cheap stuff from Trader Joe's, but it wasn't bad. He found a dinner in the freezer that he knew would be the consistency of wood chips and dirt, with a taste to match, but he didn't care. He placed the container in the microwave and turned it on.

Tony sipped his wine and checked the messages on his answering machine. Two for Josh, both from males. None for him. While he waited for the dinner to heat up, he thought about his roommate. He remembered for the first time in his busy day that he had wondered last night whether Josh was Joy's killer. Now, after a day had elapsed, he couldn't picture Josh as a murderer, but he knew

Alan Cook

the thought would nag him unless he made sure. He had to find out what Josh had been doing the night of the murder.

Josh was probably at work at the television station, but he might be coming home any time. Tony raced upstairs and into Josh's room. He turned on the light and then remembered that since Josh's room faced the carport area, if Josh drove in right now, he would see the light on in his room and become suspicious.

Damn. Tony turned off the light, went down the hall to his own room, and retrieved a small flashlight. This was going to make the job harder. Returning to Josh's room, he wondered whether Josh had left his calendar there. Tony knew that Josh had recently started using an electronic calendar at work, but he was suspicious of automation and had loudly proclaimed that he was still going to maintain his manual calendar.

Josh was messier than Tony. The bed was unmade. Dirty clothes were piled on the only chair. A distinct locker-room odor emanated from them. Tony was thankful he didn't ordinarily have to look inside this room. It was a better situation than college, when they had shared a single room. Josh did have a table, which he used as a desk. Papers were piled on it in seemingly random fashion.

Tony quickly leafed through them, using his flashlight to see, looking for a calendar. He heard the sound of an engine in the carport area. It was either Josh or a neighbor. He went to the window and peeked out between slats of the blinds. He saw Josh's car pulling into his carport. Tony figured he had thirty seconds.

He riffled quickly through another pile of papers. In the middle he found the calendar, one page per month, not exactly state-of-the-art. It was open to September. He went back one page and checked the square of August 29. Nothing was written in the square. It was completely blank. Other days had notices of appointments or social engagements, so Josh was still using the calendar.

Tony could hear Josh coming in through the unlocked door from the patio. He quickly shoved the calendar back into the stack—too hard. The whole stack of papers fell onto the floor. Frantically, Tony scooped them up with both arms and plunked them on the table. Then he took two giant steps out of the room and closed the door. At the last instant he remembered to close it softly. As he was going down the stairs, Josh started up them.

"Hey, Tony," Josh said as they passed each other. "How was your day?"

"Tiring," Tony said warily. "And yours?" At least he hadn't called him Noodles.

"Swinging. We got a scoop on network news in the case of the kidnapped little girl."

"Wonderful," Tony responded, but he was already down the stairs and headed back into the kitchen. Josh didn't seem to be in a bad mood. Now if only he didn't notice that his papers were messed up. And if he didn't bring up last night, Tony wouldn't. Tony retrieved his TV dinner from the microwave, poured himself another glass of wine, and sat down at the table in the family room, which doubled as a dining room.

Josh came downstairs five minutes later, looking comfortable in baggy shorts and a T-shirt. He opened the refrigerator. After a few seconds of searching, he said, "Looks like I blew it. Drank up all the beer. Sorry about that. You want me to make a beer run?"

"Don't do it for me," Tony said. "I'm going to bed early tonight."

"I'll get some tomorrow."

The area between the family room and the kitchen was mostly open, so Tony watched as Josh poured himself a glass of wine from the bottle on the counter and then took a package of wieners out of the refrigerator. He stabbed one with a fork and held it over the flame of a burner on the gas stove, as if he were at a wiener roast. He whistled as the wiener started to sizzle. Tony cringed as he watched the grease drip onto the burner, but he was determined not to say a word, especially one that might upset Josh.

"I haven't heard anything new about the Hotline murder for several days," Josh said. "Have you got any inside information for me that I can put on the air?"

"Nothing new."

Josh ate this wiener right off the fork and then stabbed a second wiener and held it over the flame.

Tony saw his chance. "Detective Croyden has been checking the alibis of everybody who was connected to Joy in any way. When he asked me about my alibi, I realized that I didn't have anybody to vouch for me that night." He forced a smile. "I went to a movie all alone. I don't remember where the hell you were. Where were you, anyway?" He said this in what he hoped was a jocular tone.

Josh turned his wiener over to sear the other side. With his free hand he scratched his head. "Where was I the night of the murder? I'll have to think about that."

Josh fell silent as he finished cooking his wiener to his satisfaction and ate it off the fork. Tony felt frustrated that the opportunity to get Josh's alibi had apparently been lost. If he asked again, Josh was sure to get suspicious. Josh brought his glass of wine over to the table and sat down.

He said, "Was Joy one of the girls that was here the day you had the Hotline people over when I was out of town?"

The question startled Tony. He had never told Josh that he had invited the class over and had hoped he wouldn't find out. He said, "What are you talking about?" still trying to maintain a bantering tone.

"Don't pull that shit with me. Rob told me all about it. He said the pool was full of young babes in bikinis. He and some of the other guys who live here sat around the pool, drank beer, and watched. But you did it behind your old roommate's back." Josh affected a hurt look.

Watched. Ogled. Tony remembered that well. Rob was a neighbor. Since the pool was in the common area, he couldn't exactly drive them away.

"They particularly mentioned a tall, gorgeous blonde," Josh continued. "Stacked." He placed his hands around imaginary breasts. "I kind of figured that might be Joy."

"It was Joy," Tony conceded. "In fact, that was the only time I ever saw Joy."

"You're one up on me. I have to live with the pictures we got from her parents. But I'm still pissed that you left me out."

"I didn't want you ravishing all of them. My reputation is that of a good guy, and I can't let them know I have you for a roommate. They'd probably kick me out of the Hotline."

"That might be the best thing that could happen. I don't like what you're turning into."

Josh kept score of all the beautiful girls he saw, dated, bedded. It was a contest for him. Still, he had no reason to kill one.

"In a theoretical sense, I can understand the attraction," Josh said, as if analyzing a movie. "A beautiful but unobtainable girl. If you can't have her, then nobody can have her. Kill her while she's still perfect. Then you'll have a memory that nobody else can have. Forever."

Or *did* he have a reason to kill her? Tony remembered something—the missing underwear. He needed to search the drawers of Josh's dresser. But he would have to be more careful the next time he went into his room.

CHAPTER 16

As Tony entered the Hotline, office he saw two people in the listening room. Young people on the four-to-seven shift. He signed in. It was only Wednesday, and he wasn't scheduled to work again until Friday, but he had decided to come in tonight because curiosity had gotten the best of him. He had called the office and talked to Gail, who had told him that Nathan was working the seven-to-ten tonight. Tony had decided to work with him.

Tony said hello to the two as he went into the listening room. He recognized their faces, if not their names. He admired the listening skills of the girl as she finished up a call. These kids were good. They certainly didn't fit one common stereotype of teenagers: egoists who ignored the rest of the world. Older generations might not approve of their clothes, their tattoos, and their piercings, but they had to admit that at least these particular youths had compassion. They cared.

Nathan arrived right on the dot of seven. Tony watched him as he signed in. He admired Nathan's tall, blond good looks and compared them to his own shorter, darker appearance. But there was something different about him. Tony realized that it was the first time he had seen Nathan wearing short sleeves. Well, they had been having hot weather—hotter even than in August. But this was typical in Southern California.

Nathan came into the listening room. He showed surprise as he said hello to Tony.

"I wasn't doing anything tonight," Tony told him, "and I couldn't stay away. I thought I'd keep you company."

"Good. Kyoko was scheduled to work, but I don't think she's going to show. I was going to work anyway, all alone if necessary. Who cares about the rules? I'm not afraid."

After Nathan got himself something to eat and they each took a phone call, Tony had a chance to start a conversation. He said, "Tell me about your church—what is it, Church of the Resurrected Jesus, or something like that?"

"Church of the Risen Lord. What would you like to know?"

Tony noticed, as he had before, that Nathan didn't look directly at him when he spoke.

"Well, how did it get its name, for one thing?"

Nathan finally looked at him, for a moment, as if he were trying to find out what he was driving at. "Are you a Christian?"

"You mean, as opposed to being a Jew or a Muslim? Yeah, I guess I'm a Christian."

"That didn't exactly sound like a wholehearted religious endorsement. Anyway, you know the story, right? Jesus was crucified, dead, and buried. The third day he rose from the dead and ascended into heaven, et cetera, et cetera."

"Sure."

"Okay, well the deal is that he's coming back to get us. And take us with him. At least some of us."

"The true believers."

"Uh huh."

Tony figured he had better ask his next question carefully. "Who are the true believers? Are they just the members of your church?"

"Well, there may be some others who got it right," Nathan hedged.

"How many members does your church have?"

"I don't know. A couple hundred, I guess."

"Isn't it going to be awfully lonely in heaven?"

Nathan looked upset. "Are you scoffing at my religion?"

"No, no, just trying to find out the truth. When is it going to happen?"

"When is what going to happen?"

"This…Ascension, or whatever you call it." He had almost said Day of Judgment, but that would have been quoting Reverend Hodgkins, and Tony didn't want Nathan to know that he had actually gone to the church.

Nathan clamped his mouth shut, reminding Tony of a baby Gila monster named Franklin that he had tried to raise when he was young. But Franklin, who may have missed his mother, wouldn't eat and died of starvation. Reverend Hodgkins had also clammed up when Tony had asked him the same question. They must be pledged to secrecy. Well, what did he care? Let them have their silly little secret. However, he was still curious about other things.

"What are you doing to prepare for this day?" He wasn't sure Nathan was going to answer this question either. After an embarrassing silence, Tony said, "I mean, are you selling all your things, divesting yourself of your worldly possessions, as it were?"

"Why is this any of your business?"

Nathan was getting hostile. It was too late for Tony to pretend he wanted to join the church. Besides, if he said he did, he would actually have to go to a service, and he figured if he attended a service, the roof of the church would fall in. Retribution from the Lord. It had been a long time since he had attended an actual church service. And the roof had looked pretty shaky anyway. But he shouldn't have let his skepticism show.

Tony said, "Well, if you have a good car, I might want to buy it from you." That was a flat-out lie. There was no way he was going to trade his Porsche for any other car on the road.

"I'll let you know."

Tony had a more serious reason for his questioning, but when he brought that up, he was sure it would further upset Nathan. However, he felt it was his duty to at least try to warn him. He said, "Are you…that is, are you expected to give your money or your possessions to the Church, by any chance?"

Nathan was glaring at him now, but Tony felt he had better finish what he wanted to say. "Have you at least considered the possibility that this is a scam—a way to get all your money? That the people who are running the church are fleecing the members?"

Nathan's look was more hostile than ever. Tony figured he had said enough. They finished out the shift in almost complete silence, except when they were on the phones.

CHAPTER 17

It wasn't until Tony had arrived at the Hotline on Friday and saw Shahla that he remembered that they had sent an e-mail to Paul the Poet from Shahla's address. Other challenges had crowded that out of his mind.

She was looking as fetching as ever in a skirt and top combination that bared her midriff and a few other things. But he had learned that the girls didn't dress to look sexy to others. They dressed for themselves.

Before he had a chance to ask her whether she had received a reply to her e-mail, she said, "Can we go to Las Vegas tomorrow?"

"We? Do you have a mouse in your pocket?"

"I have to go. I'm the poet, remember? Or at least I can talk about poetry in a way that he won't throw me out on my ear."

"If you received an e-mail, why didn't you forward it to me?"

Shahla looked calculating. "Because I knew what you'd say about me going."

"And now I'm saying it."

"Yes, but at least I can counter it in person. Give me a chance to explain, Tony. Here, I'll show you the e-mails."

"Plural? How many are there?"

"Oh, we've had quite a conversation."

And she had done all this behind his back. Of course, he had been doing a few things behind her back, but that was different. Shahla had printouts of the e-mails. Paul had responded to her first one by saying that he would be glad to meet her. He suggested that they meet at his house, which, Tony recalled, was really his parents' house.

Shahla had very sensibly replied that she would like to meet him in a public place. She had suggested a casino. Paul said that the Tortoise Club was a downtown casino with a nice coffee shop, and that they could meet there. Shahla asked how she would know him. Paul said he was six feet, two inches tall and would wear a T-shirt with a limerick on the front.

Tony finished reading the correspondence and tried to marshal his thoughts. He glanced at Shahla. She was sitting on pins and needles and not looking at him. If he met Paul alone, there was no telling what the man would do. He might bolt. Callers to the Hotline often had very fragile egos and the slightest thing could make them go ballistic. Having Shahla with him would be a big advantage in that respect. No, the whole thing was impossible. He would go by himself. If Paul wouldn't talk to him, he would do some gambling. He needed a mini-vacation.

"You have to be twenty-one to enter a casino," Tony said.

Shahla shrugged. "Even to go in a coffee shop?"

"No, not a coffee shop. But you can't go with me. There's a law against taking a girl across a state line for immoral purposes."

"We're not going for immoral purposes," Shahla said indignantly. "We're trying to solve a murder. Remember?"

"Your mother won't permit you to do it. And you told me you always communicate with your mother."

Shahla considered that. After spinning herself around on her chair a few times, she said, "I'll make you a deal. After we finish here, we'll go talk to my mother and tell her what we're going to do. I'll live with her decision. If she says I can't go, I won't go. If she says yes, then you've got to take me."

Tony was astonished. "You're willing to do that? Introduce me to your mother and abide by her decision? There's no way she is going to say yes."

"Then you're off the hook."

"All right." Tony found that he was looking forward to meeting Shahla's mother. And being a mother, of course she wouldn't let

Shahla go. What kind of a mother would she be if she did? So it was settled. Curiously, Tony found that he wasn't completely happy with the result. While he was wondering about that, the phone rang.

"Central Hotline. Tony speaking."

"Hi, Tony, this is Rick. I don't know if I talked to you before. I called about three months ago."

"I'm not sure, Rick." Of course he hadn't been on the line three months ago, but he didn't want to sound negative.

"Anyway, whoever I talked to helped me. I had just come here from Nebraska and needed a job bad. He told me to go to this place in Santa Monica called Chrysalis. They help homeless people get back in the job market. Well, I wasn't homeless, but close to it. So, anyway, I went there. I walked in and hadn't even registered when I met a guy in the lobby. He said he was looking for heavy equipment operators. Man, that's what I do."

"So he gave you a job?"

"Yeah. Now I'm making more money than I ever made in my life. I brought my wife and kids here. Now we're going to take a trip back to Nebraska to visit the family."

"That's wonderful, Rick." It was nice to get positive feedback from a caller.

"My wife said I should show my appreciation by donating some money to a good cause. Do you have any suggestions?"

"Well, you can make a donation to the Hotline. We rely on donations to keep us operating."

Tony gave the address of the Hotline post office box to Rick. When he hung up, he was elated. He told Shahla, "I'm going to write this up and put it on the board so everyone can see it."

Several hang ups and several calls later, Shahla signaled that she had the Chameleon on the line. Tony knew from checking the call reports of other listeners that the Chameleon was still calling the Hotline on a regular basis, using different aliases, but nothing new had been learned about him. And as far as Tony knew, Detective Croyden hadn't been able to track him down.

Shahla put him on the speaker. He was saying, "...step-mom just circumcised me. She's a doctor."

"How old are you?" Shahla asked. She was playing along with him.

"Fifteen. But when she did, I got an erection."

The voice could be that of a teenager. Or of somebody impersonating a teenager. But Shahla was sure it was the Chameleon.

"That must have been embarrassing for you."

"Yes, of course it was. She's married to my dad."

There was a pause. Tony had discussed the Chameleon with Shahla and she had agreed not to attempt to meet him. She would stick to trying to pinpoint his location. The dead air continued. He wasn't exactly voluble tonight.

Shahla broke the silence saying, "For our records, could you tell me where you're calling from?"

More silence. Then, "El Segundo."

At least he was consistent in that regard. Shahla said, "I love El Segundo. There's a cute little shop on Main Street that sells imported knickknacks. I bought some dolls there that nest, one inside the other."

Shahla had probably never stopped in El Segundo in her life. She had just driven through it to points north. El Segundo wasn't a destination. Tony had told her about it, in case this very situation occurred.

"They're called *matroshka*," the Chameleon said. "That means 'little mother.'"

"You are so lucky to live in a place like El Segundo. Do you live near that store?"

Silence. Tony and Shahla looked at each other. Tony put his finger to his lips. Outwait him. Maybe he would give something away.

"I pass it on my walks."

"When do you walk?"

"In the afternoon."

"After school?"

"When I.... Listen, I have to go."

He hung up.

"I think he was about to say, 'When I go to work.'" Shahla said.

"He broke character," Tony said. "He forgot who he was today. That may be useful. Write it up and…"

"Pass it on to Detective Croyden."

"Right."

"I knew you were going to say that." Shahla wrinkled her nose. "So far, Croyden has been a big fat zero."

***

Tony followed Shahla home and parked in the street as she pulled into the garage, which opened as if by magic as she approached, but actually in response to a remote control in her car. Tony saw that half of the two-car garage was full of stuff. He was right in thinking that they only had one car. They met on the front steps as Shahla produced a key to the house and unlocked the front door.

"Mom," Shahla yelled. "I'm home."

Shahla led the way into the comfortably furnished living room. They didn't seem to be hurting for money.

After a minute, Mom appeared through a doorway and said, "You don't have to shout, Shahla. I heard you drive in."

Shahla's mother had an accent and was a slightly darker and shorter-haired version of Shahla. In the dim light of the living room, she could have passed for her sister. She was slim and elegantly dressed, but definitely not like a teenager.

"Mom, this is Tony," Shahla said. "The one I told you about."

Shahla had called her mother from the Hotline and told her they were coming.

"I'm very pleased to meet you, Mrs. Lawton," Tony said. He didn't know whether it would be proper to shake hands with her or not.

She immediately extended her hand, however, and said, "Please call me Rasa. All my patients do. I appreciate you working with my daughter."

"You're a nurse, aren't you?" Tony asked.

"Yes, I work at Bonita Beach Memorial Hospital."

"Mom, Tony's going to drive to Las Vegas as part of Joy's murder investigation, and I need to go with him."

Shahla was diving in without testing the water. Tony expected Rasa to hit the ceiling, but she showed an amazing calm.

"Please sit down," Rasa said to Tony. "Would you like coffee?"

Tony hesitated and Shahla said, "It's American coffee. The kind you drink."

"Sure. Thanks."

Tony sat down on a soft couch that had two sections, at a 90-degree angle from each other. Shahla kicked off her shoes and sat down on the other section. She curled one leg up underneath her.

"Your mother speaks English very well," Tony said.

"She does all right. She has trouble with her articles."

"Articles?"

"A, an and the."

"Where was she born?"

"In Teheran."

"Iran," Tony said. "I have a cousin who is married to an Iranian."

"She prefers to be called Persian."

"How about your Dad?"

"He was born in Chicago."

The soft couch made Tony realize that he was tired. He found himself relaxing. Shahla had quit talking. He glanced over and saw that her eyes were closed. At least she didn't feel she had to entertain him.

They both came to attention when Rasa returned with a tray containing two cups of coffee and a glass of water for Shahla. Tony declined an offer of sugar and cream and took a sip. This would wake him up.

After they were served, Rasa sat in an armchair and said, "Tony, tell me about trip to Las Vegas."

Shahla started to speak, but Rasa interrupted her saying, "I want to hear it from Tony. You will get your chance after."

"One of our former callers is a poet," Tony said. "A few days ago Shahla and I found a poem that had been slipped under the door of the Hotline. Did she show it to you?"

"No," Rasa said and looked at Shahla, who looked only the tiniest bit contrite. "She does not show me anything."

"Since it's evidence, I felt the fewer the number of people who saw it, the better," Shahla said.

Rasa shrugged and said to Tony, "Go on with your story."

"It's a well-written poem, and Shahla felt that the only person she knows who might have written it was this former caller, Paul, who lives in Las Vegas. We sent him an e-mail, and he said he would like to meet us."

"Me," Shahla said. "He said he would like to meet me."

"Okay, but I don't think it's a good idea for Shahla to go."

"Is this not job for police?" Rasa asked.

"We don't really have any evidence that he wrote the poem," Tony said. "It's probably what my grandmother would have called a wild goose chase."

"I see," Rasa said. "Okay, Shahla, tell your side of story."

"Tony's a good guy," Shahla said, "but he's not a poet. He doesn't know how to talk to poets. He won't be able to get anything out of Paul. That is, if Paul will even talk to him. Because he has one other problem. He's not—a girl."

"Is it dangerous, meeting this person Paul?" Rasa asked.

"Not if Tony's with me," Shahla said. "We're going to meet him in a coffee shop in the middle of Las Vegas."

"Do you agree?" Rasa asked Tony.

"Er, well, no, it shouldn't be dangerous. As Shahla says, it will be in a public place. But I still don't think she should go."

"I don't think so either," Rasa said.

Shahla started to protest. Rasa held up her hand. "Tony, let me tell you little history," Rasa said. "Five years ago Shahla lost her father. She is my only daughter. I have one younger son who is asleep, that is if Shahla did not wake him by shouting when she came in. Shahla was very shook up by her father's death. It is taking her long time to recover."

Rasa paused and took a sip of coffee. "Tony, don't let anybody tell you it is easier to raise girls than boys. As a nurse, I see problems every day, not just with my own family. Girls are harder. Just look at clothes they wear."

Shahla again looked ready to say something, but Rasa continued, "It is difficult to be single mom. I try my best with children, but it is hard. Shahla misses out by not having father figure. She looks up to you. I know because she told me some things about you, and she doesn't talk about many of her friends. You are not old enough to be father figure, but you are man, much more mature than crazy teenage boys."

Tony wondered where this was going. He glanced at Shahla. She had a look of expectation on her face.

"I do not want Shahla to go, but I do not want her to hate me, either. And I don't want her doing things behind my back. It is tough decision. I trust you, Tony, perhaps more than I trust Shahla. I trust you not to hurt her and to keep her safe. If I give permission, will you take Shahla with you?"

Now he knew why Shahla was willing to leave the decision to her mother. She had her mother where she wanted her. But Rasa had made some good points. And from the trust that she placed in him, he knew that he would never be able to do anything to hurt Shahla.

He looked at Shahla. She was nodding her head vigorously. Tony swallowed his doubts and said, "All right, you can go. But you have to go to bed right now. Because I'm picking you up at seven o'clock tomorrow morning. Sharp."

CHAPTER 18

Tony upshifted smoothly as he merged onto the 105 Freeway eastbound from the 405 northbound. The 105 was a godsend to the commuter who lived near the coast and commuted inland—or vice versa. It was the newest of the L.A. freeways, and Tony drove it constantly for his work. Only infrequently did he think about the hundreds of people who had once lived along here and had been displaced during its protracted period of construction.

He glanced at Shahla, sacked out on the seat beside him. She had fallen asleep almost as soon as he had backed out of her driveway. So much for companionship. Remembering his own days as a teenager, he knew that they often didn't get enough sleep. But he couldn't play his radio or his CDs, which he would have been doing if he had been alone. Maybe she was more trouble than she was worth.

She was wearing her hair down, not in a ponytail. Her jeans were cut higher than usual on her hips and her top lower, closing the gap. The changes made her look older, and Tony knew enough about women to realize that this was a calculated look, to impress Paul. He admitted to himself that the more mature Shahla was more appealing. But he must not get carried away. She was still only seventeen.

***

"Where are we?"

Shahla's sleepy voice jolted Tony out of his reverie. The Porsche had been humming along on Interstate 15, and he had been humming under his breath, in perfect synch with it. How much better than the stop-and-go driving in town. He was only going a few miles-per-hour over the speed limit. Speed wasn't the issue. It was—freedom. Besides, he felt responsible for Shahla's safety, especially after talking to Rasa. He felt very protective of her. Almost like a father. Almost. He would have been going faster if she weren't with him.

"We're approaching Barstow."

"I've never been to Barstow."

"Neither has anybody else who doesn't drive to Las Vegas from L.A. It's not exactly the garden spot of California."

"I'm hungry."

"We're making good time. We'll stop and grab a bite to eat. How did you sleep?"

She gave him a smile. "I had a good sleep. This is closer to the time I usually get up on Saturday."

Tony downshifted as he cruised along an off-ramp. The desert community had plenty of fast-food restaurants and gas stations. It was designed for the traveler passing through. But, surprisingly, quite a few people lived here, also. It was a bustling place. What did the residents do? Besides cater to tourists. He pulled into the parking lot of the first restaurant they came to, in a space with campers on either side.

"It's hot," Shahla announced after getting out of the car.

"No cooling ocean breezes in the desert, like we get at the beach."

However, the air-conditioning was cranking away inside. They found a booth amid the weekend visitors, with their hats and loud shirts. A waitress, who had been waitressing for a long time and would continue more or less forever, took their orders. Shahla ordered orange juice and an English muffin. Tony ordered coffee and thought the muffin sounded good, so he also asked for one.

After a couple of sips of coffee, Tony said, "We need a plan for dealing with Paul. We should get there before he does, which is good."

"I thought we'd sit at separate tables, and I'd talk to him while you keep an eye on us."

"No way. I don't want to be separated from you. And I need to hear everything he says."

"You'll scare him."

"No I won't. I'll be your...brother. Don't you think we could pass as brother and sister?"

"In a dim light, maybe. But let me do the talking."

Tony chuckled. "You're really a control freak, aren't you?"

"I'm just trying to protect you, Tony. You don't know poetry. You might say the wrong thing."

"I thought I was supposed to protect you. That's what your mom wants. And speaking of, you must really have her buffaloed to convince her to let you run off to Vegas with a character like me."

"Quit running yourself down. And she exaggerates. I'm a good daughter. Especially compared to some of the others. One of the girls at school won't live at home. She lives with a friend and communicates with her mom mostly by e-mail."

"Whew. No wonder I'm not married."

"You'll make a good father."

"That'll be the day."

***

They made a nonstop run from Barstow to Las Vegas. Shahla, now fully awake, became quite talkative, commenting on the desert scenery, talking about her plans for college and life. She was in the process of filling out applications to universities. Tony reflected that she was doing a lot more planning than he had done at her age—maybe than he did now.

"Have you written a lot of poetry?" Tony asked her at one point.

"I started writing poetry when I was eight or nine. Mom sent me to my room for a time out, and I didn't have anything better to do so I wrote a couple of bad poems. I've been writing poetry ever since. I've had some published in the school paper and a few other places. I've also written articles for the paper."

"You're so busy. When do you find time to write?"

"Oh, when I'm sad. Or depressed. Or happy. I can write pretty much any time. I have a notebook full of poems."

They parked in a lot in downtown Las Vegas, near Fremont Street, and walked several blocks to the Tortoise Club. It was a typical downtown casino—loud and flashy, but without much substance beneath the facade, as Tony knew from experience. A good way to lose your money in the slots or at the blackjack tables slowly, with minimum bets, without the distraction of shows. Perfect for the businesslike gambler who didn't have a large stake. And the small gamblers were out in force today—the retirees who came on buses and lost their Social Security checks before returning home to their empty lives.

Tony steered Shahla into the coffee shop, away from temptation, a half hour before their appointment, and they sat down at a table, both of them on the same side, facing the door. A quick glance at the other tables convinced them that Paul had not preceded them here. Tony suggested they order lunch.

"Can we drive by some of the big hotels on the way back?" Shahla asked between sips of a soft drink.

Tony didn't know whether her excitement was at the prospect of meeting Paul or from the effect Las Vegas had on people. It was probably a combination. He had avoided Las Vegas Boulevard on the way in because traffic on it was so miserable—worse than in many parts of Los Angeles.

"Why not? We'll give you a look at plastic city. They've recreated some of the great places in the world here—Paris, Venice, New York, Egypt. You just have to remember that it's all fake."

"Don't be so cynical. This is all new to me."

Paul didn't appear at 1:30, the scheduled time. Tony wondered whether he was going to show up. They finished their lunches and continued to nurse their drinks.

"How much time should we give him?" Shahla asked. She sounded restless, as if she would rather be sightseeing than playing detective.

"We've driven all this way. Let's give him until two."

At five minutes of two a tall young man walked into the coffee shop, or rather eased his way in. Considering his dominating height, he looked a little timid, as though he wasn't sure how the world would treat him. Skinny as a broomstick, he wore thick-lensed glasses and had sandy hair that stuck out at odd angles. He had on a T-shirt with some writing on it and carried a notebook.

"That's him," Shahla said. She raised her arm and waved at the man.

Tony wondered how she could be so sure, but he spotted them and came toward their table with a shambling step, looking relieved. Maybe it was because they weren't monsters.

"You must be Paul," Shahla said, standing up and extending her hand. "I'm Sally. And this is my brother, Tony."

Tony stood up and shook hands with him across the table. "Sit down," he said. "Would you like something to eat?"

"Maybe a coke," Paul said, his first words other than hello.

Tony signaled the waitress while Shahla said, "So what's this limerick on your shirt?" She read it aloud:

"Now God was designing a mammal,
With beauty and grace, without trammel,
By computer, of course,
The genetics said 'horse,'
But the disk crashed and out came a camel."

"The Association for the Prevention of Cruel Statements About Camels is not going to like that," Tony said.

Paul looked uncertain, as if he didn't know whether Tony was serious. But then he smiled. He said, "I won a contest on the Internet for writing it."

"I like your sense of humor," Shahla said. "I could see it in the poems on your website. "Does that book have your poems in it?"

Paul nodded shyly.

"May I see it?"

He slid the notebook across the table to her. It was a three-ring binder, crammed full of pages. Tony wondered whether he spent all his time writing poetry. Didn't he have to work for a living? And did all poets have a similar notebook? Shahla had said she kept her poems in one.

Alan Cook

Shahla started leafing through the book, reading and commenting on some of the poems, always positively. She and Tony had agreed that if he brought poems with him—and she had asked him to in her e-mails—that they would try to look at all of them. Of course, if they could find a copy of the spaghetti strap poem, that would be a coup. If not, they would look for other poems with similar style or subject matter.

Tony was relying on Shahla to do most of the work. In retrospect, it was a good thing she was here. He would never have been able to fake enough of an interest in or knowledge about poetry to fool Paul. When Shahla excused herself to go to the lady's room, he was stuck for something to say. He decided on a subject he knew something about.

"Do you ever do any gambling?" he asked.

"People who live here will tell you they don't gamble," Paul said, "but that's not necessarily true. I like to play video poker once in a while."

"Where's a good place to play?"

"I like the New York-New York because it has some machines that pay eighty to one for four of a kind. They're hidden in a corner as you curve around from the theaters."

"Thanks for the tip," Tony said.

Shahla came back, and the discussion returned to poetry.

"I notice that a lot of your poems are about pain," Shahla said. "You use metaphors for pain."

Paul didn't immediately reply. Tony knew from his Hotline training that he and Shahla should remain silent and wait for Paul to say something. The silence dragged on for several minutes. Shahla continued to leaf through the book, looking completely at ease. Tony admired her composure.

In his calls to the Hotline, Paul had sometimes talked about an abusive aunt. Or abusive parents. Somebody had abused him. Maybe that's where the pain came from. If so, did that trauma color his feelings toward all women? Tony leaned toward Shahla and read pieces of some of the poems. The figures of speech in the poems, such as "a fire inside that makes me scream" must be the metaphors

Shahla was talking about. They were not specific as to where the pain originated.

"I'm feeling better," Paul said finally. "The pain is going away. Maybe I won't be able to write poetry anymore." He smiled.

"Has something good happened to you?" Shahla asked.

"I have a new girlfriend."

"You should have brought her with you."

"She's working today."

"When was the last time you were in Los Angeles?" Tony asked, hoping to speed things up. They didn't seem to be accomplishing anything and he was getting bored.

Paul hesitated and then said, "I've never been to Los Angeles."

"Never?" Tony said, not believing him. Everybody who lived in the West had been to Los Angeles.

"My parents don't like big cities, and I just never got there on my own."

Shahla had finished going through the book. She glanced at Tony and imperceptibly shrugged her shoulders. What now? It was time for direct action. Tony reached into his pants pocket and pulled out a copy of the spaghetti strap poem. It was folded and wrinkled.

He smoothed it out and said, "I'm not much of a poet, but I found one poem that I kind of like. He pushed it across the table and watched Paul's eyes as he read it, hoping to see a spark of something. He didn't detect anything.

When he finished reading it, Paul said, "It sounds like it was written by a teenage boy with raging hormones, but very few teenage boys can write poems like this."

"Why is that?"

"Because it takes a lot of practice and a certain amount of ability to achieve that use of meter, rhyme and organization."

"So who do you think wrote it, then?" Shahla asked.

Paul pushed his glasses up on his nose. He did that frequently. He said, "It was probably written by an older man who wishes he were still a teenager."

After some further discussion about the poem, Paul excused himself to use the restroom.

Tony said, "Well, do you think he wrote it?"

"Definitely not," Shahla said.

"Then we have no more use for him. Let's get rid of him."

"Tony. You know as well as I do that our callers have fragile psyches. We can't just dismiss him."

"Well, what do you suggest then?"

"I read about an art exhibition at one of the hotels. We could invite him to accompany us to see that."

Was she falling for this geek, just because he was tall and wrote pretty words? Tony caught himself before he said anything he would regret. "Great idea."

When Paul came back, Shahla brought up the subject of the exhibition.

Paul said, "I'd…really like to, but I'm meeting my girlfriend after she gets off work. If fact, I should be leaving now. It was really nice to meet both of you."

He picked up his notebook. Tony shook his hand. Shahla gave him a hug, which apparently surprised him. He turned and almost ran to the door of the coffee shop. As he went through the doorway, he turned and looked back at them, giving a tentative wave. Then he was gone.

CHAPTER 19

"There's the Sahara. The Riviera. Oh look, Circus Circus." Shahla excitedly craned her neck and read the names of the hotels as they crawled past them, stuck in the Saturday afternoon traffic on Las Vegas Boulevard. "Can we go inside just one?"

"You know you have to be twenty-one to gamble," Tony said. He had put the top of the Porsche down to enjoy the sun. It was easier to cruise slowly along in the car than to face the hassle of parking and walking in the heat.

"What are they going to do, card me? It didn't look as if they were watching too closely at the Tortoise Club."

"But we didn't do any gambling there."

"I can look older. I brought a dress with me. It's in the trunk, er, the front."

"We're stuck in traffic, and there's no place to change."

"I can handle it. Open it up so I can get my bag."

Shahla started getting out of the car.

"Shahla. What are you doing?" When he saw she wasn't going to stop, he said, "Stick your fingers under the hood to release it. And when you shut it use two hands." And do it gently.

Shahla went around to the front of the Porsche, oblivious to the stares of the other motorists stuck in traffic. Tony had no choice but to unlatch the hood. Shahla grabbed her small traveling bag and brought the cover down hard enough to make Tony wince. She was back in the car in thirty seconds.

"What are you going to do now?" Tony asked as he inched forward.

In answer, Shahla unzipped the bag and pulled out a dress. "It's my mom's. We wear the same size. Don't you think it will make me look older?"

"Yes, but as you can see there's no place to change."

"Don't look."

To his amazement, she pulled her top up over her head in one fluid motion. Sure, she was wearing a bra, but all the tourists in their SUVs, towering over them, had a good view of her as they looked down at the little Porsche. And telling him not to look? She might as well tell a bear not to hibernate.

"I saw the ads for the nudie shows," Shahla said as she unzipped her jeans. "Las Vegas is a pretty casual place."

It was no easy job for her to wriggle out of her tight jeans in the enclosed space. She had to lift her legs and place her bare feet against the windshield of the car in order to accomplish it. Some senior citizens in a tour bus watched her, fascinated. Maybe they thought she was part of the entertainment on the Strip. Several guys in a van opened their windows and cheered. It was a good thing Tony was stuck in traffic, or he would have been in danger of wrecking the car.

She had an easier time getting on the dress. She pulled it over her head and worked it down, slowly, until eventually it reached her knees, and she became the picture of modesty.

"There," she said. "How do I look?"

"Like a million dollars. You should be on display in a casino to show what a million looks like."

"I'm not through."

Next, Shahla took her long hair and wrapped it into a bun. Then she applied a little more lipstick and some eye shadow to what had been an almost makeup-free face. She turned to face Tony.

"What do you think now?"

"Okay, I give up. We'll go to New York-New York. I heard they have some video poker machines that have a good payoff."

It took a while, but Tony was eventually able to park within walking distance of the hotel. Shahla took his arm as they knifed their way through the crowds of pedestrians outdoors, despite the September heat, and finally made it into the air-conditioned interior of the hotel.

"It's so big," Shahla said, craning her neck in all directions, as they strolled through the gaming area, which was like an irresistible force that oozed its way into all corners of the building not taken up by restaurants, theaters, or shops.

They stopped beside one of the blackjack tables, where a bored dealer was dealing out of a shoe to a couple of bored players.

"Can we play this?" Shahla asked as one of the players displayed an ace-king combination and collected his reward from the dealer.

"Not here," Tony said. In spite of her transformation, it wouldn't be wise to let Shahla be scrutinized by a dealer and the unseen employees who watched all the games on video monitors. In addition, the minimum bets were far too high to allow her to play just for fun.

They wandered around, looking at the other games. They watched the roulette wheel spin, and Tony explained some of the bets at the craps table. They read the information about the shows that were playing. Shahla was interested in everything.

Finally, Tony realized that the afternoon was moving along, and they would be very late getting home. He told Shahla they had to go.

"We haven't tried gambling yet, ourselves," she said. "You promised."

"We'll play a little video poker."

Tony led her to the area that as nearly as he could tell was where Paul had talked about. After some wandering around, he spotted a cluster of video poker machines in a relatively isolated place. He checked the payoffs on one of them. Sure enough, it paid eighty to one for four of a kind. It also had a slot that accepted bills. He inserted a five dollar bill and twenty credits appeared on the monitor.

"Do you know how to play poker?" Tony asked as he figured out which buttons to press.

"No."

"Your mom is never going to forgive me for corrupting you, but here goes. This kind of poker is called five-card draw because you get dealt five cards, and then you can draw to replace any or all of them. Aces are high, deuces, that is twos, are low. You have to get at least a pair of jacks to win. Other winning hands, in order of increasing value, are two pairs, three of a kind, straight, flush, full house, four of a kind, straight flush."

"Now tell me that in English."

"In English, what we're always trying for on this machine is four of a kind, because it pays eighty to one, which is better than most machines. We use our other wins to maintain our capital so we can go for the big one."

Shahla caught on much too quickly. Soon she was pressing the buttons herself, and playing with minimal guidance from Tony concerning how many cards to draw. After ten minutes, she hit four eights and screamed as the credit counter tallied up the score.

"Congratulations." Tony pushed the button to get the cash out of the machine. Quarters came gushing into the tray. He picked up one of the paper containers available for that purpose and scooped all the coins into it. He said, "Now we can go home."

"Already? We've only just begun."

"Any time you hit a sizeable jackpot, you cash out and start over. That way you keep your perspective. Even when you're only playing for quarters. But this is a good time for us to leave. We've got a long ride."

When they exchanged the quarters for bills, Tony figured they were about seventeen dollars ahead. Not much, but winning was better than losing.

Shahla said, "Of course, that money belongs to you because we were playing with your money to start with. Now I want to play a little with my own money so I can keep the winnings."

She pulled a five dollar bill out of a small purse she carried.

"What if you lose?" Tony asked, but Shahla was already returning to the machine, where she inserted the bill in the slot.

"This is a good experience for a listener on the Hotline," Shahla said. "After all, many of our callers have addictions of one kind or another, or compulsions, as they call them. I want to see what it feels like to lose. Will I want to throw good money after bad?"

Tony decided to let her lose her five dollars, and then they would leave. There wasn't going to be any testing of compulsions. He stood by her side while she sat in front of the machine.

After playing a dozen hands, Shahla got an interesting deal. "Wait," Tony said as she pressed the buttons to hold all her cards. "Let's take a look at this."

"I've got a flush," Shahla said. "Five spades."

"I know, but look at what else you have. You have the ace, king, queen, and ten. In other words, you are one card short of a royal flush which pays 250 to one."

"Ooh," Shahla said, taking another look at the cards. "So I have one chance in…"

"Forty-seven of drawing the jack of spades because five cards have already been played from a fifty-two card deck."

"I want to go for it."

They stared at the cards for a while, not wanting to spoil the anticipation. Finally, Shahla drew one card.

"I can't look," she said. "Tell me…"

Tony peeked at the credit counter. It was going crazy. She had drawn the jack of spades. "You did it."

Shahla jumped up and down screaming. Then she threw her arms around his neck and lifted her legs off the ground.

"Calm down," Tony said laughing, as he tried to keep his balance. When she let go of him, he pressed the button to cash out and scooped the quarters into the cup. "If you look too much like a teenager, you'll blow your cover." He started toward the cashier.

"Where are you going?"

"Now, we're really going home."

"But I might win some more."

"You'll get the opportunity to know what it feels like to quit when you're ahead. That will give you empathy for your callers who can't do that."

Shahla grumbled, but Tony was adamant. He pocketed the three twenty dollar bills, plus a five and a couple of ones that he received from the cashier, telling Shahla that he would give the money to her when they got home.

She threatened to take more money out of her purse, but Tony said, "I'm leaving, and I've got the car." He walked away.

Shahla caught up to him and said, "You are really mean. I'm never going to Las Vegas with you again."

"Shhh," Tony said suddenly, turning to face her. "Look over my right shoulder."

Shahla peeked over his shoulder and said, "It's Paul. And he's got a girl with him. Should we go talk to them?"

"Wait. Describe the girl." Tony kept his back to Paul and the girl.

"She's blonde. She's quite tall. And pretty. She looks something like…Joy."

"That was my impression, too. Of course, it probably means nothing."

"That he likes girls who look like Joy? Or maybe he really hates them."

"What are they doing?"

"They're going over to where we just came from, where those video poker machines are. He's got his arm around her neck, as if he's aching to strangle her."

Tony turned his head and could see the pair, walking diagonally away from them. Paul did have his elbow resting on the girl's shoulder, with his forearm curled in front of her neck. Innocent though it might be, if you could picture him as a killer, it looked scary.

"We should follow them," Shahla said urgently, taking the thought right out of his brain.

"But if we want to learn anything, we need to be incognito."

"I look different from what I did at the coffee shop. Turn your T-shirt inside out."

Tony glanced down at the front of his shirt, which had the words "San Diego" on it and a picture of a beach and palm trees. If Shahla could undress in public, he could too. He pulled the shirt over his head and put it back on wrong side out.

"Now put on your dark glasses."

He took them out of the case in his pocket and put them on. He glanced at Shahla. "Put on yours, too, so he can't see your eyes if we get close to them. They're a dead giveaway."

Shahla took her dark glasses out of her purse and put them on. She said, "One thing more. I'm going to change your hairstyle. Sit down there." She pointed to a chair in front of a slot machine.

Tony did as he was told. She took a comb out of her purse and fooled with his hair. She chuckled and said, "There. He won't know you now."

"What have you done?"

"Don't worry. It looks good. I got rid of your cowlick." She put away the comb and said, "How shall we do this?"

"It would be nice if we could get close enough to listen to what they say."

They approached the video poker machines and saw Paul sitting in front of one. The girl stood beside him with a hand on his shoulder. The adjoining video poker machine was free.

"Do you think we can sit at that machine without being recognized?" Tony asked, speaking softly.

"You sit down, and I'll sit on your lap, facing away from them. If we don't say anything, Paul won't recognize us."

Tony took a few quarters out of his pocket that were left over from their play. He approached the machine from behind Paul and sat down in the chair while Paul was engrossed in a deal. Shahla quickly jumped up on his lap with her back to Paul. All Paul would be able to see of Tony if he looked over was a profile. Tony noisily threw his quarters into the tray and put one in the slot. He would play slowly so they could mostly listen.

He had to play with one hand because the other one was around Shahla's waist. He was conscious of Shahla's closeness to him. At first, Paul and the girl said nothing. He could tell from the noises of their machine that Paul was playing steadily.

After a couple of minutes, Paul said, "I'm not having any luck today. I found an interesting cliff overlooking the city. Come on, I'll show it to you."

Paul got up and walked away with the girl.

"He's going to push her off a cliff," Shahla said, jumping down from his lap. "We've got to stop them."

CHAPTER 20

"I left some money in the machine," Tony complained as they tried to keep the two in sight.

"Hurry up," Shahla said, taking his hand so they wouldn't get separated while navigating their way through a line of people who were waiting to see a show. "We don't want to lose them."

"This might be totally innocent."

"Or it might not be. The way he talked about the cliff...."

Paul and the girl went out the door of the hotel. Tony and Shahla followed them as fast as possible. Outside, swarms of people walked along Las Vegas Boulevard in the light of the still-hot setting sun.

"Which way did they go?" Shahla asked.

"I don't see them. Oh, there they are." Fortunately, Paul's head stuck up above the crowd. "They've turned on Tropicana."

Tony and Shahla weaved their way through the pedestrians, trying to regain visual contact with Paul and the girl, who had disappeared around the corner. The pursuers also turned right onto Tropicana Avenue and saw the other couple again, loping along at a swift pace. The girl seemed to have no trouble matching Paul's long strides.

"Maybe they parked in the same lot we did," Tony said. He slowed down as the traffic thinned, away from the Strip. Fewer people between them and the pursued made their chances of being spotted greater. Shahla dropped his hand and slowed down beside him. He noticed that she wasn't even breathing hard. She must be in good shape from cross-country.

Paul and the girl walked past the lot where Tony's car was parked.

"We're going to need a car if we want to follow them into the hills," Tony said, hesitating as they approached the entrance to the parking lot. "But if we get the car now, we'll lose them."

"You get the car," Shahla said. "I'll stay behind them."

"How will I know where you are?"

"I'll call you. My cell phone is in my purse. Give me your number."

Tony always carried a pen with him. He scribbled the number of his cell phone on the back of a business card he pulled from his pocket and gave it to Shahla. He said, "Be careful. Don't let them know you're following them."

"Don't worry."

She took off at a trot to regain the distance she had lost. Tony hoped Shahla wouldn't attract too much attention by running in a dress. He had misgivings about leaving her and almost called her to come back. He'd better get the car as fast as he could.

He ran to the car and started it. Another car was backing out of a parking space behind him—and the driver was taking his sweet time. Tony fumed, but he knew that blowing his horn would only aggravate the situation. When he finally drove out onto the street, Shahla and the other couple had disappeared. Where were they? He had promised Rasa to protect her. He warded off a surge of panic. He had to trust her. She was a smart girl.

He drove slowly, looking for a sign of any of the three. When he figured he had driven farther than they could have walked by now, he circled the block. Five minutes went by without a sighting. Why hadn't he written down Shahla's cell phone number? He stopped the car to work on a plan.

His cell phone rang. He punched the talk button and said, "Tony."

"They've gotten in a car and driven toward the hills."

"Where are you?"

Shahla gave an intersection. Tony remembered that one of the streets she named crossed the street he was on. He was only a few blocks from her. Relieved, he gunned the engine and took off. He spotted her within two minutes. He pulled the car up beside her, and she jumped in.

"Quick, write down their license plate number before I forget it."

Tony took the card she was still holding and wrote the number Shahla dictated.

"Which way did they go?"

"Toward the hills." Shahla pointed. "They're in a gray Honda."

"So is the rest of the world."

"I think I'll recognize it."

Tony drove as fast as the traffic would allow. The sun was just setting behind the hills they were approaching, so spotting the car would be that much more difficult. Still, there only seemed to be one road that went up into the hills. And Paul had to go in that direction if he was going toward a cliff. The traffic was heavy enough so that Tony doubted that he could catch Paul. Maybe it was just as well. They would drive uphill for a while and then turn around and go home.

The views got better as they drove. This must be the right direction. Paul had mentioned a view of Las Vegas. But what chance did they have of actually spotting the car?

"I think I just saw it," Shahla said.

"Where?"

"Parked beside the road."

She must have sharp eyes. It was now quite dark. Tony said, "Do you want to check?"

"Yes."

It took him several minutes before he found a place wide enough to allow them to turn around. He pulled off the road, waited for traffic to go by, and swung a sharp U.

"Go slowly," Shahla said, as they rounded a curve. "I think it's near here. There it is."

Tony stopped opposite the car Shahla pointed at and pulled off the road as far as possible. They got out and crossed the pavement to a turnoff where the car that Tony now could identify as a gray Honda was parked. He compared the license plate number to the one he had written down. They matched.

"Good work," he told Shahla. "Now where did they go?"

"There's a path," Shahla said. "It leads up that hill."

The dirt path disappeared into the desert foliage and the dark.

"You wait in the car," Tony told Shahla. He handed the keys to her.

She refused to take them. "I'm not going to let you go up there by yourself."

He knew from experience that she meant what she said. "Okay, this is what we'll do. There should be enough light from the moon to follow the path. I'll go first. If I hold up my hand, stop."

"All right."

At least she didn't argue. Tony started up the path, slowly, avoiding rocks and roots that made the footing tricky. He was relieved that it wasn't especially steep. The night air was chilly—it cooled off rapidly in the desert—but he wasn't going to take time to go back to the car for the sweatshirt he had brought. And Shahla wasn't complaining. They walked uphill for several minutes in silence. Then the path leveled off, and Tony saw an open space ahead. And moving shadows; they must be people. He held up his hand. Shahla obediently stopped.

He beckoned for her to come up beside him. He bent down and spoke into her ear. "There are at least two people there. In order for us to get close enough to hear them, we'll have to get behind that rock." A rock large enough to hide them stood fifty feet ahead. Tony moved toward the rock, staying silent and close to the ground, to keep from being silhouetted against the moonlit sky like the two figures he was watching. It was difficult work. He crouched as low as he could, but sometimes he had to get down on his hands and knees, amid small but sharp stones. He kept looking back at Shahla. She remained at his heels, stuck to him like a tick. He hoped her dress—Rasa's dress— wasn't getting too dirty.

Several times he saw a flash of light coming from the direction of the two people. The first one startled him, but then he realized that they must be taking pictures.

He could hear voices, but he couldn't make out words. Probably a man and a woman. When they got to the rock, he felt more secure. At least they weren't exposed. Tony put his finger to his lips as Shahla hugged the rock beside him. He inched forward so that he could see around it.

What he saw almost made him gasp out loud. A girl—she was now lit well enough by the moon so that he could tell—was standing right at the edge of a cliff. Behind her he could see city lights—Las Vegas. It looked to him as if one step and she would be over the edge.

Shahla leaned against his back so she could see. She put her mouth to his ear and said, "She's going to fall over the cliff. And what is she wearing?"

Not much, as Tony could see now. It looked as if she was wearing a bra and panties. She must be cold. He spotted Paul—the angular silhouette could only be Paul—a few feet away. He had something in his hands, probably a camera.

"Now the bra," he heard Paul saying.

The girl didn't argue; she immediately took off her bra. Paul was aiming the camera. There was a flash. Another flash. Each flash momentarily lit up the girl. It was the blonde, no question about it—and she was beautiful.

After taking several pictures, Paul told her to take off her panties. And she did. Without any fuss. Tony was perplexed. This was too easy. Especially for someone he had said was a new girlfriend. Paul took more pictures.

Shahla said, with her mouth to Tony's ear, "He's got her underwear. Now he's going to push her off the cliff."

Was he? Was this what Paul had done to Joy? Convince her to pose for him in the nude? Pretty girls were vain about their figures and susceptible to flattery, but Joy hadn't even known him—had she? What was going to happen next? Should he intervene?

They heard Paul say, "That's enough of that."

Paul placed his camera on the ground and started to walk toward the girl.

Shahla spoke into Tony's ear, loud enough to hurt his eardrum. "He's going to do it now. Stop him!"

Tony sprang to his feet and ran toward Paul. The girl screamed. Tony lowered his head and hit Paul with his shoulder, at waist level, the full weight of his body behind the blow. Paul crumpled to the ground, and Tony fell on top of him. Tony lay dazed for several seconds. Paul didn't move either.

Then he realized that the girl was standing over him, yelling at him. "What are you doing?" she shouted, again and again. He was aware that she had picked up something. A rock. She was going to hit him with a rock. He staggered to his feet and raised his arms. She threw the good-sized rock at him with both hands. It was a weak throw, and he evaded it.

"He was going to push you off the cliff," he told the girl.

"You idiot. He wasn't going to push me off the cliff."

"How do you know? You just met him."

"I've known him all my life. He's my brother."

"Your brother?" He looked from the girl to the still horizontal Paul. There was definitely a family resemblance. This was terribly wrong. Tony couldn't sort it out, but he knew he had to get out of here. Right now. Before Paul got up. And Paul was stirring.

Tony started running toward the path. Where was Shahla? Then he saw her running ahead of him. He came to the downhill portion. He was going too fast in the dark. He tripped over a root and went flying. He landed hard. He couldn't breathe. The wind had been knocked out of him. He lay there for several seconds, wondering if he was going to die. He gasped for breath and then realized that since he could gasp, he could breathe.

He climbed slowly to his feet. He hurt all over. He continued down the hill, looking over his shoulder, expecting to see Paul coming after him. But there was nobody in sight. Tony limped down to the street, waited for a car to pass, and then crossed to the other side. Shahla was standing beside the car.

"Are you all right?" Shahla asked anxiously. "I was about to go back and look for you."

"No." But he had to get them out of there before Paul identified them. He belatedly fumbled for the keys in his pocket—found them. His hands were shaking as he tried to press the remote that unlocked the car. He finally heard the click and then managed to open the door. He fell into the car. Shahla was already in her seat. He started the engine and ground the gearshift into first. The car jolted forward.

***

"You look terrible," Shahla said as Tony stiffly got out of the car.

"Thank you."

They had stopped at a diner outside of Las Vegas. Shahla had insisted on it. They hadn't eaten anything since lunch. And Tony's hands, elbows, and now he realized, his knees were ground up like raw hamburger from his fall. He admitted he couldn't drive home until he ate and got cleaned up, but he refused to go to an emergency room, thinking that if Paul reported the attack he would be linked to it.

"They won't let me in there looking like this," Tony said, surveying his wounds.

"I'm going to get some paper towels to clean you up."

Shahla went into the diner. Now that the initial shock had worn off, Tony wondered how he would be able to hold the steering wheel for 300 miles with his mangled hands. And his pants were ruined, torn at the knees. He sat back down on the car seat as he became conscious of increasing pain.

Shahla returned a few minutes later with damp paper towels and a knife.

"I borrowed this from the kitchen," she said, referring to the knife.

"Are you going to put me out of my misery?"

"I'm going to cut off your pants above the knee so we can get at your knees."

In order for her to do that he had to stand up. He was afraid she'd cut his legs off, but she was careful. And skillful. She fashioned him a new pair of shorts. Together they cleaned up the worst of his injuries. By the time he walked into the diner, he was confident he wouldn't attract too many stares.

"Go into the restroom and finish cleaning yourself off," Shahla ordered.

"While I'm doing that, call your mother and tell her you're all right." It wouldn't be a complete lie.

Tony emerged from the restroom a few minutes later, feeling almost human. They ordered dinner, and he realized how starved he was.

"What do you think was going on between those two?" Shahla asked, after the waitress took their order.

"Well, I think that's what you call an incestuous relationship. When I tackled Paul, he was starting to take his shirt off."

"Incest? I've heard callers talk about incest, but I thought they were fantasizing."

"That didn't look like a fantasy to me."

***

"I can't stay awake. If I try to keep driving, I'm going to kill us." Tony took the off-ramp into a rest area and parked the car. It was past midnight, and he hadn't had any sleep since 5:30 that morning. Even the pain from his injuries couldn't keep him awake. He had been driving all over the road. His left knee was stiffening up, too, making it difficult for him to shift, although not much shifting was required on the Interstate. It was the sleep factor he couldn't overcome.

"I'll drive," Shahla said.

"Have you ever driven a stick shift?"

"No, but I can learn."

"Not in my Porsche. Besides, you must be as tired as I am."

"I got an extra couple of hours sleep. Remember? And I'm younger."

"Call your mother again and tell her you're still all right."

The car was not designed for sleeping. The seats didn't tilt back. Tony slid down in his seat to try and get comfortable, but his left knee hurt when he bent it. He closed his eyes. At some point

Shahla bridged the gap between the seats and placed her head on his shoulder.

Tony spent a restless night, but every time he woke up he fell asleep again and had dreams with violent but undefined movement. Finally, he opened his eyes and saw that dawn was breaking.

CHAPTER 21

Tony didn't feel up to working on the Hotline Monday evening. His body ached, his wounds had not healed, and his left knee was still stiff, making it difficult for him to shift his Porsche. He had been evasive in telling Josh what had happened to him, admitting that he had gone to Las Vegas, but not that anybody had accompanied him. His injuries had occurred when he tripped on a crack in the sidewalk.

He told essentially the same story to Mona. She was sympathetic, even offering to make him dinner at her place. He declined, feeling that it wasn't a good precedent to set, and told her that he was working on the Hotline that evening, knowing that she would respond positively. Rather than turn himself into a liar, he went.

Tony left his office late and picked up a pizza he had ordered by phone on his way to the Hotline. The door was unlocked when he arrived, which immediately made him feel irritated at Shahla. He would chew her out, especially if she were there alone. She wasn't. As he walked in the door, he could see Shahla and Nathan in the listening room.

Nathan was on a call, but Shahla came out when she saw him and asked, in a stage whisper, "How are you feeling?"

" Like sh…. Like I've just spent an hour in a clothes dryer with spikes on the tumbler."

"I'm sorry. I feel responsible for what happened. I wasn't sure you were coming tonight."

"Were you going to work alone?" He was still looking for a reason to be mad at her.

"I called Gail, and she said Nathan was signed up to work. I thought it would be a good chance for me to ask him about this church he belongs to."

"I don't want you doing any detective work by yourself."

She turned her back on him.

He *was* being rather snarly. There was no reason to take his pain out on Shahla. He admitted to himself that he had enjoyed having her along on the trip. If only the climax had been different. And that hadn't been her fault. He had bought into the idea that Paul was going to push the girl off the cliff. Paul had lied to them about his girlfriend. Or at least not told them the truth. But when you're committing incest with your sister, what story are you going to tell people?

Tony said, "I asked Nathan some questions about his church, but he wasn't very forthcoming. In fact, I made him mad. I'm surprised he'll even work a shift with me on it."

"Let me try."

As long as Tony was there, he was willing to let Shahla ask questions. He signed in while Nathan was ending his call and then limped into the listening room.

Nathan looked up and said, "My God, Tony, what happened to you?"

In addition to his limp, he had wrapped his hands in white gauze to cover the ugliest scrapes. "I got caught in a cement mixer."

"Ha ha. Listen, if you'd like to take the night off, Shahla and I can handle the phones."

That was exactly what was not going to happen. Tony sank into the remaining chair and vowed to stay there until the shift ended. He opened the pizza box, selected a piece, and took a big bite out of it. "Have a piece," he said with his mouth full, including Shahla and Nathan with a gesture.

Nathan declined; Shahla took a piece. Within a minute, the phone rang. Tony picked it up, figuring that talking to a caller might improve his mood. A repeat caller was on the line who liked to talk sports. Tony could handle this call with half a brain. And eat his pizza at the same time. He pressed the mute button when his chewing was loudest. And he could keep an eye on Nathan and Shahla.

He wished Shahla weren't wearing such a short skirt—the shortest one he had seen her wear. Nathan wasn't just another high school boy. He was older, and older men could be lecherous. Josh was a good example. And, if he was honest, Tony couldn't exempt himself.

Tony listened in on the conversation between Nathan and Shahla with one ear, while the other ear listened to the caller.

"May I ask what religion you are?" Nathan asked Shahla without looking at her.

"My dad was Protestant, my mom originally was Muslim, and I have Quaker ancestors. What does that make me?"

"A mess. Let me tell you a little about my church."

Tony frowned. Was he proselytizing her? Shahla looked at Nathan attentively. With his usual shiftiness, Nathan didn't look directly at her.

"Our church is based on Christianity," Nathan said, "but we differ from other Christian sects in one important respect."

"What's that?" Shahla asked.

"We know when Jesus is returning to earth to take the believers with him into heaven."

"Oh, when is that?" Shahla asked, as if she were asking what time the next bus left.

Tony had to answer a comment made by his caller at this point. He missed the next few sentences of their conversation.

When he tuned in again, Shahla was saying, "You can tell me, Nathan. I won't tell anybody."

"Would you like to attend one of our services? Since you're not strongly committed to any religion, that means you have an open mind. You would get a chance to learn the truth. And you would get into heaven with us. I would hate for a pretty girl like you to be left behind. Our services are on Thursdays at seven."

So, Nathan wanted Shahla to go to heaven with him. Tony had an almost overwhelming urge to grab Shahla by the scruff of her neck and yank her away from him. He gave a head-fake and quickly and quietly told his caller that he had to take another call. He told him he could call back tomorrow. Tony hung up, surreptitiously, so that Nathan wouldn't be aware that he was listening to their conversation.

Shahla was mumbling something, apparently looking at her appointment book. Tony knew she carried one. She was one of the most organized teenagers he had ever known.

"Thursday. Why Thursday?"

"You mean, as opposed to Sunday? Because on the weekends we're too busy getting ready for the big day. Some of us still have jobs, you know, and can't do that during the week."

"How long do the services last?"

"Often several hours. But you wouldn't have to stay for the whole thing. People come in and out. Would you like me to pick you up?"

"No, I think I can get the car. Where is this church?"

Tony wanted to scream. From the comments he heard them making behind him, he knew that Nathan was writing down the address and drawing a map for her. But Shahla was never going to make it to the church service because Tony was going to strangle her first.

Two calls came in simultaneously. Shahla took one and Nathan the other. Tony sat and fumed and finished eating his pizza. He couldn't wait to get his hands on Shahla. Then the phone rang again, and he answered it. It was a man. When Tony routinely asked his name, the man wouldn't tell him.

The man said, "I used to work on the Hotline as a listener. I know all about you people."

Tony was instantly alert. He asked, "How long ago was that?"

"I left about a year ago. Because I couldn't stand it anymore. The listeners on the Hotline are all stuck-up jerks. Especially the girls." He rambled on for several minutes about how mean everybody had been to him.

"What did you say your name was?" Tony asked.

"You people pretend that you're performing a great service, but you're really ripping off the callers. You don't help them. You laugh at them. The kids would put the calls on the speaker and everybody in the room would make fun of the callers."

"The calls are confidential. And only three listeners at a time are allowed in the listening room."

"Bullshit. I was there. On the weekends, at night, it was party time. Beer and orgies."

"Alcoholic beverages are not allowed in the office. Listen, if you have a legitimate complaint, I'd like to follow up on it, but I need to know your name."

A click told Tony that he was not going to learn the caller's name. Shahla and Nathan were still on the phone so he couldn't talk to them about it. He wrote a detailed call report, mentioning that the caller had a slight accent and sounded older than a teenager. He painfully got up, walked into the administration office, and placed the report on Gail's desk. She had been volunteer coordinator with the Hotline for years and knew all the listeners. Maybe she could figure out who it was.

It wasn't until an hour later that all three of them were off the phones at the same time. Tony didn't want to hear any more talk about Nathan's church, so he told them about the call from the former listener.

"You were here a year ago," Tony said to Shahla. "Does my description ring any bells with you?"

"No. But of course we don't know all the other listeners. Gail is the best bet because she knows them all."

"That's what I thought, too."

"From what you said about him, I sense hostility," Nathan said, looking out the window rather than at them. "He's one of those people who never quite fit in. He's a little bit different, a little bit odd. He doesn't get the girls. Of course, he blames them for his problems. And you have to admit that some of the girls here are stuck up."

"Does that make him a candidate for murder?" Tony asked.

"It might. It depends on how bad it gets and how long it lasts. The feelings of anger and alienation build up inside him until they reach a flash point. And then…pow."

"Pow," Shahla said, "meaning…?"

"Anything can happen. But he'll feel justified in whatever he does. Because he was wronged."

Tony winced. "So people like this stockpile guns and ammunition and then one fine day they walk into the place where they experienced humiliation and shoot everybody there."

"Don't talk like that," Shahla said, looking at the outside door apprehensively. "Is the door locked? We don't want that guy to come busting in here."

Tony couldn't remember whether he had locked it. He started to get up, but Shahla said, "No, I'll go. I can get there in less than half an hour."

"That was a cruel thing to say," Nathan said when Shahla returned and confirmed that the door was locked. "You sound like the girls the caller was talking about."

"I'm sorry," Shahla said sounding sincere. She put a hand on Tony's shoulder. "Tony, you know I would never humiliate you."

"I know," Tony said, feeling better than he had all evening. It was amazing the power a girl could have over a man. "I just have one question. Nobody told me about the weekend orgies."

"You'll only find them in your dreams," Shahla said.

CHAPTER 22

Tony was feeling a little better by Tuesday evening. Some of the stiffness had left his body. His wounds were beginning to heal. He felt good enough to whip himself up a mess of spaghetti for his dinner. His Italian mother had taught him how to do it. Of course, she made her own tomato sauce, whereas Tony got his out of a bottle. He also used store-bought hamburger and spaghetti, but he added basil, oregano, and garlic, just as his mother had showed him.

As he sipped a beer and spun the spaghetti worms (as they had seemed to him in his youth) on his fork, he remembered that he had been going to check Josh's drawers for women's underwear. Except that no opportunity had presented itself. Until now. This morning, Josh had said he would be home late tonight. He had some function he was going to attend, related to his job.

Tony decided he had enough time to eat his dinner before he conducted a search. His body still complained when he tried to rush into anything. He ate all the spaghetti he could manage, saved the rest, and rinsed his dishes. Then he went upstairs to Josh's bedroom. He opened the door and turned on the light. He remembered that if Josh came home while the light was on, he would see it as he drove into the carport, but Josh wouldn't be home for a while. Searching with a flashlight was difficult and time consuming. Tony wanted to get this over with.

Where should he start, amid this mess that constituted Josh's possessions? The dresser drawers presented an obvious location to check. He would search the easy places first; he might get lucky.

He quickly went through the drawers. He found socks, T-shirts, handkerchiefs, boxer shorts (one difference between him and Josh—he wore briefs), a bathing suit, a jockstrap, baggy shorts for outerwear, but nothing that a girl would consider wearing. Well, he remembered when girls had worn boxer shorts for a season, but not this size.

The closet was next. Sweaters and sweatshirts were stacked on two shelves at the top. He checked between them and underneath them. Nothing. Dress shirts, sport shirts, sport coats were hung on hangers. Nothing unusual here. Josh had a lot of clothes. More than Tony did. And yet he always looked as if he wasn't quite put together.

A pile of dirty clothes lay on the floor. Tony went through this pile, one piece at a time, carefully, restacking the pile in another spot in reverse sequence. When he was through, he flipped the pile over and reset it in the original location—just in case Josh was more observant than he gave him credit for.

The bending over and kneeling hurt his knees. He wasn't going to be able to do this much longer. What was left? A two-drawer filing cabinet. Tony pulled open each drawer, in turn, being sure to look in the open space in the back of the drawers. He found nothing unusual. All that was left to search was a bunch of brown, cardboard boxes—boxes that Josh had carted around with him for years, containing all his other possessions. Keepsakes, mementoes, souvenirs, books, whatever it was that Josh saved.

Tony didn't relish the idea of going through the boxes in his present condition, especially since they were heavy and stacked three high. He looked at his watch. It was after nine. He didn't know when Josh would be home. He'd better wrap this up soon. He could look inside the boxes on top while standing up. He decided to do that and then quit for the evening.

The first box contained books. Tony lifted several out to see what was underneath. More books. He gave a pass to that box and went on to the next. This one contained papers, tickets, programs. It was definitely a souvenir box. He had to lift each item individually and that took time. Near the bottom of the box he felt something soft, something that wasn't paper.

He pulled it out and stared in shock. A pair of white panties. This was what he was looking for, but now that he had found it, he couldn't believe it. He had been trying to clear Josh, not convict him. How long he stood there with the wispy piece of lingerie in his hand, he didn't know. It suddenly came to him that he should find the bra. He searched the rest of the box, feverishly, but there was no other piece of clothing.

There was no time to search the other boxes. He interleaved the flaps on the top of the box together the way he had found them, just as the sound of an engine came from the carport area. If that was Josh, he had already seen the light on in his room. Tony would have to bluff his way out of this. He stuffed the panties into his pocket, turned, and headed for the door. He never made it.

He forgot about Josh's swivel chair; he had moved it into the middle of the room during the search. He tripped over one of its metal supports and felt flat on his face. And his bad knee.

Tony let out a yell as the pain hit him like a Freightliner truck. After a few seconds he tried to get up, but his leg collapsed, and he was back on the floor again. He was still there when Josh found him a minute later.

"Holy shit. Tony, what happened?" There was real concern in Josh's voice.

"I was trying to check your calendar." Tony forced the words out, between spasms of pain. "I can get tickets to the SC football game on Saturday."

"But what happened to you?"

"My knee. I fell on my knee."

"Can you walk?"

Josh helped, or rather lifted, Tony to his feet. If it hadn't been for Josh's continued support, he would have fallen again. Tony put his left arm over Josh's shoulder and leaned against him.

"Help me get to my room."

"I'm taking you to a room all right—the emergency room."

"I'll be all right. I just need to sit down for a few minutes."

"Don't argue with Uncle Josh. You can't even stand up, for crissake.

Josh practically had to carry Tony down the stairs. When they reached the ground floor, Josh became his left leg as they slowly made their way out to the carport. He bundled Tony into his SUV and went around to the driver's side.

On the way to the hospital, Tony tried again to explain why he had been in Josh's room. Josh didn't listen. He concentrated on his driving—accelerating and stopping slowly, easing his way around corners, as if Tony were Humpty Dumpty. Tony wanted to tell him to drive normally, but he didn't. He felt protected, just as he had when he first met Josh in college, and Josh had taken him under his wing.

***

"I don't think there's any permanent damage," the young-looking emergency-room physician, whose name Tony had never caught, said, surveying the X-rays mounted on the wall. But you've got a helluva bruise and some lacerations to boot. I'll bet you didn't get those falling down in your house."

"No," Tony agreed. "I got those falling down a hill." A paraphrase of the old nursery rhyme kept singing in his head: "Jack and Jill went up the hill, to see two siblings playing. Jack fell free and broke his knee...."

"I'm going to give you a pair of crutches," the doctor continued, "and a flexible knee brace. But I don't want you putting much weight on that knee for a couple of weeks."

"Will I be able to use that leg to shift gears in my Porsche?"

"I don't want you even bending your knee as much as it takes to get into a Porsche. You need to be driving something big and roomy, with automatic transmission, that will allow you to keep your leg straight. And you're lucky this isn't your right knee or you wouldn't be able to drive at all."

Lucky? How was he going to work? How was he going to do anything?

"I know what we'll do," Josh said. "We'll swap cars. You can drive my Highlander and I'll drive the Porsche."

"If he hadn't volunteered to trade you, I would have," the doctor said smiling. "It's always been my dream to own a Porsche, but with a wife and two kids...."

Tony had never let anybody drive his Porsche, and he would have rated Josh near the bottom of his list of possibles. But Josh had taken care of him tonight; he had not only driven him here, but stayed with him for hours while the paperwork ground slowly, and sicker and more seriously injured patients gained priority over him.

"Will you promise to drive it the same way you drove me here tonight?" Tony asked Josh.

"Scout's honor."

Josh had never been a boy scout, but there was another reason Tony was willing to consider it. The pair of panties was still in his pants pocket, which at the moment hung on a peg on the wall of the examining room. Fortunately, his wallet had been in another pocket, so he was able to retrieve his insurance information without pulling them out, but he was feeling a fair amount of guilt at violating Josh's privacy.

CHAPTER 23

Tony remembered the way to Carol's apartment so well that he could have driven it blindfolded. As it was, he was driving it with one leg. He was thankful for Josh's SUV. At least he didn't have to rent a car, in addition to making hefty lease payments on the Porsche. He forced himself not to worry about what Josh was doing with his car.

During his few free moments at work, he had used the time to worry about something else: what to do with the panties. He couldn't bring himself to turn them over to Detective Croyden. He couldn't rat out Josh, especially since he would have to drive Josh's car to the police station to do it.

Josh had been super nice to him ever since their little "talk," during which Josh had said he would move out within thirty days. He hadn't mentioned moving out since, and there was no evidence that he was looking for another place to live. He hadn't violated Tony's rules about having loud visitors over on work nights. He was still a slob, but Tony could live with that. At least Tony knew Josh's habits. And he always paid his rent on time. What would life be like with a new roommate he didn't know anything about? It would be risky, to say the least.

While he was driving to Carol's apartment, Tony thought some more about the panties. Even though he had finally opened his mind to the probability that Josh was somewhat of a misogynist, he still couldn't picture him as a cold-blooded murderer. Josh might have looked up the address of the Hotline office in Tony's notebook.

He might have gone to the office out of curiosity. He might have seen Joy come out. He might even have accosted her, verbally, perhaps tried to make a date with her. But murder her? Tony couldn't picture it.

But this line of reasoning fell apart as Tony thought once again about the panties stuffed into the bottom of his attaché case. He couldn't explain them. And they badly needed an explanation.

Here was Carol's apartment building. Fortunately, a parking place appeared, on demand, on the street close to the entrance. Unfortunately, Carol lived on the second floor and there wasn't any elevator. Tony had practiced using the crutches on his own stairs; going up last night, coming down this morning. It had not been easy.

He was glad that none of the apartment dwellers was watching as he made his way up the stairs, trying not to fall, trying not to look too awkward. It was like attempting to play a new sport at which one has no experience. That he made it to the second floor without disaster was a major relief to him.

As he rang the bell to Carol's apartment, he realized that he was looking forward to seeing her. That quickening of his pulse, that feeling of glad anticipation—they returned as he waited for her to open the door. When she did open the door, she looked as good as he had pictured her, except for the expression on her face.

"Tony, what happened to you?"

"I, uh, fell down."

"You didn't tell me. Oh, you poor dear. Are you all right?"

She gave him a gentle hug, which he couldn't return because his hands were holding the crutches.

"It's just my knee. It'll be all right in a couple of weeks. I can make it through the doorway."

Carol was trying to help him, but she didn't know how to do it. He smiled a wry smile. Perhaps he should have gotten hurt while they were dating. Then she might have had more sympathy for him.

"Dinner is all ready. Here, would you like to sit in this chair?"

"That should work. I just need room to stretch out my left leg. There's a bottle of wine in my fanny pack."

Carol laughed as she extracted the Merlot.

"I can always count on you to bring the right wine, even when you can barely walk."

He had been using the fanny pack to carry essential papers and other items today because his hands were tied up. Carol had the small table set intimately for two, with candles and even cloth napkins. When he had called her, asking for a little of her time, he hadn't expected her to invite him to dinner. But he also hadn't been able to refuse the invitation. What was the occasion? He knew he shouldn't ascribe any special meaning to it.

Tony sat down in the proffered chair, and Carol took his crutches—and placed them out of his reach. He almost protested; he felt like a prisoner. He watched her as she opened the wine in the adjacent space that was the small kitchen and placed the food on the table. She looked unbelievably good in form-fitting white pants and a purple silk blouse. A blouse that he was sure he could see through in the right light.

And then when she passed through a beam of light pouring in the window, courtesy of the setting sun, he had the revelation that not only could he see through the blouse, but she wasn't wearing a bra underneath it. He had a sudden and overwhelming urge to bury his face in that blouse. It was a good thing he couldn't get up. None of the outfits he had seen on the teenage girls even approached this one in sensuality. All his libidinous feelings for her came back. How long had it been since their liaison had ended? How long had he been celibate?

Tony barely noticed what he was eating. The Caesar salad, the barbequed ribs, the mashed potatoes, the wine; he ate and drank them automatically, but didn't taste them as they entered his mouth and slid down his throat. Carol chatted about various things, and he agreed with everything she said—for a change. Until she started talking about the Hotline.

"You know that Josh called me because he was worried about what had happened to you since you started working at the Hotline."

"Yes. Remember, you called me and told me."

"But I didn't know what he was talking about until I saw you with that teenybopper at the Beach House."

"I work with her on the Hotline." He kept his voice even. And if it was Shahla that concerned her, he knew that her concerns were different than Josh's.

"Right. But as I recall, it was rather late at night. And she had the kind of innocent good looks that men can't resist."

Tony decided that silence was his best option at this point and was thankful once again for his Hotline training. He put a large bite of mashed potatoes into his mouth so that he couldn't say anything.

"Okay, I'll get off it." Carol smiled a thin smile. "After all, it's none of my business anymore."

"Let's talk about the reason I wanted to see you," Tony said after swallowing the potatoes.

"You said you wanted to show me a poem that might have something to do with the girl's murder. What was her name?"

"Joy."

Carol had been an English teacher for a few years before she became disgusted with principals who didn't back her and the lack of discipline that made teaching difficult. She had quit teaching and gone into the computer industry. She was making far more money than she would ever have made as a teacher. Tony explained the circumstances of finding the poem but not the fact that Shahla had been with him. Don't borrow trouble.

"If you gave the poem to the police, how is it that you still have a copy?"

"I entered it into a computer, being careful about fingerprints, of course."

"Were there any fingerprints on it?"

"Only a couple of mine before I started being careful. Whoever wrote the poem was even more careful than I was."

"So, as I understand it, what you want me to do is to read the poem and then tell you who wrote it."

"Yes, please, if you would be so kind."

They both laughed. This was more like it.

"All right. But before I perform this feat, let's have dessert."

Tony had several more opportunities to observe the enticements inside Carol's blouse while she cleared the table. He saw the mole on her breast that had bewitched him once upon a time. He realized that he badly needed to find himself another girlfriend.

Carol did something behind the counter that separated the table from the kitchen. It involved matches, as Tony could tell from the smell. He wondered whether she was going to add to the two candles already on the table. Then she lowered the lights, leaving the room lit mostly by the candles. She came back to the table, carrying a cake with birthday candles on it and singing "Happy Birthday."

Tony was flabbergasted. He had completely forgotten that his birthday was only two days away. Carol placed the cake in front of him and gave him a light kiss on the lips.

"Make a wish and see if you still have enough wind in your ancient body to blow out the candles."

Tony did. He didn't count to see if she had gotten the number right. At some point, you had to stop counting. He cut the cake and they ate it in an atmosphere as amicable as that of the best day they had spent together, while drinking crème de menthe in miniature glasses with silver stems that Tony had given Carol for a Christmas present. Time stood still.

When they had finished, Carol broke the spell saying, "Okay, let's see the poem. And move your chair back from the table. Will I hurt your knee if I sit on your lap? I think I can get the best perspective from there."

God. What was she trying to do? She was temptation personified. How was he going to keep his hands off her blouse? Tony realized that he would be the sourpuss if he refused her, so he backed his chair up and guided her to a safe position on his lap. He put his arms carefully around her waist, that being the most innocuous place for them. Carol picked up the computer printout of the poem, which Tony had placed on the table when he arrived, and read it through, seemingly concentrating on the words to the exclusion of everything else.

Tony read the poem again over her shoulder:
> She wears a summer dress, spaghetti straps
> to hold it up, or is this so? Perhaps

it's gravity, the gravity of con-
sequences should it fall. If she should don
her dress one day but then forget to pull
them up, those flimsy wisps of hope so full
of her ripe beauty, do you think the weight
of promises within, or hand of fate,
would slide it down, revealing priceless treasures?
If so, would she invoke heroic measures
to hide the truth, for fear this modest lapse
would air the secret of spaghetti straps?

When she was finished, Carol said, "That poem was written by somebody who has written a lot of poems. It was not an amateur effort."

"What else can you tell me about it?"

"There are not many people in the world who can write a poem like this. Technically, it rates an A. It has images, meter, enjambment, clever rhymes. As to the subject matter, my first inclination is to rate it a C minus and say it must have been written by a horny teenager."

"Except that a horny teenager couldn't write it."

"Exactly. Unless he had previously written a few hundred poems and had some talent to boot. If that person exists, I never saw him in any of my classes. And, in addition, although the subject matter is suspect, the way it's handled, in a poetic rather than a voyeuristic fashion, would probably prompt me to give it a higher grade than a C minus. I can imagine one of my students writing something like, 'What if her boobs flopped out of her dress?'"

"Okay, we've settled the grading. I'm sure the author will be pleased. But who did write the poem?"

"Somebody with talent and a lot of poetic experience. Somebody who remembers what it's like to be a horny teenager."

"Or somebody who is a horny adult," Tony said, his thoughts about Carol's blouse still heavy on his mind.

Carol turned toward Tony so that her mouth was not more than two inches from his and said, "Do adults still get horny?"

Tony couldn't say anything. She kissed him. At first he sat there, not responding, wondering what was going on. Then, before he could return her kiss, she jumped up from his lap and said, "This brings us to my present for you. Or perhaps it's for me."

"Present?" Tony said dumbly.

Carol brought Tony's crutches to him and said, "We have to go into the bedroom."

Tony slowly got up and followed her into the bedroom, still not clear about what was happening. He noticed that the bed was unmade, which wasn't like Carol. The bedspread, the blanket, even the top sheet, all lay on the floor at the foot of the bed, leaving it covered by the bottom sheet.

"I didn't figure on your injury," Carol said. "I don't suppose you can kneel on that knee."

"No."

"Well, turn around." She turned him so that his back was to the bed and said, "Sit."

He sat.

"Give me your crutches. Now lie down on your back."

He lay down, partly as a result of a push from Carol. She helped him scoot his body up until he was completely on the bed.

"All right," Carol said, unbuttoning her blouse. "I can do most of the work, but you have to help me some. For starters, how about unbuckling your belt and unzipping your pants."

***

"Time for you to go," Carol said, raising her head from Tony's chest.

Her naked body was lying on top of his naked body, and Tony would just as soon stay like that forever. She rolled off him and sat up.

"How much help do you need getting into your clothes?"

"Oh, I think I can manage if you put them within arm's length." Tony was still in a euphoric daze and was having trouble coming back to reality. However, having no choice, he started putting on his clothes. Carol did the same.

"There are a couple of things I need to tell you," Carol said. "I will be moving in with Horace next weekend."

"You're moving out of the apartment?"

"I won't need it anymore. Horace has a beautiful house on the beach. Not only is he rich, he loves me to pieces. And he listens to me. Even better, he pretty much agrees with everything I have to say."

Ouch. Well, Tony had not come here expecting anything different. Still, this was a quick reversal. "You said you needed to tell me a couple of things. What was the other?"

"If Horace is lacking in one thing, it's…I guess you would call it, libido. Something you never lacked. I just wanted to experience what it was like between us one more time. But the upshot is, this was the last time. If I'm going to live with a man, I'm going to be faithful to him."

"I wish you every happiness," Tony said. "And thank you for a nice evening." What else could he say?

CHAPTER 24

As Thursday afternoon advanced inexorably toward evening, Tony became more and more worried about Shahla. Although he had been upset with her on Monday for talking to Nathan about the possibility of attending a service at the Church of the Risen Lord, he hadn't really believed she would do it. But the more he thought about it, the less sure he was of this conclusion.

Shahla was impetuous, and if she thought she could find out something about Joy's murder by attending the service, she would go. In addition, Tony had seen her writing in a spiral notebook in the car while they were driving home from Las Vegas. When he had asked her whether she was writing poetry, she had said no, she was taking notes. For what? She said for the true-crime book she was going to write. So now she pictured herself as a reporter. And reporters went wherever there were stories. And the premise of this Church might be enough of a story to entice her to attend one its services.

Tony called Shahla's cell phone number about 4:00. When she didn't answer it, he didn't leave a message, figuring that if she was planning to go to the service, she probably wouldn't return his call. By 5:00 Tony had become so anxious that he was no longer able to work. He left his office and walked—limped—to his car. He was becoming more adept at using the crutches, but they were a damned nuisance, and he would be glad to be rid of them.

He decided to drive to Shahla's house and deal with her face to face. On the way there, he thought about Carol and last night. What an ending to that romance. Had she spoiled him for other women? If all their evenings had been like that one, they would still be together. He was going to have a hard time getting over her.

Tony pulled Josh's SUV to the curb in front of Shahla's house and was carefully negotiating his way out of the vehicle when Rasa drove into the driveway. She was undoubtedly coming home from her work at the hospital. Uh oh. He wasn't sure whether she would be happy to see him. After all, he had driven her daughter to Las Vegas and not returned for over twenty-four hours.

Better to face the situation head-on. He limped up the driveway and greeted Rasa as she got out of her car. He was struck again by how much she looked like a short-haired and darker version of Shahla.

She looked at him and said, "Tony, what happened to you?" He was certain that Shahla hadn't told her everything about their trip, so he said, "I had a fall, but I'll be all right. I just have to be on crutches for a week or so."

"Did you see doctor?"

"Yes. In fact, I went to the emergency room at your hospital."

"Good. They have good doctors there. Are you here to see Shahla? She has cross-country practice in afternoon, but she should be home soon."

"All right, but I'd like to talk to you for a minute, if I could."

"Sure. Come into house."

Rasa collected the mail from the curbside mailbox, and Tony followed her carefully up the driveway and then up several steps to the front door. Once inside, she waved him into the living room and excused herself. He sat on the couch and thought about what he should say. Five minutes later she returned, having shed her work clothes and donned a dark blue sweat suit that made her look even younger than she already did.

She sat in the chair she had sat in when he had been here before and said, "Shahla told me nothing happened on Las Vegas trip. Since you were gone so long that is hard to believe."

"It is a bit of an exaggeration," Tony agreed. "We talked to this guy, Paul, who is the poet. We went into one of the hotels so Shahla could see what it looked like. And then we...well, we followed Paul and a girl. But we did it carefully and were never in any danger."

Then how come he was on crutches?

"Shahla said you fell asleep on drive home."

"Well, fortunately, I stopped before I fell asleep, and I took a nap. But that's why we didn't get home until Sunday morning."

"Thank you for keeping Shahla safe."

"You're welcome." He wasn't sure he deserved her thanks. "Let me tell you the reason I'm here. When Shahla and I were on the Hotline Monday evening, another listener was there who talked about a church he belongs to. They have a service on Thursday evening, and he invited Shahla to attend the service."

"What church is this?"

"It's called the Church of the Risen Lord. It's a sort of Christian Church, but it has kind of a funny idea."

"We do not go to church. I have not had faith since my husband was murdered. Did Shahla tell you about that?"

"Yes."

Rasa paused, as if contemplating whether to say more about her husband. She apparently decided against it.

"I have not raised Shahla in religious environment. Sometimes I feel little guilty about this. If she wants to attend church, it is all right with me."

"Well, this church is at least ten miles from here and not in a great part of town. I don't think Shahla should be driving there alone—especially at night."

"I see." Rasa frowned. "Thank you for telling me. I think I hear Shahla now. We will talk to her together."

Shahla had apparently received a ride home from a classmate, because Tony heard the sound of a car driving away at the same time as the front door opened.

"Shahla," Rasa called. "We are in living room."

Shahla appeared a few seconds later, her hair in a ponytail, wearing running shoes, shorts, and a white athletic bra. Tony knew that the cross-country team had uniform shirts, but on warm days, the girls often took off their shirts and ran in just their bras, at least in practice.

"Tony," she said startled. "What are you doing here?"

"Tony has come because he is concerned about your safety," Rasa said.

"Where's your car? And what are you doing with crutches? You didn't have crutches on Monday."

"Long story," Tony said. "But it can wait. Right now, we want to know whether you were planning to go to Nathan's church service tonight."

Shahla looked from one of them to the other, as if they were conspiring against her. For a moment, Tony thought she would explode, and then as he watched in admiration, she deliberately got herself under control. When she spoke, she was completely collected.

"You two look like parents, sitting there in judgment."

"One of us is your parent," Rasa said. "But we are both concerned about you."

"Let me tell you the reason I want to go," Shahla said. She paused, perhaps for effect. "The police have not solved Joy's murder yet. I think everything should be done to solve it. Nathan is a queer duck. Being a queer duck is not enough to go to the police with. I want to see if I can get enough information about him to make it worthwhile to go to the police."

"Tony says church is far from here and in dangerous part of town."

"How do you know?"

Tony said, "Because...I've been there."

"You didn't tell me."

"I haven't told you everything." Tony held up his hand, as if to ward off her anger. "I talked to the minister. I didn't get all the answers I wanted. I agree with you, there is something strange about it. And about Nathan, for being a part of it. Which is all the more reason you shouldn't go. I'll tell you what I'll do; I'll go to the service tonight."

"I'm going with you."

"There is no need for that. I can handle it."

Shahla took a visible breath, again appearing to calm herself down. Then she said, "There is a good reason. You are on crutches.

You have helped me. Now I can help you. It isn't safe for you to go alone on crutches."

Rasa nodded. "Shahla has good point. But if church is in dangerous part of town, neither one of you should go."

"It isn't that dangerous," Tony said. "Nathan goes there. I would be all right."

Rasa turned to Shahla. "What is your homework situation?"

"I worked for two hours after class and before cross-country practice. I only have a little more to do."

"You do rest of homework while I make dinner for all of us. Then you may go to service. But I want you back by ten."

"Agreed," Tony said, before Shahla could say anything.

This was the second night in a row that Tony had been invited out for dinner. He could get used to this. He helped Rasa in the kitchen while Shahla showered, changed her clothes, and finished her homework. He and Rasa chatted about her job as a nurse, and he told her about Bodyalternatives.net. She was intrigued with the concept, especially for weight loss, and said that she had several patients she would refer to his company. Tony gave her a bunch of his cards.

When dinner was about to be served, a boy of ten or eleven materialized from a stairway that led to the basement. Tony hadn't even known he was in the house. Rasa introduced him as Kirk. He had Shahla's coloring and a slight build. Tony shook hands with him and said, "Hey, Kirk, glad to meet you. What do you do in the basement, plot the overthrow of the world?"

"Yeah, stuff like that. I play computer games and surf the net."

"I hope you don't go to any of the bad sites."

"Aw, Mom got some computer geek to put a lot of controls on the computer to keep me out of those sites. I haven't found a way to get around all of them yet."

"Good. It can be dangerous out there."

"Yeah. Right. Say, are you Mom's boyfriend?"

Rasa overheard and said, "Tony works with Shahla on the Hotline."

"You're too old for Shahla. And I'd say you're too young for Mom."

Kirk was still trying to figure out where Tony fit in when Rasa called them to dinner.

CHAPTER 25

"There's something else I haven't told you," Tony said as he and Shahla drove to the church. Actually, there were several things he hadn't told her, but he figured it was better to spring one at a time.

"How can I ever trust you again?" Shahla asked, but in a way that told Tony she wasn't serious—or at least not completely serious.

Shahla was wearing a fairly modest dress, which was her version of what to wear to church, along with a light jacket against the chill of the evening. She wore her hair in a bun. She looked good, but then she was one of those disgusting women who looked good wearing anything.

"I have been doing some more investigating on my own," Tony said, stalling a little. If he opened Pandora's box, he wouldn't be able to close it again. "I had some reasons, which I won't go into right now, to take a look at…my roommate."

"Your roommate? I haven't met your roommate. In fact, the only friend of yours that I have met is that woman—what's her name?"

"You mean Carol?"

"The one who said snotty things about me. Have you seen her recently?"

Had he seen her recently? How could he answer that with a straight face? "Yeah. I ran into her. She's living with that man who was with her."

"I guess you won't be dating her anymore."

"I guess not. Anyway, as I said, I was taking a look at my roommate, and I happened to search his room. And I found something."

"What did you find?"

"I found…well, I found a pair of panties."

"Panties?" Shahla almost screamed. "What did you do with them?"

"Nothing yet. I just found them. I have them with me. They're in the attaché case on the seat behind me."

Shahla unbuckled her seat belt, turned around and retrieved the case, which she brought to the front seat. She reached in and, after searching briefly, pulled out the white panties. She held them up and looked at them by the light of the streetlights they passed.

"Do you think they could be Joy's?" Tony asked.

"I don't know. The size is okay. But they're a little…"

"Conservative?"

"Yeah. I mean, not all girls wear thongs all the time, but these are, like, for an older woman, or perhaps a style of a few years ago."

"So you think they might be too old-fashioned for Joy." Tony was willing to grasp at any feather of hope that would clear Josh, to paraphrase an Emily Dickinson poem that Shahla had recited to him.

"Maybe. I need to see them in a better light."

"I'll bring them to the Hotline tomorrow. We can study them there." Anything to delay taking them to Detective Croyden.

"You didn't find a bra with them?"

"No."

"It's easier to tell whether a bra belongs to someone."

Tony was immensely relieved about Shahla's uncertainty. For a few minutes he had been second-guessing his decision to show the panties to her. He made sure that she put them back into his case. He wanted to keep them in his possession.

***

Parking was at a premium near the Church of the Risen Lord. Tony pulled into the small parking lot, but there was not a space to be had.

"It doesn't look like a church," Shahla said. Some of her enthusiasm for the project seemed to have dissipated.

Tony wasn't willing to double-park and block another car because he wanted to keep a low profile. He carefully backed out of the lot into the street and finally found a space a block away that he could ease the Toyota into. He parallel-parked and then hesitated.

He said, "Do we really want to do this?"

Shahla was also hesitating. Perhaps the reality of walking at night on a dark street in a strange part of town was giving her pause.

"Can you walk that far on your crutches?" she asked.

"Of course."

Tony didn't want his infirmities to be the excuse for their failure. He opened the door and carefully stood in the street, with the help of the crutches. He navigated to the narrow sidewalk and laboriously started along it. Shahla walked two steps behind him, staying out of his way. He watched in the dark for cracks in the concrete that might upset him and felt empathy for disabled people who faced these problems every day of their lives.

They passed small, older houses with small but tidy front yards, perhaps built right after World War II. Lights shone in some of the windows, but there was nobody else on the street.

As they neared the church, Shahla said, "I hear singing."

"The service must have started already," Tony said.

It was after 7. The singing grew louder as they came to the front of the church and started up the walk to the door. A wheezy organ backed the vocal. Tony thought he recognized a hymn from his youth, but this version of it was livelier and more melodic than he remembered. They must have paid their electric bill. Lights were on inside the church.

When Shahla opened the door, he could pick out distinct voices, from bass to soprano, with some singing harmony to the melody of the others. The notes reverberated off the walls and ceiling and filled every corner of the room. Their religious practices might be suspect, but their music was top-notch.

Tony went through the doorway first. He saw that most of the pews were filled. The congregation was standing. The men and women and a few children swayed to the music, adding the impact of their bodies to that of their voices. The Reverend Luther Hodgkins stood in front leading the singing, and Tony could clearly hear his booming bass voice over those of everybody else. The voices of the robed members of the choir also penetrated to the back of the room. Shahla came in behind Tony and stood beside him, looking awed.

Tony felt a presence on the other side of him. He turned his head and saw a man smiling and holding out a program toward him. Tony nodded his thanks—there was no point in trying to talk over the singing—and took it, being careful not to lose control of his crutch. He led Shahla to the back row of the pews, which, fortunately, was empty on one side. She went past him, and he stayed on the aisle.

They didn't try to join in the singing. They did find themselves joining the congregation in moving their bodies as the music engulfed them. Tony surveyed the other parishioners. His guess was that the majority of them were of African descent, with a sprinkling of Europeans and at least one woman he could see who looked Asian. He did not see Nathan.

The singing went on for another five minutes. Just when Tony wondered whether it was ever going to end, it came to a conclusion with a final amen. Reverend Hodgkins motioned for the congregation to sit. In order for Tony to have enough room to stretch out his left leg, he had to sit somewhat sideways. He sat facing toward Shahla so he wouldn't lose contact with her. What to do with his crutches was another problem. He finally laid them on the floor.

Reverend Hodgkins was giving announcements of the kind made in many churches. News of congregation members who were sick and one who had died. He said of the deceased, "He has preceded us into Glory, where we will be joining him soon." Tony wondered how soon "soon" was.

He heard the Reverend saying, "We have two guests with us tonight. It is customary for our guests to give their names and tell

Hotline to Murder

what prompted them to come to our church. Would you please stand and be recognized?"

The Reverend had sharp eyes. So much for trying to stay incognito. Shahla clearly wasn't going to stand unless Tony did, and for Tony to stand again after he had just sat down would have taken a major effort. Everybody had turned around and was looking at them. Tony felt growing embarrassment.

He said, in what he hoped was a voice loud enough for everybody to hear, "It is difficult for me to stand because of a recent injury, but I want to thank you for welcoming us here tonight. My name is Tony and this is Shahla. We are friends of Nathan Watson, whose talk about your church has made us curious." Realizing that "curious" wasn't a good word, Tony said, "We are on a spiritual quest, and we have been led to your door."

"Nathan," Reverend Hodgkins said, focusing his eyes near the front of the congregation, "Do you acknowledge these guests?"

Nathan stood up from the third row and looked back toward Tony and Shahla. "They are my friends, and I take full responsibility for them."

Tony detected a certain lack of conviction in Nathan's voice and suspected that his presence, rather than Shahla's, caused it. But Nathan couldn't admit that he had screwed up in front of the congregation. Apparently, not just anybody could wander in off the street and attend a service.

Reverend Hodgkins had them bow their heads in prayer. Tony was thankful that the spotlight was off them. He glanced at Shahla, whose return look showed doubts about what they were doing here. Perhaps they would leave during the singing of the next hymn, when the attention of the parishioners would be focused elsewhere. Tony was plotting their escape when the words of the Reverend's prayer caught his attention.

"It is written that the Day of Judgment is coming," Reverend Hodgkins said. "Others have tried to pinpoint this day and have failed. With your divine guidance, oh Lord, we, your humble servants, have been privileged to discover the correct date. Let our hearts be light as we divest ourselves of our material possessions and use them for the greater glory of your Church."

Then he started to talk about the wonders of heaven. To hear the Reverend tell it, heaven was indeed paradise, with amenities to suit every fantasy. If you liked tropical beaches, you would be on a heavenly Bora Bora. If you liked mountains, you would be surrounded by them. If you had been unhappy in love in this life, wait until the next one. Reverend Hodgkins made the possibilities sound better than the seventy-odd virgins promised to every Muslim suicide bomber.

Then he came back to this world. It sounded to Tony as if the Reverend was telling them to turn their possessions, or the proceeds from selling their possessions, over to the Church. He looked around and wondered whether these people were really buying into this. He wondered whether Nathan was buying into this.

When the length of the prayer threatened to put Tony to sleep, he remembered he had a printed program and looked at it for the first time. If he was correct about where they were in the service, the offering came next. And then the sermon. Who knew how long the sermon would go? Reverend Hodgkins was a strong-looking man who could probably talk for hours. Tony's attention was also called to the fact that he had not had a chance to pee since leaving Shahla's house, where he had drunk a bottle of beer with dinner. How long could he hold on?

The prayer finally ended, and Reverend Hodgkins asked the men and women who were going to collect the offering to come to the front. He presented them with bowl-like containers, larger than the offering plates Tony was used to seeing in churches. He wondered why. He soon found out. People were dumping in large envelopes, presumably containing cash, as well as checks. This was evidence that the members of the congregation were taking the Reverend seriously about divesting their assets. Tony almost felt guilty about putting in only ten dollars. But why? What was going on here was a sophisticated form of robbery.

And when the sermon started, Tony discovered that it wasn't an ordinary sermon, building on a quotation from scripture or something similar. It was more of a planning session. Planning for the big day. Except that the Reverend didn't say when the big day was. He went through the congregation, person-by-person, family-by-family, having them stand and tell how they were progressing concerning divestiture of their possessions. If they owned a house, had they sold it? Was it in escrow? Did they have a place to live, temporarily, after the sale closed? He wasn't satisfied with the money they had already contributed. He wanted more.

After their interrogation, some people remained in their seats, but others stood up and wandered around, talking to fellow members of the congregation. A few left the building, staring at Tony and Shahla on their way out. Tony had a whispered consultation with Shahla and they decided to leave after they heard Nathan speak.

Nathan's turn came about thirty minutes into this phase of the program. His only significant possession appeared to be a car. He stated that he thought he could sell his car, but that he needed it as long as he was working. The Reverend suggested that he stop working because the Great Day was at hand. Nathan seemed hesitant. Reverend Hodgkins admonished him saying that only true believers would be admitted to heaven. And they had to demonstrate their belief with actions.

"Let's get out of here," Tony whispered to Shahla. He laboriously turned his body around to face the aisle and just as laboriously rose to his feet. They attracted more attention as they walked out of the church. The man who had given Tony the program on their way in smiled at them and said, "Have a glorious evening."

They went down the church walk to the street and were turning onto the sidewalk when a voice behind them called, "Wait."

They turned around and saw Nathan running after them. When he caught them, he stood panting for a moment, looking at the ground. When they didn't say anything, he said, "Isn't he wonderful?"

Was Nathan serious? Tony was speechless. He began walking toward the car. Shahla and Nathan followed him. He hoped Nathan would get lost. He didn't want this weirdo around Shahla.

When they had gone a few feet and had separated themselves from other people who were leaving, Shahla said, "Nathan, don't you realize that this is a scam to get all your money?"

At least she had her head screwed on straight. Tony listened for Nathan to respond.

After a few seconds, Nathan said, "No. No. You don't understand. You don't understand."

He seemed incapable of saying more. Tony said, "The Reverend never said when this big day was going to take place. When is it?" When Nathan was silent, he continued, "You don't know, do you? He's going to announce it after he has all your money. And then, while the faithful flock gathers on the hillside and waits for the chariots to come for you, he takes off to Bora Bora or one of the other paradises listed in his prayer."

They were at the car. Tony unlocked it with the remote and opened the passenger door for Shahla. As she got into the car, Nathan fell on his knees beside it and actually raised his head and looked her in the eyes.

"It's not true," he said. "You believe me, don't you? You want to go to heaven, don't you?"

"I want to go home," Shahla said. "I've got school tomorrow."

She shut the door in Nathan's face. Tony limped around to the driver's side, stowed his crutches in the backseat, and slid behind the steering wheel. As he maneuvered out of the parking place, he saw Nathan standing there, looking at Shahla, with a strange expression.

"He's as crazy as some of our callers," Shahla said as they pulled away.

"I'm glad to hear you say that," Tony said. "I'm almost as relieved as your mom will be that you're not getting mixed up with Nathan. But in addition, I don't think I could have any part in a religion where you have to be a member of the elite to get into heaven. I guess I'd call that the religion of the smug."

Shahla laughed. "You know, you're a pretty smart guy."

"Thanks." Maybe he was smarter than he thought he was.

CHAPTER 26

Detective Croyden listened to Tony's story while doodling with his Mont Blanc pen on his pad. He didn't take any notes that Tony could see. When Tony was finished, he said, "That's not our jurisdiction. That's LAPD."

"Then why did you let me talk so long?"

"I wanted to see if there was anything about this Nathan character that we should be looking into. He sounds like a harmless kook, however."

"He may be harmless, but he's about to lose all his money."

"As I said, you'll have to tell that to LAPD. I can't do anything about it."

"If I go to them, what do you think they'll say?"

"They'll ask you if you have suffered a loss. Since you haven't, they'll ask whether you know of anybody who has. You will mention Nathan and the rest of the congregation. They will ask why none of those people has complained to them."

"By the time they complain, it will be too late. This Reverend Hodgkins will be long gone. With their money."

"Tony, it isn't illegal to contribute money to the nonprofit organization of your choice. It's not even illegal to contribute *all* your money."

"Unless the leader of the nonprofit absconds with it."

"Which hasn't happened yet."

Tony felt thoroughly frustrated. "What you're telling me is that there's nothing the police can do."

Detective Croyden shrugged. "Believe it or not, I'm sympathetic to your point of view. We see this all the time. But until a crime is committed, our hands are pretty much tied."

"These people are going to be wiped out. And when the big day comes and they don't get lifted up into heaven, they're going to be homeless and starving."

"You're welcome to go to the police station nearest the church and tell them what you told me."

"But you don't think it will do any good." Tony considered. While he was here, should he tell Detective Croyden about the panties he had found in Josh's drawer? No, he wasn't ready to do that yet. Shahla had said she wanted to look at them again. He clung to the hope that she would reject them as evidence.

"Have you got any leads?" he asked.

"We're working on a number of possibilities," Detective Croyden answered, enigmatically.

"In other words, no. Thanks for your time, Detective." Tony carefully got to his feet and swung his crutches into position. He was able to bear some weight on his bad leg now and hoped he could discard the crutches soon.

"Always a pleasure, Tony. By the way, what's with the crutches?"

"I fell and hurt my knee."

"Well, try to keep your balance."

"I always do."

***

Tony went to the Hotline after leaving the police station. On the way there, he bought a gyro to go at the drive-through window of the Beach House. He was eating on the run more and more lately. He knew that wasn't good for his attempt to control his weight. Too much fat and too many empty calories. Or was it too many carbs? He had to get back to his days and nights of relative leisure, before he had started working at the Hotline. Well, that wasn't going to happen tonight.

Shahla was already there when he arrived. She almost ran to meet him as he came through the doorway. The first words out of her mouth were, "Did you bring the panties?"

Tony quickly looked around the office to see if anyone else was there.

"Tony, don't be so squeamish. We're alone. Did you bring them?"

"I...er, they're in the car."

"Give me the keys, and I'll get them. It will take you all night to hobble down to your car and back. At least I'm not a cripple."

"But you are showing your usual sensitivity. My knee is actually feeling better, thank you for asking. I should be able to get rid of the crutches soon."

"Sorry, but we're running out of clues." She held out her hand for the keys. "I want to make sure we follow up on the ones we have."

"Bring the whole attaché case so that we'll have something to keep them in, just in case somebody else shows up."

Tony was on a phone call when Shahla returned, having eaten no more than two bites of his gyro. He watched Shahla take the panties out of the case, while at the same time trying to concentrate on his caller. She looked at them from all angles and then another call came in, tying her up. She placed the garment on the table. Tony spent the next twenty minutes listening with one ear for the sound of somebody unlocking the outside door of the office, in which case he was prepared to put his caller on hold, even though she was talking nonstop, rush over to Shahla's table, grab the panties and stuff them into the attaché case. Until he remembered that he couldn't rush anywhere in his current condition.

Fortunately, that eventuality didn't occur and when Shahla ended her call thirty minutes later, Tony was examining the panties, himself, while attempting to fathom the vicissitudes of life that found him looking at a woman's underwear from the point of view of a detective rather than a horny man. He didn't see anything unusual about them. They didn't contain any obvious tears or stains. As to their age, how did one tell? Could they use carbon dating on panties?

Shahla finished writing her call report and said, "Tony, we've got to turn these in."

"To the police?"

"No, to the Goodwill. Of course to the police."

"I was hoping that you would be able to prove they didn't belong to Joy."

"So was I, for your sake, but I can't. They're too generic. Both the size and the style."

"You said they were conservative."

"So? It proves nothing. Maybe Joy's mother bought them for her."

The shit was really going to hit the fan. If his relationship with Josh had been stumbling a little, now it was going over the cliff. Tony had a strong impulse to destroy the panties, perhaps to burn them. But that would be tampering with evidence. And what if Josh had actually killed Joy? No matter how many times he thought about it, he couldn't rule out that possibility.

The phone rang. Tony answered it. He thought he heard somebody breathing before he heard the click. Hang up. He and Shahla chatted about their adventure of the night before while he finally finished his sandwich. They concluded that Nathan was a harmless dupe, as were the other members of the congregation.

Tony said he was going to spend part of his Saturday telling the story to the Los Angeles Police Department, if for no other reason than to clear his conscience. Shahla said she would go with him. Tony said it was unnecessary, and he didn't want to waste the time of both of them. He thought she looked a little disappointed, but that may have been wishful thinking on his part.

The phone rang again. Shahla answered it. After a few seconds, she signaled to Tony and put the call on the speaker. The voice wasn't immediately recognizable to him, but then he hadn't had as much experience with the Chameleon as Shahla had. And the Chameleon was a master of voice disguise, sometimes even using some sort of mechanical means to change it.

The voice was saying, "If you're too busy I'll call back another time."

Tony looked a question at Shahla. This couldn't be the Chameleon.

Shahla saw his face and pressed the Mute button. "This is part of his act," she said. "It puts us off guard." Into the receiver she said, "I'm not busy. You can talk to me."

"Well, this problem is kind of embarrassing. There's a girl who lives next door. She's in high school. She has tattoos."

The caller paused and Shahla prompted, "She has tattoos?"

"Yes."

Another pause. Shahla pressed the Mute again and said, "Sometimes you even have to drag it out of the masturbators." And to the caller, "Have you seen them?"

"I was talking to her one day. She mentioned that she had tattoos."

Another pause. This time Shahla waited him out, while making circles in the air with her hand, a gesture meaning, let's get on with it. Tony stifled a laugh.

"I asked her where her tattoos were. She said she'd show me one."

Pause. The Chameleon—Tony was certain by now that it was the Chameleon—was really milking this.

Shahla said, "And did she?"

"Did she what?"

"Show you her tattoo."

Shahla cradled the phone on her shoulder and put out her hands, palms up, in a gesture of supplication. Tony almost laughed again.

"She told me to look out my window at ten o'clock that evening. My window faces her bedroom window. When I did, she had her drapes open. I saw her undress. When she took off her bra I saw the tattoo. It's on her breast."

"So what happened then?"

"I watched until she closed the drapes. Now I look out my window every evening, but her drapes are always closed. I can't get anything done. I'm obsessed with her tattoo."

"But you haven't been able to see it again."

"No. What do you think I should do?"

"Would you like to see another tattoo?"

Tony frowned. Shahla put her finger to her lips. He wanted to end the call, but something in her demeanor prevented him from disconnecting it.

Shahla broke the silence saying, "I'm a high school girl, and I've got a tattoo. Would you like to see it?"

Tony was almost positive that Shahla did not have a tattoo. More silence followed while he hoped that the Chameleon would hang up, as he had done before.

"Where is it?"

The Chameleon was hanging in there and not hanging up. Tony was pulled in two directions, wanting to protect Shahla on the one hand and wanting to see if she could hook him on the other.

"It's on my butt. I would have to take down my jeans to show it to you."

Now who was making the obscene call? Tony started to say something. Shahla put up a hand and stopped him.

The Chameleon said, "When you said before that you'd meet me, a man came instead."

He remembered her name, or at least her Hotline name—Sally. Now he would surely hang up.

Shahla said, "I'll come alone. I really want to see you."

"The man drove a Porsche. What kind of car do you have?"

Shahla pressed the mute button and looked at Tony. "What should I tell him?"

"Uh…tell him you have a black Toyota Highlander."

Shahla got back on the phone and repeated the information.

"Can you come to El Segundo tonight?"

"Yes."

Silence. They scarcely breathed. Had she hooked him? Or would the next sound they heard be the click of a disconnect?

Shahla pressed the Mute again and said, "Should I ask him where to meet him?"

Tony shook his head and put a finger to his lips. He knew that their only chance was to say nothing. Seconds passed. A whole minute. It was the longest minute of their lives. Tony gave a couple of head-fakes. Shahla fiddled with her hair.

The caller said, "Meet me at Zook Sheeting at 11:30." He gave an address. Then he said, "Ring the bell at the front door. I'll know if you're alone because there are surveillance cameras trained on the outside of the building."

"Will you be the only one there?" Shahla asked.

"Yes."

The caller hung up before she could say anything else. Tony and Shahla looked at each other. Then Shahla jumped up from her chair and threw her arms around his neck, almost knocking his chair over.

"We know where he works," she cried. "We know where he works."

"Good job," Tony said, grimacing as her leg hit his bad knee. "We can give that information to Detective Croyden, along with the panties."

Shahla leaned over him with her hands on his shoulders, her face close to his. She said, "He'd better not screw it up."

CHAPTER 27

The meeting with Detective Croyden proceeded badly, as far as Tony was concerned. Croyden met Tony and Shahla in the conference room just off the waiting room of the police station. Tony reluctantly gave him the panties and told him how he had found them. In answer to Croyden's questions, he tried to explain why Josh might be a suspect. His arguments sounded weak to himself, and he wondered whether he was accusing his roommate for no reason.

Croyden took notes with his Mont Blanc pen and said that he would investigate Josh. In answer to Tony's sudden plea, he promised that he wouldn't use Tony's name unless he had to.

Next, Tony and Shahla told about the call from the Chameleon. When they got to the part where he agreed to meet Shahla at 11:30, Croyden asked Shahla how she had elicited this information. She told him about the discussion of tattoos.

"I thought you weren't supposed to give personal information," Croyden said.

"I did it to try to get his address," Shahla said. "I don't have a tattoo."

"It worked," Tony pointed out.

"That remains to be seen," Croyden said. "He's a pretty tricky guy."

"It's still worth a try," Tony said. "Zook is only a couple of blocks from where I saw him before. He must live nearby. You are going to follow up, aren't you?"

"That address is in the jurisdiction of the El Segundo Police Department," Croyden said. "We'll have to coordinate with them."

There was no sense of urgency in his voice.

"You're not going to do anything tonight?" Shahla asked.

"Don't worry; we'll check it out. If he is the night guard there, we'll find him. That will be easy enough."

"But not *tonight*," Tony said.

"There's no hurry. If he's working there tonight, he'll be working there tomorrow night. We'll check with the management at Zook and get all the information on him." Croyden looked at his notes. "His story doesn't ring true. If he's working nights as a security guard, how could he be looking out his window at the tattoos of the girl who lives next door?"

"That's a fantasy," Shahla said. "A real girl probably won't even talk to him, let alone show him her tattoo. Our callers fantasize a lot."

"You shouldn't be talking to weirdoes like that," Croyden said.

"It's part of the job."

"That's what I mean. This whole concept of the Hotline is a bad one. Putting teenage girls on the phone with these guys who are the scum of society. I don't like it at all."

"Not all the callers are like that," Shahla said hotly. "We help a lot of people."

"If I had a daughter, I wouldn't let her work in a place like that. If this…Chameleon calls again, I want you to hang up on him. I'm going to talk to your boss, Nancy, about this. I want all the girls to hang up on him."

***

"I feel so frustrated. I wanted to take one of those old hatpins and stick it up Croyden's ass to get him to do something."

Shahla *must* feel frustrated. This was one of the few times Tony could remember her using language that was even slightly off-color. He had followed her home to make sure she got there safely. He had even pulled into the driveway behind her to make sure she went into the house and didn't take off for El Segundo. It was too late, anyway. His watch said 11:30.

She stuck her head through the window of his SUV and said, "Croyden doesn't appreciate that I got evidence for him. He doesn't want girls working on the Hotline. I read a book that talks about men who want their women barefoot and pregnant. I'll bet he's one of them. And I don't think he's going to find Joy's murderer, whoever he is. Croyden is incompetent, and I suspect the rest of the Bonita Beach police are the same way."

"They'll get him," Tony said with more confidence than he felt. "They know what they're doing." He lifted his hand to give her a reassuring pat, but she turned quickly away and walked toward the front door of the house. He watched until she went inside and shut the door. An upstairs light told him that Rasa was awake.

Tony backed out of the driveway, intending to drive home. But instead of going directly home, he went to Pacific Coast Highway and turned north. North toward El Segundo. He didn't know what he was going to do there, but he did remember the Chameleon saying previously that he got off work at midnight. Traffic was light. Tony would get there by midnight with no problem.

***

Tony didn't have a better plan when he drove past Zook Sheeting on Grand Avenue in El Segundo at five minutes to midnight. One problem was his lack of mobility. Another problem was that Shahla had told the Chameleon that she was driving a black Toyota Highlander—on his advice. That was a mistake. If he parked anywhere near Zook, the Chameleon would spot it as soon as he walked out of the building.

Tony drove around a corner and made a U-turn, with the help of a driveway. He parked under a tree, away from the streetlights. Another car was between him and Grand. He suspected that the Chameleon walked to work. He had been on foot when Tony saw him before. If he lived in one of the nearby apartments, he should walk along Grand in this direction to get home.

What did the Chameleon think when Shahla didn't show up? Was he disappointed? Or relieved because he couldn't handle contact with a real girl? Just his job, night security guard, indicated that he preferred to be alone. Why had he told Shahla where he worked? Because he was delusional enough to believe that a girl returned his...desire? Lust? Or whatever?

Tony wondered what he was doing here. What could he possibly accomplish? The impulse that had brought him—stemming from the frustration he and Shahla felt about Detective Croyden's lack of action—had dissipated in the dark of the night. He should go home. And he would. Soon. But first he would wait a few minutes, just to see if he could catch a glimpse of the Chameleon. That by itself would be useful information and tend to confirm that the man did work at Zook.

Since there were no pedestrians about and very little auto traffic, the Chameleon should be easy to spot. And he was; his baseball cap and his rapid, slouching walk with his hands in his pockets gave him away. Tony recognized him instantly as he crossed the street where the SUV was parked. He looked neither to the right nor to the left—thankfully.

Well, that's it, Tony thought. Mission accomplished. I'll wait a few minutes for him to get away from the intersection and then drive home. But maybe he could do more. What if he could find out where the Chameleon lived? After a minute, he cautiously drove to the intersection and looked to the right. He could see the Chameleon by the light of the streetlights, walking away from him.

Tony looked away for a moment, and when he looked back, the Chameleon had disappeared. Had he seen a mirage? No, the man must have turned a corner. Tony drove along Grand to where he had seen the Chameleon. A side street went off to the right. He stopped just short of the intersection and looked along the street.

At first he saw nothing moving. Just shadows, parked cars, trees, and the gray shapes of apartment buildings. Then he saw movement. Someone was climbing the outside stairs of one of the buildings. Tony had trouble seeing him in the dark, but he was positive the man was wearing a baseball cap. At the top of the stairs he opened a door and went inside.

Tony waited thirty seconds and then drove to the building. He pulled out one of his business cards and wrote the address on it. Now he should leave. But his adrenaline was flowing again. He couldn't leave yet. He'd love to get a good look at the Chameleon, get inside his apartment. How could he do it? Not with crutches, that's for sure. Could he walk up those steps without crutches? His knee was feeling better.

Tony parked the car far enough away from the Chameleon's building so that it wasn't visible from a window. He opened the door and swung his body around so he could place his right foot on the ground. He stood up on his right leg and gingerly shifted some of the weight to his left leg. It hurt, but it was bearable. He shut the door and walked slowly toward the Chameleon's building, favoring his left leg.

It was still warm. Some of the warmest LA nights occurred in September. It would be a pleasant night for a walk if one wasn't limping. Tony was wearing a short-sleeved shirt, and he wasn't cold. Just a little chilly. He remembered watching fireflies on summer nights back home. And catching them in bottles. In days long gone.

When he came to the wooden stairs, he climbed up one step with his right leg and then brought his left leg up to the step. It was slow, but it worked. He climbed the fifteen or so steps in this manner and found himself facing a door. A plain wooden door that could use a coat of paint. The door the Chameleon had gone through. There was a window beside the door, but the blinds were closed. However, a light was on inside.

Tony suddenly remembered that he didn't have a gun with him. And he was certainly in no position to make a fast retreat down the stairs. In his favor was the fact that there was no evidence that the murderer had used a gun. But there was also no evidence that he hadn't. Would the Chameleon recognize him? He had looked at him for about a tenth of a second in the dark several weeks ago. Surely, a memory couldn't have been imprinted on his brain.

Tony didn't see a doorbell. He knocked on the door. He listened but couldn't hear any movement inside. He called out, "Pizza man."

In a few seconds footsteps sounded on the other side of the door. A bolt slid open. Then the door opened.

"I didn't order any…" The man stopped talking when he saw that Tony wasn't holding a pizza.

"Sorry," Tony said. "That was the only way I could think of to get your attention. I saw your light. I-I'm looking for a friend, but I must have his address wrong."

"What's his name?"

"Uh…Sam. Sam Jones."

"I don't know any Sam Jones."

He started to close the door. Tony saw a large picture on the wall beside the doorway.

"Is that Britney? Britney Spears? I love Britney."

The door stopped closing.

"Yeah, that's her. She's great, isn't she?"

"For sure. You don't by any chance have a phone book do you?"

"Come on in."

Tony carefully walked through the doorway, trying not to spook this man who looked as if the slightest sound or movement would make him jump. An unpleasant stench hit him in the nostrils. It smelled like rotting garbage. The Chameleon was thin and short and his head was narrow, with a pointed nose that reminded Tony of a ferret. He was bald in front, and what hair he had in other places was overgrown, like a bush that needed trimming. He wore jeans and a stained T-shirt.

"I'm T…I'm Ted," Tony said. He couldn't give his real name or the Chameleon might recognize him from the Hotline. He was sure that some of his hang ups had been from the Chameleon. He tentatively offered his hand.

"Fred." Fred gave him a quick, clammy shake and then withdrew. "I've got a phone book here someplace."

A look around convinced Tony that it might be hard to find. The apartment was a filthy mess. The sparsely furnished room was piled high with magazines and notebooks. Newspapers littered the floor, along with uneaten food, some on plates, some just lying on the worn carpet. This was the source of the stench.

A wave of sadness went through Tony. My God, what kind of a life is he living, was the first thought that occurred to him. And then fear. This could have been me. A couple of wrong turns, and this could have been me. He had a sense of how thin the barrier was that separated the two of them. And he desperately wanted to get out of here. But he couldn't—just yet.

Fred was methodically going through the piles of written material, hunting for a phone book. Tony lifted his gaze. Hundreds of pictures were taped to the walls. Pictures of girls. Almost every square inch of the walls was covered. Most had evidently been cut out of magazines. A few, like the one of Britney, were posters. Tony recognized some of the pictures of models, actresses, and singers. Others were unknown to him. All were young and beautiful. Tony didn't see any nudes among the pictures. No *Playboy* centerfolds, such as had graced the walls of his fraternity in college. All the girls were at least wearing swimsuits.

"Great pictures," Tony said, for lack of something better to say.

"Yeah," was all Fred said, but he did smile for the first time.

"You must know every pretty girl in the world."

"Not quite."

There was only one other window in the room, in addition to the one beside the front door. An inside door led to another room, probably a bathroom. But that couldn't have a window because its outside wall abutted the wall of the next apartment. The windows didn't have a good view of another building. So Fred wasn't looking at any tattoos out his windows. Shahla was right; that was a fantasy.

"Where do you sleep?" Tony asked.

Fred nodded toward the side wall opposite the internal doorway. "Hide-a-bed."

The bed folded into the wall. Tony could make out its outline. It was covered with pictures. That's why he hadn't noticed it before.

"Here," Fred said, pulling a phone book out from one of the piles. He handed it to Tony.

"Thanks." Fred didn't look at him when he handed him the book. In fact, he hadn't looked him in the eye since he first opened the door.

Tony noticed a cell phone for the first time. The cell phone from which Fred made his calls to the Hotline? It was sitting on top of some magazines, on an end table beside a dilapidated chair, which was also covered with junk. There was a plastic gizmo beside it that looked like a toy. Tony had never seen anything like it. It occurred to him that it might be the voice-altering mechanism that the Chameleon used.

Tony pretended to be looking through the phone book. He said, "Are you a writer? I see you've got some notebooks."

"No. I just use them to put...put pictures in."

More pictures. "So you don't write poetry?"

"Not a chance. I'm the world's worst poet. Excuse me for a minute."

Fred went through the doorway leading to what Tony assumed was the bathroom and closed the door. Tony took a step and picked up one of the loose-leaf notebooks sitting on the chair. He quickly riffled through it. Sure enough, it was crammed with more pictures of girls, taped to the pages. He didn't see one word of writing.

Tony replaced the notebook before Fred returned and resumed his perusal of the telephone directory. It was time for him to make as graceful an exit as possible. But first, was there any way to figure out whether Fred had the potential to be a killer? He remembered his Hotline training regarding noninvasive questioning.

"You must really love girls," Tony said as Fred returned to the room.

Fred shrugged without looking at him.

"Do you ever get irritated with them?"

Fred thought about that for a moment, still without looking at Tony. "Yeah. They don't pay much attention to me."

"And you wish they would."

"Yeah."

But he said it wistfully. Tony could not detect any undertone of anger.

"Apparently my friend isn't in the phonebook. Thanks for letting me look at it." Tony walked the couple of steps to the door, carefully, both to avoid the piles on the floor and to protect his knee.

He had been standing since he had left the car, and his knee was beginning to ache.

Fred glanced up almost to Tony's eyes and said, "You're welcome."

He didn't say anything more. He stood in the middle of his room and seemed to be looking at the pictures on one of the walls. As Tony closed the door, he was still standing there, motionless.

Tony went slowly down the stairs, leaning on the railing with his arm to support much of his weight, each time he lowered his left foot from one step to the one below. He limped to the SUV and settled himself into the driver's seat. He drove home at a leisurely pace, while thinking about Fred. And being glad that he wasn't Fred.

CHAPTER 28

The next morning as Tony prepared his version of an omelet for breakfast, he thought some more about Fred. He couldn't picture Fred as a killer. A masturbator, yes. He was obviously that. The pictures, the phone calls, the voice-altering mechanism. The girls had been trained to hang up on him whenever he started talking dirty—and rightly so. But he didn't appear to have any normal sexual outlets. Whatever normal meant.

Not only did he show no signs of anger or pugnacity, he wasn't as big as Joy. And Tony couldn't picture him wielding a knife to subdue her, let alone strangling her. When Tony had gone to meet him the first time, Fred had fled before he even knew that Tony was a man instead of a girl. It had probably taken all the guts he had just to go to the meeting place. He had undoubtedly persuaded himself that Shahla—Sally—wouldn't show up, and so he was safe. But when someone did show up, he couldn't face the situation.

And last night, Shahla had again talked him into meeting her. This invitation was so different from the usual hang ups he received from the girls that he had been flustered enough to give his work address. He had grasped at a thread of hope, while probably dreading what would happen if she actually came. But when she didn't come, it cemented his self-image. He was a loser, and girls wouldn't have anything to do with him.

One more thing. Fred undoubtedly had an alibi for the night of the murder. He had probably been working. And although he worked alone, didn't he have to punch time clocks and leave other tracks during his shift?

That sealed it. Tony was not going to talk to Detective Croyden about Fred. For one thing, he didn't want to take Croyden's shit about doing police work and interfering with the law. He hadn't interfered with anything. Croyden would be able to verify Fred's employment, his alibi, and anything else he wanted to know. And nothing Tony had done would stop him. Fred didn't associate him with the police or with the Hotline. He was sure of that.

The doorbell chimed. Who could that be at 10:00 on a Saturday morning? Tony glanced at his attire, relieved that he was wearing shorts, even though he was shirtless. At least he was presentable enough to answer the door. He padded slowly into the living room, without his crutches. He didn't intend to use them anymore. He didn't bother to look through the peephole in the front door. The sun was shining and nothing bad could be lurking outside. He opened the door and found himself looking at the crooked nose of Detective Croyden.

It was a shock to see the man he had just been thinking about. Tony stared at him for a moment before he found his voice. "Good morning, Detective Croyden," he said. "Do you work twenty-four hours a day?"

"Thirty, sometimes. I've come to talk to Josh."

Josh. Tony was horrified. When he had given the panties to Croyden, he had known at some level that Croyden would have to talk to Josh. But he hadn't actually pictured how this would take place. In his house. And so soon.

"Josh is still asleep." He had come home even later than Tony.

"Well, wake him up. This is official police business. And I want to talk to him alone."

That did sound official. Tony stepped back so that Croyden could enter. He pointed to the couch in the living room and said, "I'll get him."

As he went slowly up the stairs, still favoring his left leg, Tony dreaded what was going to happen. Croyden was carrying a briefcase. He could guess what was inside. He pictured Croyden whipping the panties out of the case and saying, "Where did you get these?"

Croyden hadn't had time to perform any tests on the panties. But what could he test for? If there wasn't any blood on them, how could a test connect them with Joy? Tony reached the top of the stairs and looked at Josh's closed door. He was a grumpy riser. And being faced with the prospect of talking to the police would make his mood that much fouler.

Tony decided to go to his athletic club and work out, something he hadn't done since his knee injury. Get good and sweaty. And not return for a while. He gritted his teeth and knocked on the door.

***

In fact, Tony didn't return home until late that afternoon. After he finished his workout he went to his office to catch up on paperwork. He sometimes did that on weekends when there was nobody around to disturb him. It was peaceful, and he was very productive. He found that he really liked this job, and he wanted to do well at it. He was sure that what he did helped people. Just as the Hotline helped people.

Toward the end of the afternoon, he remembered that he had been going to tell the Los Angeles Police Department about the church scam. It would be a long drive to a police station near the church. And then back. And Croyden had been pessimistic about how much good it would do. He decided to skip it.

He hadn't thought about Josh and Detective Croyden for several hours when he turned into the car park of his townhouse development. He had driven the Porsche for the first time in several days, and it felt good to be behind the wheel of the responsive car, even if he had to be careful shifting because his left knee was still sore.

As he drove down the row of carports, he saw that his was filled with large cardboard boxes. What the hell was going on? He saw Josh's SUV, which had been backed into the adjoining carport, and then he saw Josh, methodically loading the boxes into it.

Tony stopped the Porsche outside the carport and got out, not bothering to close the door. He limped over to Josh, who had not ceased work, and said, "What are you doing?"

Josh placed a box carefully into his car before he replied. He looked at Tony and said, "Remember, I told you that I'd move out within thirty days? I'm well within that time period, I believe."

"I didn't think…I didn't think…." He didn't think what? "I didn't think you'd really do it."

Josh looked very cool. He said, "An agreement is an agreement. Now if you'll excuse me, I have work to do, although I'm almost finished. This is the last load. Then I'll be out of your hair for good." He picked up another box and shoved it into the car.

"Where are you going?"

"What do you care? I'm going; that should be all that matters to you."

"It was Detective Croyden, wasn't it? What did he tell you?"

"He didn't have to tell me anything. When he showed me the panties that were a souvenir of my first affair in college, I knew the whole story. I knew that my buddy had double-crossed me. I knew he was trying to set me up—for what reason I don't know. But it's definitely time to make a break with the past. So sayonara, Noodles. It's been fun."

"But I didn't remember the panties. I'm not trying to set you up. You know that." Tony sputtered, not knowing what to say.

"After all we've been through together, you don't trust your roommate. That's what hurts the most."

Josh shoved the last box into the back of the SUV and slammed the door down. He walked around to the driver's side, pushing Tony out of the way when he tried to stop him. He climbed in, slammed that door, started the engine and pulled forward out of the carport. He took a left turn, then another, and disappeared around the row of townhouses.

***

Tony had just finished looking into Josh's room and verifying that everything "Josh" was indeed gone when the phone rang. It was Rasa, Shahla's mother. She was speaking rapidly and Tony had trouble understanding her.

"Could you repeat that?" he asked.

"It's Shahla. She has disappeared."

CHAPTER 29

"When did you last see Shahla?"

Tony tried to ask the question in an even voice, hoping that his example would help to calm Rasa down enough so that he could understand what she was saying. Upon receiving her call, he had immediately driven to her place, knowing that he would never be able to communicate with her by phone. When he had arrived, she had started talking as soon as she opened the door, so rapidly that he still couldn't understand her accented words. He had suggested they sit down in her living room. She appeared to be a little calmer now as she answered.

"This morning. She came down about eight o'clock and had something to eat."

That was better. The act of sitting had slowed the flow of words; they were now intelligible to Tony. He said, "And then what happened?"

"She said she was going to study with her girlfriend. Her girlfriend lives short distance from here so she walked." And Rasa's car was in the driveway.

"And she was supposed to come home at a certain time?"

"That is too much to ask. I told her to call me at noon and tell me where she was. She did not call so I called her cell phone. I got message."

"Did you call her girlfriend?"

"Yes, I called girlfriend. There was no answer."

"And you haven't heard from her since."

"No. I called again and again and always got message. She must not have phone with her. Otherwise she would return my calls."

"What do you think happened to her?" As soon as he asked it, Tony wished he could withdraw the question.

Rasa sobbed, "I think Joy's murderer has kidnapped her."

He wasn't used to all this emotion, except from the callers, and with them he had the safety of a phone line between them. At least Rasa didn't say she thought Shahla was dead. But she did look close to collapsing. Tony reflected that in the days before cell phones, it wasn't unusual for a teenager to be out of touch with her parents for several hours, or even all day. Now, parents expected instant access to their children. He didn't know whether to be worried or not. If it weren't for the fact that a murder had been committed....

"Let me try her," Tony said. He pulled out his own phone. God. The world was being run by them. He called Shahla's number and waited. It rang twice and went to voice mail. After the beep, Tony said, "Shahla, it's Tony. Please give me a call at your earliest convenience." He gave his number and hung up.

"What should I do?" Rasa asked wiping her eyes with a tissue.

She was looking to him for guidance. Because of the circumstances, immediate action was called for. And maybe it would get her to stop crying. "I think we should call the police."

"Do you think police will help?"

"That's their job."

***

It was after 9 when Tony got back to his townhouse, emotionally exhausted and starving. He hadn't had anything to eat since about noon. He rummaged through the refrigerator and found some leftover chicken that Josh had bought at a fast-food restaurant and not finished. A parting gift from his ex-roommate. He gave it the sniff test, and it passed, so he ate it, along with a potato and some frozen corn that he microwaved.

It had been a thoroughly bad day. First Josh and then Shahla. After Tony had called the Bonita Beach Police, the desk officer had called Detective Croyden who was at home. Tony had actually been shocked that Croyden wasn't working. And then he realized that he expected Croyden to be on duty all the time. And it almost seemed as if he was. When Shahla and others badmouthed the police for not solving the murder, they were ignoring Croyden's work ethic.

Croyden had come to Rasa's home. She had repeated her story to him. Tony had told him about his meeting with the Chameleon. Otherwise, he would have been withholding evidence. Croyden hadn't even chewed him out. He just took notes with his Mont Blanc pen and looked properly concerned. An officer Croyden had brought with him started calling friends of Shahla from a list supplied by Rasa.

Tony belatedly told Croyden that Josh had moved out. Croyden made a note and looked at Tony for a moment with what was almost a compassionate expression. He said, "You still did the right thing. It's hard to rat out your buddy, but sometimes to have to do it."

"You don't think he's involved in this, do you?" Tony asked, shocked by Croyden's serious tone.

"His story about the panties sounds legit. We're checking on his alibi for the night of the murder."

Tony couldn't recall that Josh had given him an alibi. But he felt relieved. Even if Josh never spoke to him again, he didn't want him to be convicted of murder.

A female friend of Rasa's arrived to comfort her. Detective Croyden was using the house as a temporary command post while he coordinated the efforts of several officers in the field. In between phone calls, he asked Rasa questions about Shahla's friends and habits.

After watching him in action for a while, Tony began to see him in a better light. He really was a good policeman. It relieved Tony's mind a little. He still wasn't convinced that Shahla had met with foul play, but whether she had or whether she hadn't, Croyden was doing his best to find her.

Eventually, Tony began to feel expendable, like a disposable razor. So he left. He decided to conduct his own search. He drove slowly, up and down almost every street in Bonita Beach—the streets that crossed Pacific Coast Highway and ran downhill to the water, and the cross streets parallel to PCH and the coastline. He did this for two hours—until his gas gauge registered empty.

What else could he do? The more he tried to think, the more his brain wouldn't function. It was then he realized that he was exhausted and starving. He drove home and parked in his carport. After staring at the empty space where Josh's car used to be, he dragged himself into the house and went to the refrigerator.

***

Tony leafed through the pages of the Green Book at the Hotline office on Sunday morning, concentrating on the inactive callers at the back of the book. Detective Croyden had considered all of the active callers as possible suspects, and as far as Tony knew, he had discarded all of them except Fred the Chameleon. And Tony had discarded Fred as a suspect. Tony was sure that Croyden had also looked at the inactive pages, but because there was no way to contact the people who were no longer calling the Hotline, he really didn't have any leads to follow.

Tony wasn't sure he could do any better, but he read the description of each caller, looking for something—he didn't know what— that might set off an alarm in his brain. He read the information for each inactive caller and then went back and reread it for just the male callers. Then, for some reason, he came back and read the page for one caller a third time.

This was a man who had given a variety of names, none of which had any special meaning for Tony. His Hotline nickname was Cackling Crucifier. He had called for several years and apparently stopped calling very abruptly about nine or ten months ago. He was given the name because of his weird laugh and because he liked to talk about religion. He appeared to carry a lot of guilt. He talked as if he thought he had personally crucified Jesus. He asked listeners about their religions. He always had a television set on in the background. The page on him said not to discuss religion or give him any personal information.

Tony had come into the Hotline office because he wanted to feel as if he was doing something to help find Shahla. Besides, he couldn't stand the quiet in his townhouse with Josh gone. He had called the Bonita Beach police first thing this morning to get an update on the search for her. No news. Now that he was here, he realized that this was where he usually saw her. He missed her. It occurred to him for the first time that if something had happened to her, he might never see her again. He shuddered.

He was sitting at the white table in the outer office. A girl named Anne was in the listening room. Tony knew she had been a listener for a couple of years. When she hung up from a call, Tony carried the Green Book into the listening room and said, "Anne, did you ever speak to this guy called Cackling Crucifier?"

"Several times," she said. "He was what I would call a Jesus freak."

"Did he ask a lot of questions?"

"Yeah. He wanted to know if I went to church and if I had accepted Jesus as my personal savior. I didn't tell him I was Jewish."

"Did he ever ask where the Hotline was located?"

"He may have, but if he did, I didn't tell him."

"What else can you remember about him?"

"He had a distinctive laugh. Kind of a cackle. That's how he got his name. I'd recognize his laugh anywhere."

"Anything else?"

"He asked what I looked like and whether I'd go out with him. He got pretty personal. I blew him off. Once or twice he became abusive, saying that I was immoral and would go to hell. When he did, I hung up on him."

"The book says he lives in Los Angeles. Did he ever tell you anything more specific than that?"

"I don't think so. I imagine he lives somewhere within fifty miles of here."

He and a few million other people.

CHAPTER 30

When Shahla left Jane's house, she walked to the beach. One of her friends from school, Lacey, lived in a three-story house right on the beach. Lacey's parents were away for the weekend. Lacey had decided this was the ideal opportunity to throw a party.

Rasa didn't allow Shahla to attend parties that weren't supervised by adults. So Shahla hadn't bothered to tell her about this party. Doing schoolwork with Jane was her excuse to go out. And she and Jane had done schoolwork, Shahla rationalized, as she felt a twinge of guilt. But she also deserved a little fun.

It had been exactly one month since Joy had been murdered. A month during which she had grieved for Joy while she attended school, filled out college applications, and run cross-country. And hunted for Joy's killer. A month of unrelieved stress. Except for the trip to Las Vegas with Tony. That had been fun, at least until Tony got hurt.

She wouldn't stay at the party long, only an hour or so. Just long enough to relieve her tension. It was a beach party, mostly outdoors. During the day. What could happen?

The party was already swinging when Shahla arrived. She heard it while still a block away as she turned onto the concrete beach path at the end of a street. Music blared from strategically placed speakers and inundated passersby. As Shahla approached the house, she saw teenagers strewn across the back patio: bikinied girls and bare-chested boys. They were eating, drinking, and shouting at each other over the din of the music.

Shahla stepped onto the stone floor of the patio from the beach path and threaded her way among the bodies, saying hello to several of them, although her voice was drowned out. She entered the house through wide open doors and spotted Lacey ladling some liquid concoction out of a large punch bowl.

Lacey, who was dressed in the skimpiest bikini Shahla had seen for a while, gave Shahla a hug and shouted in her ear, "Have some punch. It's better than beer because the cops patrol the beach path and might see it. And get out of those clothes."

The cops should be looking for Joy's murderer, not underage drinkers. Shahla picked up a cup of the yellowish liquid and looked for a spot where she could stow her daypack. Various articles of clothing were lying along the wall. She picked a corner of the spacious living room, dumped her pack, and took off her jeans and top. She was wearing her own bikini underneath.

She took a sip of the punch as she headed for the patio. It had a sweetish taste. She understood that it contained alcohol, but it couldn't be too potent. She wouldn't drink much. Meanwhile, she was hungry. She headed for a table covered with food.

***

A ray of sunlight slanting in through the open doors and into her eyes brought Shahla back to reality. She sat on one of the jumbo-sized leather couches while a boy regaled her with a tale about a wild weekend spent in Tijuana. The sun was setting over the ocean. She hadn't noticed time passing. The party had gravitated indoors as the afternoon grew cooler, but she had talked, danced, eaten—and drunk. She had not thought about Joy or her mother or the necessity for going home for several hours.

Muttering an excuse, Shahla jumped up from the couch. She stumbled as a wave of dizziness overcame her, and she almost fell back down in a heap. Blinking her eyes to clear her head, she searched for her clothes and pack. Fortunately, they were in the corner where she had left them. As she struggled to pull on her jeans without falling, she experienced a moment of fear as she thought about what her mother would say.

At least she hadn't gone upstairs. Reports had drifted down from the upper two floors—reports about girls losing their tops. And other things. She hoisted her pack onto her shoulders and walked unsteadily out the still-open doors. The cooling evening air helped to sharpen her senses. She needed to call her mother.

Shahla practiced talking to herself as she pulled her cell phone out of the pack, to make sure her voice sounded normal. At least one walker heading the other way on the beach path looked at her strangely. She turned off the path and headed up the hill on one of the residential streets—where the folks lived who couldn't afford a McMansion adjoining the beach. She was about to place the call when the phone rang. Her mother had beaten her to the keypad.

She pressed the "talk" button. "Hello."

At first she didn't hear anything. This couldn't be her mother. Her mother would have started in on her immediately. She said hello again.

"Where are you?"

The voice sounded unnatural. She couldn't decide whether the caller was male or female. It sounded like one of the voices the Chameleon used. But of course it couldn't be him.

"Who is this?"

"I need to talk to you."

She looked at the number of the caller. She didn't recognize it. It certainly wasn't a friend of hers, unless a joker was playing a trick on her. Could a listener on the Hotline who was familiar with the Chameleon be getting his jollies?

"Who is this?" she asked again, more forcefully.

"I'm trying to help you," the voice said.

"If you don't tell me who this is, I'm going to hang up."

"Wait. I'm really trying to help you."

"Is this Fred?" Shahla asked, using the name she had called the Chameleon.

The voice on the phone didn't deny it. "Where can I meet you? When are you going home? You haven't been there all afternoon?"

How did he know that? Shahla's hands began to shake. She was within ten minutes of her house. Was it safe to go there?

"Where are you now?" Shahla asked, trying to keep the fear out of her voice.

"I'm cruising along Sandview Street."

Sandview was the street where she lived. It ran most of the length of Bonita Beach, parallel to the ocean. Shahla was just now coming to it, preparing to turn right, toward her house. She quickly looked both ways on Sandview. None of the cars in sight was moving; all were parked. Instead of turning onto Sandview, she ran across it and continued to trot up the hill. Jane's house was just two blocks from here. She had to get there. Jane and her father would help her.

She heard a car behind her, and looked over her shoulder without stopping. This action made her a little dizzy. After a second or two, she could make out an older couple in the car. No danger there. She swiveled her head back to the front just in time to see a lamppost looming right in front of her eyes. Instinctively she threw out her hands to keep herself from crashing into it. As her left hand hit the post, she heard a sickening crack. The phone had crunched between her hand and the scalloped metal.

There was no time to check for damage, so she shoved the phone into her pocket. She was panting freely as she turned the corner onto the street where Jane lived. As she approached Jane's house, she didn't see any lights on inside, and it was now quite dark outside. She ran along the driveway, which sloped downhill, and then up several steps to the front door. She rang the bell. She heard the chime, but no other sound came from within the house.

Then she remembered. Jane and her father had taken an overnight trip. They had been going to leave soon after Shahla left the house. There was no help here. She started shaking again. What could she do? She turned and faced the street. Nothing was moving. But she wasn't safe here. The driver of any passing car would spot her.

The house sat on a hillside lot that slanted down toward the ocean. It had a lower floor with an entrance in the back of the house. The rest of the floor was underground. Shahla quickly walked around the house toward the back. She felt minor relief when she was no longer visible from the street.

He must be lurking nearby. He would be looking for her. She had to stay out of sight. The entrance to the lower floor of the house was a sliding glass door. She gripped the door handle and tried to slide the door open. It didn't budge. What now? There was a window beside the door. A screen covered it. Shahla looked through the screen and saw that the window was open. Thank Mother Nature for warm weather.

First she had to get the screen off. It was set into grooves on either side of the window, but it could be slid horizontally out of one groove at a time. If only she had something to hold onto. The screen was smooth on this side. She had to slide it by putting pressure on the screen and her shaking hands had trouble applying any pressure.

She put her body weight behind her hands to exert more pressure. Just when the screen started to move, her weight caused its mesh to pull away from the frame. Now she owed Jane's father a new screen. Since the screen was ruined anyway, she pulled out enough of the mesh so that she could stick her hand through the gap. Then she was able to grip a tab on the inside of the screen and pull the screen out of one of the grooves. And then the other.

Shahla opened the window wide enough to admit her body, dropped her pack inside, and then crawled through. Her feet found the floor, and she stood up. She reached back through the open window and picked up the screen, which she had left leaning against the house. She replaced it in the grooves and flattened the damaged mesh as much as she could. At a glance, nobody could tell it had been tampered with, especially at night, which was fast approaching. She closed the window and locked it. She also closed the curtains.

She felt momentarily safe. She pulled a sweatshirt out of her pack and put it on. Now she had to call her mother. Drapes covered the sliding door, so it was dark inside the room. She wasn't about to open the drapes. She tried to picture the layout of the room. Jane had brought her down here from the upstairs once. This floor was used primarily for storage of furniture. There was a bathroom at the other end. The bathroom had a light. She needed to use the bathroom anyway.

She started walking gingerly toward the bathroom. Not gingerly enough. Her toe hit something hard. "Shit." Trying to ignore the pain, she continued, using her hands to help her locate pieces of furniture she had to navigate around.

After what seemed like a cross-country trip, during which she was careful not to look behind her because something might be following her in the dark, she reached the bathroom and found the light switch by feel. Being able to see again calmed her a little. After using the toilet, she retrieved the phone from her pocket.

One glance convinced her that it was damaged beyond repair. What had been an intelligent electronic device was now an inanimate mixture of scrap plastic and metal. She threw it savagely into a wastebasket. What alternatives did she have? She was sure there wasn't a house phone on this floor, but to make sure, she opened the bathroom door wide and used the light that came into the main room to scan it for a phone.

The piled-up furniture blocked her view of all the corners, but she didn't see a phone in any of the logical places. She did see the stairs to the upper floor and those gave her an idea. She would use the phone upstairs. She found another switch that operated a light that lit up the stairs. She padded up the stairs slowly—her toe still hurt—and turned the latch of the door at the top.

The door wouldn't open. It was locked from the other side. Shahla would have screamed, but there was nobody to hear her. Instead, she hit the door and hurt her knuckles. She plodded slowly back down the stairs. She was cut off from the world.

She saw a third switch and flicked it. A light in the ceiling came on. She immediately turned it off. It might be visible from the outside, even through the drapes. She walked over to the sliding door by the indirect light coming from the bathroom and the stairway. She peeked through the drapes.

It was almost dark outside. Maybe she could make a run for it to her house. She removed a security stick from the slide and was about to open the door when she saw something move out there.

She froze, momentarily, and then quickly pushed the drapes back into place. Even the dim light could silhouette her. She was panting as if she had just run up the hill from the beach. She went to the wall beside the door and pressed her body against it. She didn't move for a few seconds. But she couldn't stay here. She inched sideways slowly, and peeked through the drapes again.

At first she didn't see anything except a last glow of daylight over the ocean. The house that was directly behind was too far down the hill to see, and apparently fences blocked lights from the houses on either side. As her eyes adjusted to the dark, she could see shapes of trees and bushes in the yard. One of the bushes was large enough for someone to hide behind. It was located approximately where she had seen something move.

Shahla dropped to the floor and quickly crawled in front of the door, until she could reach the security stick, beneath the drapes. She replaced it in the track of the sliding door. Then she got up and ran back to the stairs, dodging furniture, and turned off that light. Next she turned off the light in the bathroom. She leaned against the wall, trying to get her breathing under control. No way was she going outside in the dark.

One of the pieces of furniture stored in the room was a couch. Once again in the dark, she carefully felt her way to the couch and sat down. She would spend the night here. It was large and soft, and she felt somewhat protected by it. A noise outside made her jump. It sounded like the howl of a cat. After a few seconds of panic, she determined that it was probably just that.

Her mother would be worried about her. That couldn't be helped. She hoped the caller wouldn't go to her house. If he knew what street she lived on, he must know her address. Were her mother and Kirk safe? He was apparently after *her*, and he knew she wasn't at home. That didn't make her situation any better, but at least it relieved her mind a little concerning her mother.

She could see the outline of a heavy lamp on a table beside the couch. If necessary, she could use that as a weapon. She intended to keep her ears open all night, but she soon became very sleepy. What had been in the punch? And how much had she drunk? Maybe if she rested for a few minutes, she would feel better. She put her head down on the couch.

CHAPTER 31

Tony couldn't stay still. After he had left the Hotline, he had conducted another search of Bonita Beach by car. It was more difficult on a sunny Sunday morning than at night because a lot of people had apparently decided to go to the beach, perhaps for the last time this summer. Automobile traffic was heavy, as was pedestrian traffic, so if Shahla did happen to be walking, he could easily miss her.

He finally parked the car at the northern boundary of Bonita Beach and decided to walk the beach path the couple of miles to the south end and then back. He walked slowly on the concrete path, still favoring his left leg, attempting to observe everything that took place within sight and hearing.

A lot was taking place, what with the bicyclists, inline skaters, joggers, and walkers on the path. In addition, hordes of unconscious beachgoers constantly crossed the path without looking, intent on getting to the sand. As a result, near-accidents occurred regularly.

In addition to scanning the traffic on the path, Tony tried to check out all the girls on the sand catching the late summer rays. However, the beach was so wide that he couldn't possibly get a good look at all of them. One of the attributes that made this beach desirable now worked against him. To help him concentrate, he scored the girls, depending on their looks and what they wore. He scored one for a pretty girl in a nice bikini. Using his system, he could score an additional point for an unfastened top or a thong.

Some of the best-looking girls were competing in a beach volleyball tournament. Competing here in the birthplace of beach volleyball, which was appropriate. Tony slowed down as he walked past the courts. He recognized Martha, Joy's friend to whom he had spoken about her murder. She was partnering with another girl. She had a good figure. And her volleyball playing wasn't bad, either. She couldn't be the murderer. Especially if the murderer had kidnapped Shahla.

Shahla. He had to keep focused. He had to find her. He wondered if he would ever see her again. No, don't think like that. Think positively. He would find her. Or somebody else would. He kept walking.

***

Shahla awoke because somebody was pounding on her head with a hammer in time to her heartbeat. She didn't want to move, but she couldn't stand not to. She had to make him go away. How long had she been asleep? She opened her eyes. There was a film over them, but she could see objects, however blurry they looked. It must be daylight outside. A little light was seeping through the drapes. She looked at her watch and blinked her eyes, trying to focus. As the watch hands slowly became clearer, she read the time as quarter to eight. She had slept all night. She sat up and immediately felt nauseated.

She sat on the edge of the couch, wondering whether she was going to vomit. The pounding in her head continued. She thought about trying to get to the bathroom, but was sure she wouldn't make it. She sat motionless, waiting for the nausea to pass. After a few minutes, her stomach steadied, although her headache continued. She got up, feeling wobbly, and made her way to the bathroom.

After using the toilet, she thought about what she could do to make her body livable. She didn't have any pills with her. She didn't have any food or drink. Water. She needed water. She turned on the sink faucet and placed her mouth under it. She sucked in the lukewarm liquid and swallowed it until she couldn't drink any more. She straightened up and felt a little better.

She determined that the only food she had eaten since yesterday morning was whatever she ate at the party. She had snacked on chips and dip and other so-called food that Lacey had randomly pulled off the shelves of a supermarket, but nothing substantial. What Shahla needed more than anything else was a good meal.

And to call her mother. She suddenly realized that her mother must be frantic by now. Where was her cell phone? Then she remembered. Well, she'd better get home, on the double. She took the security stick out of the track of the sliding door and opened it. Once outside she closed it again. She took a look around, but of course nobody was there. Had she imagined that she had seen something last night? She might have seen an animal. Maybe the cat that howled.

The route to her house was two blocks downhill and then relatively level along Sandview Street. At least it wasn't uphill. Shahla walked slowly, in time to the throbbing pulse in her head. Food would help, she knew. There was food at home.

She arrived at her house and opened the door with her key. Inside she was greeted with silence. "Mom," she called. No answer. She looked at her watch. It was a little after eight. At least her mother should be up by now, even on a Sunday morning. She went into the kitchen. A few dirty dishes sat on the counter, but they were not breakfast dishes.

Shahla went upstairs. Her mother's bed was made. She went into Kirk's bedroom. His bed was also made. That was indicative. He wasn't known for making his bed in the morning. That bed hadn't been slept in. Where had they gone? As of yesterday morning, her mother had not had any plans to go anywhere.

She checked for messages on the house answering machine. There were none. She picked up the phone and called her mother's cell phone number. She got voice mail. She said, "Mom, it's me, Shahla. I'm home. Give me a call." Then she checked the garage, just to make sure. The car wasn't there.

Her mother apparently hadn't been very worried about her, but she should at least have left her a note. Shahla looked around, but there definitely wasn't any note. Well, she wasn't going to worry about them, either. She would get a call from her mother or they would show up, sooner or later. Meanwhile, she would fix herself something substantial to eat.

Maybe her mother had told a neighbor where she was going. They were good friends with the Thompsons, who lived across the street and three doors north. Shahla didn't know their phone number, so she walked over to their house and rang the bell. There was no answer. Nobody was home this morning.

Should she call Detective Croyden and tell him about the phone call last night? He wouldn't be working today. She didn't want to deal with anybody else. She would call him tomorrow. Anyway, the caller was probably just one of her friends playing a joke on her. Who else would know her cell phone number and her street? She had probably overreacted last night.

***

Shahla had a desire for action. She had been sunning herself on the beach since early afternoon. She was all alone. Jane was out of town. Lacey's house had looked empty when Shahla walked past it. She had rung the doorbell, just in case, but there was no answer. Her mother and Kirk were who knew where. She had come to the beach because she wasn't going to stay in the house alone any longer on a beautiful late summer day.

She should go for a workout run for cross-country, and she had worn her running shoes with that in mind, but she still had a headache, although it was improving. And she didn't feel like doing any more homework. She felt naked without her phone, but she had left tracks so that her mother could find her. She had written a note, saying where she was. Her mother couldn't accuse her of disappearing again. In fact, she could accuse her mother of that very thing.

She looked north along the beach and saw people playing beach volleyball, near the long pier that provided a walking path out over the water. She was too short to be good at volleyball. She was much better at running. It looked as if all the players were girls. She remembered something about a beach volleyball tournament for amateur females this weekend.

Some of the players were undoubtedly from the Bonita Beach High team. Joy should be playing. But Joy would never play volleyball again. Shahla wondered whether Martha was playing. Martha. The question of whether Martha had anything to do with Joy's murder was unresolved. Shahla had talked to Tony about it, but nothing had ever been done, as far as she knew.

She walked along the beach path to the volleyball courts. She saw a couple of girls from the Bonita Beach team, girls she barely knew. Then she saw Martha. Martha was playing a match. She was teamed with another girl from Bonita Beach, whose name Shahla didn't know. Martha's bikini was too small, but Shahla had to admit, grudgingly, that she had a better figure than Shahla had previously given her credit for. In spite of the acne on her face. She and her partner seemed to be holding their own against another team.

Shahla watched the match for a few minutes. In two-person beach volleyball, it was necessary for each player to be able to do everything well: serve, dig, set, spike and block. There were no specialists here. Martha's game had a lot of room for improvement, but she showed promise as she sprawled in the sand after digging out a hard spike with one arm. She got up in time to run to the net, jump, and hit her partner's set for a winner.

Martha was playing better than she had any right to be. Shahla walked to a table set up on the sand. A lady at the table must be in charge of the tournament. She was doing several things at once; talking to players clustered around her, writing down scores that were being relayed to her by the referees, and making occasional announcements concerning court assignments, using a megaphone.

When she was relatively free of her duties for a moment, Shahla asked her, "How are the Bonita Beach girls doing?"

"Not bad." The woman smiled at her. "They've won a couple of matches already." She referred to her score sheets. "Dembroski and Fulton won their first two matches."

Martha's last name was Dembroski.

The woman continued, "It's such a shame that Joy Tanner was killed. She and Martha were signed up as a team for this tournament. They would have been the favorites."

Shahla was startled. Joy and Martha a beach volleyball team? But of course. They had grown up together. They knew each other's every thought. It was logical. In fact, Joy had said something about that to Shahla. Shahla had immediately repressed it, as she had tried to do whenever Joy mentioned Martha.

Most upsetting was that it probably destroyed any motive Martha had for murdering Joy. You didn't murder your beach volleyball partner, especially when she might be your ticket to greatness. Shahla turned away from the table in disgust. She had willed Martha to be a murder suspect, but what one wished for and what one received were often two different things.

Shahla turned around and walked back toward the beach path. Fifty yards down the path she saw somebody who seemed familiar. The short, dark hair, the compact figure. He looked like Tony. He was walking away from her so she couldn't see his face. And he wasn't on crutches. It couldn't be Tony. Her imagination was playing tricks on her.

CHAPTER 32

Tony didn't know whether all this walking was good for his knee, but he couldn't stop himself. After he walked the length of Bonita Beach twice, he drove home and checked with the police. Still no news of Shahla. He ate something—he didn't notice what—in his empty townhouse. So empty he imagined he heard echoes as he moved through the rooms. Maybe he should call Josh and apologize. He didn't know where Josh was staying, but at least he had his cell phone number.

After staring at his own phone for a while, he decided not to call. He couldn't face any more rejection right now. Without a plan, he walked out his front door. He went toward the Hotline office. Distances were not great in Bonita Beach. He walked to the building that housed the Hotline, and then he walked around it, observing the shoppers who were patronizing the adjacent stores. He didn't go up to the office, itself. That morning, when he had been perusing the Green Book, it had felt eerie without Shahla there. If something happened to her, he was sure he could never go to the office again.

He walked back to his townhouse, getting home after dark. What now? There was no place he wanted to go. His knee was too sore to walk anymore. He couldn't even watch television because Josh had taken the TV set. He forced himself to get a pad and pen and sit at his table to formulate a plan of action. He covered the pages with doodles, but nothing intelligible.

***

Shahla ate a dinner that she fixed at home. Most of it consisted of leftover lasagna, nuked in the microwave. It didn't taste great, but it would keep her alive. She knew some of the rudiments of cooking, but it wasn't much fun to cook for one person.

She turned on the TV but couldn't find a show that interested her. It was dark now and her mother and Kirk still weren't home. The feeling of unease that had been gnawing at her became a full-fledged worry. What if they had been in an accident?

She decided to go back over to the Thompsons' house. They must be home by now. And if they weren't, she would call Tony. He would know what to do. As she walked out the front door, she could see Thompsons' driveway. The car that was usually parked there wasn't. Well, perhaps somebody was home, anyway.

She walked north along her side of the street until she was opposite the Thompsons' house. She was about to cross the street when she saw a car coming from the south. She waited to let it pass, but it slowed down and blinked its lights. Considerate California drivers sometimes stopped for pedestrians, even in the middle of a block.

Shahla waved at the driver as the car stopped, even though the car's headlights prevented her from seeing who was inside. She had reached the middle of the street when the car suddenly lurched forward, directly at her. Confused, she jumped back toward the curb, trying to get out of its way. It screeched to a halt beside her and the driver's door flew open, narrowly missing her. A man jumped out of the car and grabbed her before she could react.

Shahla screamed as the strong arms attempted to pull her toward the car. But the car was still rolling slowly. He let go of her with one hand and grabbed the open door frame of the car with his other hand, apparently to try to stop it. He was holding her by the right wrist. She tried to jam the fingers of her left hand into his throat. It was a glancing blow, at best, but she felt his grip loosen on her wrist. She jerked her whole body as hard as she could.

Her wrist pulled free, and she ran north along Sandview Street. Out of the corner of her eye, she saw the man chasing the car, which was rolling toward the far curb. She was running away from her house, but in the other direction the street ended in a cul-de-sac. He must have been waiting for her there. At the first intersection, she turned in the downhill direction, toward the beach. She had to get out of his line of sight.

She went one block downhill and stopped behind a lamppost, panting. This wasn't a good hiding place, but she didn't hear any sounds of pursuit. A car went by, but not that of the kidnapper. What should she do? She couldn't go back to her house as long as the man was in the neighborhood.

She decided to go to Jane's house. Jane's father should be there now, and he would protect her. Their house was several more blocks north and three blocks uphill from here. Shahla crossed the hilly street and ran along the street parallel to her own. She would go another block north and then cut uphill. She slowed down to a jog, wanting to conserve her energy. It was a good thing she ran cross-country. Training in the hills had greatly improved her wind.

At the next intersection, Shahla looked uphill. A car was moving farther up, but it was harmless. She started up the hill at a fast walk. Before she had gone halfway up the block, a car went through the intersection above, on Sandview Street. It was *his* car. She stopped, frozen. Then she heard the sound of a car backing up. That thawed her. She turned and ran back downhill.

In a few seconds, she heard the sound of the car approaching her from behind. She kept running downhill, trying not to go so fast in her panic that she tripped and sprawled on the steep sidewalk. Her speed didn't matter much because he could drive much faster than she could run. But here, close to the beach, cars were parked along the curb and he couldn't get near her without leaving his car.

He drove alongside her. Shahla didn't look at him. She hoped he didn't have a gun. Then he pulled ahead and stopped the car in the middle of the street. He opened the door and jumped out. She was on the right sidewalk so he had to run around the back of the car to cut her off. Her first instinct was to try to outrun him, but he squeezed between two parked cars and blocked her path.

He was wearing a baseball cap. Shahla couldn't see his face in the dim light. Was this the Chameleon? He was an apparition, more ghost than real, with his arms up and his body braced to intercept her, like a football player. She couldn't reverse direction and go uphill. By the time she stopped her forward momentum and turned around, he would be able to grab her.

She had a strong desire to barrel into him at top speed. She was within a few feet of him, close enough to see him flinch at the prospect of impact. At the last possible instant, she put on the brakes and slowed enough so that she was able to slip between two parked cars. She headed out into the street to go around his car.

Caught by surprise, the man went through the next space between the parked cars and reached for her as she ran by. He got hold of her arm. Desperate, Shahla tried to keep running, dragging him with her. As she steered just to the left of his car, he was off balance and hit the back of it. He released his grip on her. She lurched forward and thought she was going to tumble head over heels.

She desperately tried to get her center of gravity over her legs and regain her balance. She bounced off a parked car and careened through a complete 360-degree turn before she got her body under control. Then she found herself running down the middle of the street, almost to the dead-end at the beach.

She ran past the end of the street for a few feet to the concrete beach path and turned right on it, heading in the opposite direction from her home. She didn't hear footsteps behind her, so she looked over her shoulder. The man wasn't in sight, and a beach house blocked her view of the street she had come down.

Shahla continued north on the beach path at a slower pace and immediately saw the benefit of being here. The path was well lit by lights on poles, and there were other joggers and walkers going in both directions, even at night. She didn't think he would dare to follow her here.

But where could she go? She might be safe on the beach path, but she couldn't stay here all night. She couldn't go home because the kidnapper might stake out her house. The police station was too far away from the path to get to safely. She couldn't call anyone because she didn't have her cell phone or any money. Could she try to borrow a phone from another jogger? That meant a long explanation and the strong possibility that she would be labeled as a weirdo.

She continued on at a slow jog for a few minutes, breathing the cool night air and being thankful that she was free. However, each time she went past one of the streets that came down to the beach, she looked for the kidnapper's car. She didn't see it. A few minutes more and it occurred to her that she must be getting close to where Tony lived. She knew his townhouse complex was near the water in the northern part of Bonita Beach.

Tony would help her. But she had to find him first. She wished she had her phone. His home number was in her directory. Of course she hadn't memorized it, and of course it was unlisted. He had told her that he had gotten an unlisted number because some women made crank calls to Josh, his roommate.

His development had a name. What was it? Something to do with the ocean. Duh. Ocean View? Ocean Air? Ocean Potion? Shahla almost laughed, in spite of herself. Something to do with the Pacific Ocean. Ocean Pacific? No, that was a trademark. She was getting close to the northern boundary of Bonita Beach.

She stopped where the next street came down to the beach and looked carefully up the pavement but didn't see the dreaded car. A jogger was coming down, about to turn onto the beach path.

"Excuse me," Shahla said, stopping him in mid-stride. "Do you know of a townhouse development called something like Ocean Pacific?"

The man, who was dressed in sweats, stopped his forward progress and ran in place as he thought. "How about Peaceful Ocean? It's just a few blocks from here."

"Yeah, that's it."

"Go up this street and take the second left. It's quite big. You can't miss it." He took off in an easy lope.

"Thanks," she called after him. Shahla took one more look up the street before she started to walk along it. The coast was clear. As soon as that thought entered her head, it occurred to her where it had originated. The seacoast. Idioms, expressions, sayings, words, and their meanings—all fascinated her.

But she had to concentrate on the present. The two blocks went fast and soon Shahla was walking roughly north again on the cross street in this relatively level part of the city. A few blocks more

Alan Cook

and she could see a sign at the entrance to a residential development. Please let it be Peaceful Ocean, she prayed. She hadn't prayed since her father had died.

As she approached, she could make out the letters. Peaceful Ocean. Thank God. Shahla turned into the entrance road and was faced with a number of almost-identical townhouses. Which one was it? She looked to the left and the right and realized that there might be a hundred of them.

She remembered Joy's description—the pool was in its front yard. Where was the pool? Not in sight so it must be in the center of the complex. She continued on the entrance road, which went between groups of the homes.

She heard a car engine behind her. It was probably a resident, but she turned around to make sure. Her breath caught in her throat. It was *him*. Panic overcame her. She ran. When she passed the first row of buildings, she looked to the right. There was an open grassy area. She looked to the left. She saw the pool.

Shahla ran toward the pool on the sidewalk. The road didn't go in that direction. After a few seconds, she heard footsteps running behind her. She ran like she had never run before. As she approached the fenced-in pool, she realized that three units qualified as "having the pool in its front yard," and they were at the other end of the pool from her.

Would he dare follow her that far? She ran past the pool. The footsteps were gaining on her. Three houses. Which one was it? She didn't have a clue. She ran up two steps to the door of the first one and knocked loudly. She turned her head and saw him a few feet away. He had stopped.

If nobody answered, Shahla was sure he would try to grab her. She leapt off the steps and ran through a small garden area to the second house, trampling flowers. She jumped onto its steps and knocked on that door. Then she continued through another garden to the third house and did the same.

Again she turned and faced her would-be kidnapper. He had retreated a few feet but was still near the first door. It hadn't been opened. Uncertain now, Shahla stayed on the steps of the third townhouse. What if none of them were home? Would she end up running around the pool with him chasing her?

She planned to beg for help from the person who opened the first door—whether it was Tony or not. The door in front of her opened. It was a middle-aged woman.

"I need your help..." Shahla began, and then she saw the second door open. It was Tony. "Tony, thank God," she cried. She jumped off the woman's steps and ran over to Tony. At least she remembered to use the sidewalk instead of the flower garden. She leapt up his steps and into his arms.

CHAPTER 33

To say that Tony was surprised to find Shahla in his arms would have been the understatement of the century, but before he could say anything she cried, "That man is trying to kidnap me."

She pointed past the pool where the running form of a man was visible, heading at top speed away from them.

"I'm going to get him," Tony said, releasing her. He jumped off the steps, but as soon as he landed, his face contorted in pain, and he almost fell. He let out a yell and croaked, "I forgot about my damn knee."

He grabbed the knee and stood bent over. All they could do was watch as the man, now some distance away, reached his car and got into it. A few seconds later, the car disappeared behind the buildings of Peaceful Ocean Townhomes.

As Tony turned to hobble back up the steps, he saw his neighbor watching them with her mouth open. "It's okay, Muriel," he called to her. "Everything's fine."

"Are you sure?" she asked. "Do you want me to call the police?"

"We've got it under control. We'll handle it."

Muriel looked dubious, and she continued to watch them as Tony herded Shahla into the house, limped in behind her, and closed the door.

"She's a busybody," he said. "This will be all over the development by tomorrow." Before he could say anything more Shahla came into his arms again and started crying on his shoulder.

"Are you all right?" he asked, awkwardly, as he could feel her body racked with big sobs. She couldn't talk, so he just stood and held her, forgetting about the pain in his knee. At least she was alive and in his arms. He was thankful for that.

Several minutes passed before Shahla could say anything. When she had calmed down a little, Tony led her to the couch in the living room and sat her down. Then he got her a glass of water. He coaxed the story of the attack out of her.

"Did you recognize him?" Tony asked when she told about the man getting out of the car.

"No. He was wearing a baseball cap. I never got a good look at his face."

"Like the Chameleon. How big was he?"

"Tall—and fairly thin—but he has a strong grip."

Shahla showed Tony what looked like a burn mark around her right wrist, which she had received when she pulled free of him.

"Your hands are cut too."

"I hit a car when he tried to get me the second time."

"My God. How many times did he attack you?"

"Three, including just now."

"Jesus. But that doesn't sound like a description of the Chameleon. He's short, and I wouldn't credit him with a lot of strength, in spite of his job as a security guard."

Shahla was talking more freely now. The words tumbled out as she told the rest of the story. But she told it backwards, and it took Tony a while to figure out that the attack had started near her house.

"So you were home," he said. "Have you talked to your mother?"

"My mother isn't home."

"No, she's with her sister in Carlsbad."

"She didn't leave me a note."

"We'd better call and let her know you're all right," Tony said. "Then we have to go to the police."

Tony was still confused about what had happened to Shahla, but he could sort out the facts later. He had the number of Rasa's sister written down. Rasa and Kirk were staying with her sister because she was too freaked out by Shahla's disappearance to remain in her own house. He called that number. A woman answered who sounded something like Rasa. Tony asked for Rasa. The woman asked who was calling. Tony said, "Tell her it's Tony."

"Tony?" Rasa said, emotion in her voice. "What is happening?"

"Shahla's safe."

"Oh, that's wonderful." She repeated the word "wonderful" several times, her voice breaking. Finally, she asked, "Where is she?"

"She's right here. I'll let you talk to her." Tony handed the phone to Shahla.

"Mom? I was worried about you. I went home, and you weren't there." Shahla was crying on the phone.

There had obviously been a royal mix-up. Rasa had driven to Carlsbad last night. The police hadn't wanted her to go, especially in her distraught state, but she had said she couldn't stay in her own house. But at least the police knew where she was. And she had left her sister's number on Tony's answering machine.

"I called your cell phone, but you didn't return my call," Shahla said through her tears. And after a pause, "You forgot to take it with you?"

"I can't stay in the house tonight," Shahla told her mother. "The kidnapper knows where I live." After listening, she said, "No, don't come home tonight. We don't know where he is. Nobody should stay in the house." And after a short pause, "I'll stay with Tony."

Besides, Carlsbad was a couple of hours away, by car, near San Diego. Shahla told Rasa that Tony had an extra bedroom. They talked for another minute, and then Shahla said, "I love you," and hung up.

"Are you okay?" Tony asked Shahla.

Shahla nodded. She said, "I was worried about her."

"That must have been very difficult…"

"If you complete that sentence, I'll punch you in the nose," Shahla said, smiling through her tears.

Tony was relieved. He asked, "Are you up to going to the police now?"

***

They arrived at the police station ten minutes later and found out from the female officer at the desk that Detective Croyden wasn't on duty. Tony thought for the second time that at least he didn't work twenty-four hours a day.

"I'll get Lieutenant Stone," the desk officer said, perking up after they told her who Shahla was. She had looked bored when they came in. "She's the officer in charge." And then to Shahla, "I'm glad you're all right. We were worried about you."

"You were?" Shahla turned to Tony after they entered the conference room and said, "Were the police looking for me?"

Tony nodded.

"But I was right here all the time."

Lieutenant Stone walked into the conference room. Although she wasn't exceptionally big, she looked impressive in her blue police uniform, with the full belt, attached to which were a gun, handcuffs, a nightstick, a cell phone, and a number of other implements of the trade that Tony couldn't identify. That belt must weigh plenty. And the lieutenant looked as if she could take care of herself.

Lieutenant Stone shook hands with both of them. She said to Shahla, "Your hands are cut. Do you need medical attention?"

"It's nothing. I'm okay."

"Be sure to clean them up and disinfect them. I'm glad you're safe. Sit down and tell me what happened."

"The first thing is that a man attempted to kidnap her within the last half hour," Tony said. "He may still be in the area."

The lieutenant flashed into action and asked key questions. When she asked what kind of car he was driving, Shahla said, "It was silver, not too big. I don't know what kind." Tony, who had seen it only at long range, couldn't identify it any better. Shahla's description of the suspect was a little more helpful, but not much.

Lieutenant Stone said, "That isn't much to go on, but I'll put out an APB and tell everybody you're safe."

She went out of the room. Tony ached to question Shahla some more, but he would hear it all soon enough. He felt a great sense of relief that she was all right. She looked okay, if a little bedraggled, except for her wrist and hands. He wondered whether the broadcast went out to more than just the two or three cars that he imagined were patrolling in Bonita Beach, but when Stone came back, she was all business, and he didn't get a chance to ask.

"They're keeping an eye on your mom's house," she said to Shahla, "and yours too, since he knows where you live," indicating Tony. "We can have a car drive you home, Shahla."

"I'm staying with Tony tonight," Shahla said. "My mom's out of town, you know."

Stone looked dubious. "Is that all right with her?"

"I talked to her. She said it was okay."

Tony didn't want to get involved in this discussion. He had that guilty feeling he got when he thought he was going to be accused of doing something immoral.

Stone said, "Maybe that's for the best. I suspect some news crews may be on their way to your mom's house now. It's probably better if you can avoid them for one night. We just gave out your picture a short time ago. They'll pick up the APB and know you're safe, so they'll want to talk to you. But they can do that tomorrow. For now, tell me what happened to you since yesterday morning."

Shahla hesitated and then blurted out, "I went to a party."

"An all-night party?"

"No. I left before dark. But then I got a phone call from him."

"Who's him?"

"Probably the man who tried to kidnap me. I didn't recognize his phone number. And then I broke my phone. I don't remember what it was."

When, in response to probing from Lieutenant Stone, Shahla said that the caller sounded something like the Chameleon, the lieutenant said, "An officer from El Segundo talked to the Chameleon last night at his apartment. He was home with all his girlie pictures. So I can tell you for sure that he wasn't out harassing you. In fact, he doesn't even own a car. And he has an alibi for the night of Joy's murder."

Shahla told how she had been too scared to leave Jane's basement. When she started telling what she had done that morning,

Stone asked her why she hadn't contacted the police after she found her mother gone.

"Because I didn't know you were involved," Shahla said. "I just thought my mother and Kirk had taken off to someplace."

"You're greatly undervaluing yourself by thinking your mom wasn't worried about you," Stone said. "She's been calling here every hour since last night to see if we have any information on you. I don't think she slept at all."

"Why didn't you at least return my phone call?" Tony asked.

"Like I said, I broke my phone. I didn't know you called. My mom said she left a message on my phone about going to my aunt's house. I didn't get that one either."

"Can't you retrieve your messages from another phone?" Stone asked.

Shahla looked puzzled. "I don't know. I've never been without my phone before."

Tony said, "Your mom must be in the same boat because she didn't get the message from you."

Lieutenant Stone nodded. "We get situations like this all the time. You would think that since we're in the age of communication, people would be able to communicate with each other. But we depend too much on technology. However, I want to give you kudos for foiling your kidnapper. It's a good thing you're not a docile little doll. If you were, you wouldn't be here right now. Of course you shouldn't have gone to the party without telling your mother. But this whole thing sounds like one of those old slapstick comedies where everyone is in the wrong place at the wrong time."

Stone was an adept questioner, and she wrung every possible bit of information out of Shahla, including as much of a description of the kidnapper and his car as she could give. Shahla answered readily, but she was getting visibly tired. Finally, it became evident that she had nothing new to add to what she had already said.

"We'll let you go and get some sleep," Stone said, looking meaningfully at Tony. "Let me see if any reporters are here."

She went out and returned within a minute. "They're starting to gather. Do you want to speak to them tonight, Shahla? You are one terrific story, and they're going to hound you until they get it."

Shahla shook her head. "I can't take any more tonight."

"Okay. Tony, is your car parked in front? Drive it around to the back. I don't think they know you, do they? I'll distract them and then sneak Shahla out the back door."

***

"How did you know I had a spare bedroom?" Tony asked as they went from the carport through his back door.

"I didn't," Shahla said. "I didn't want to tell my mom I was going to sleep on the floor. She wouldn't have liked that."

"So you didn't know that Josh left."

Shahla looked surprised. "What happened?"

"He didn't like the fact that I turned him in."

"Oh, Tony, I'm sorry. Is he still a suspect?"

"Not really. It seems those panties are about ten years old. They date from college. I vaguely remembered something about them after he accused me of betraying him."

"I guess I can't say that the situation must be difficult for you."

Tony laughed shortly. "No more than I can say it to you. We have to make up the bed in what was Josh's room for you. Fortunately, I actually do laundry once in a while, and I have clean sheets."

"May I take a shower? I haven't had one in a couple of days. And I need to wash off his touch. And my clothes are dirty."

"We should have gone by your place and picked up some clean clothes."

"And fight the reporters? No thanks. I'll manage. But my leg started to hurt when we were at the police station."

Shahla pulled up her shorts and pointed to a bruise on her upper thigh. But when that didn't uncover all of it, she impatiently pulled her shorts down. She was wearing a bikini bottom underneath. Tony forced himself to concentrate on the colors of the ugly blotch, ranging from red to black and blue, like a poorly executed abstract painting.

"How did you get that?"

"When I was trying to get away from him, I hit a parked car. That's when I hurt my hands."

"I have some disinfectant for the cuts," he said. "But I don't know what we can do about the bruise. Do you want to put ice on it?"

"No. It will be okay as long as nothing touches it. May I take a shower now? I'll wash it off."

Tony gave Shahla towels and a washcloth and made up the spare bed while she was in the shower. He felt like a housewife. He was glad he had a cleaning lady who came on a regular basis so that the house wasn't too dirty. He also found a first aid kit.

He had an urge to open the bathroom door and ask her if she needed her back washed, but he was the parent here, and he couldn't do that.

He was in the spare bedroom when Shahla poked her head out of the bathroom door and yelled, "Do you have a T-shirt I can wear?"

He had forgotten about nightclothes for her. He limped down to his bedroom, passing her on the way and came back with a T-shirt. She reached out a bare arm and took it from him, then closed the door. Tony retreated to his bedroom so she would have a clear path to her room when she came out.

However, several minutes later she appeared in his doorway and said, "I borrowed your comb. Do you have an extra toothbrush?"

The T-shirt was long enough on her so it served as a mini-dress. Tony said, "My dental technician always gives me a toothbrush when I get my teeth cleaned. I think I have a couple of extras."

He went into the bathroom and saw her clothes sitting on the toilet seat. He said, "I have a washer and dryer. I'll wash your clothes for you."

"I see this is a full-service hotel," Shahla said, really smiling for the first time since she had shown up at his doorstep.

"Do you want the swimsuit washed?"

"If you don't mind. That's my underwear until I go home."

Tony took her clothes downstairs and put them in his washing machine. The washer and dryer were located in a small utility room off the kitchen. When he came back five minutes later, Shahla had gone into her bedroom but left the door open. He waited until the wash cycle ended and placed the clothes in the dryer. Then he went to bed. It had been an exhausting day. And his knee hurt.

He was trying to settle himself down to sleep when he felt, rather than heard or saw, something in his doorway. He turned his head and barely saw Shahla's silhouette against the dark background of the hallway.

"I don't want to sleep in there alone," she said. "It's too dark with the light out. I'm afraid."

"Do you want a nightlight?" Tony asked.

"No, I want to sleep in your bed."

"You mean, you want to trade beds?"

"No."

"That's not a good idea. I'm just down the hall from you. You can call if you need me."

"The stairs are between us. He might…come up the stairs.

"The police are watching the house." Tony was getting a little perturbed. He needed a good night's sleep. He said, "I guess I could sleep on the couch downstairs."

"No, I want you nearby. Stay in the bed. I won't take up much room."

Shahla lay down on the bed beside him and pulled the sheet and light blanket over her. She lay on her side, facing away from him. He normally slept in his briefs and a T-shirt. Sometimes he took the briefs off if they were too constricting. Fortunately, he hadn't done that tonight. It was an old-fashioned double bed, not queen or king-size. There was no extra room. Tony turned his back to her and found himself on the edge of the bed.

"After my father was killed, I sometimes slept with my mom, and we would cuddle together like spoons," Shahla said.

It was clear what she wanted him to do. He turned over and carefully arranged his body so that, although they were touching, it didn't go beyond that. He tentatively placed his arm over her. She snuggled against him and then lay still. He felt tense and wondered how long he could stay like this. He would never fall asleep. At least not for a long….

CHAPTER 34

When he awoke, Tony was facing his window, which faced toward the east. And the rising sun. Which had already risen. There was something wrong with this. Oh yes, it was a workday, and he hadn't set the alarm. He was late already. He carefully got out of bed, trying not to disturb Shahla. It had been a while since he had slept with a woman. What was the proper etiquette? Let her wake up at her own speed.

Shahla was curled up in roughly the same position in which she had gone to sleep. She had let out a muffled scream several times during the night. Her legs had twitched, as though she were running. Tony had patted her back and said soothing words, trying to calm her. She hadn't woken up, and each time she had quieted down after a few seconds.

Tony went to the bathroom and attempted to bring some coherence to his thoughts. Today was Monday. Monday was a workday. And a school day. But was Shahla in any shape to go to school? She was probably all right physically, but emotionally? And was it safe for her to go to school, with the kidnapper on the loose? He had acted boldly, but in a risky manner. He wanted her badly. He might try to snatch her again.

Tony put on a pair of shorts and went downstairs. While he made coffee, he wondered whether he should take a vacation day in order to stay with Shahla. Or he could just call in sick. But he didn't like to lie.

Rasa had gone to her sister's house for comfort and support. She had said she was returning to Bonita Beach today, but she might not be here until noon or later. She apparently wasn't going to work, and Shahla's brother, Kirk, wasn't going to school.

Tony was making himself toast when Shahla appeared, still wearing his T-shirt. Her hair was uncombed, and her eyes were a little bleary. She looked vulnerable, but sweet. And although her mood was subdued, she didn't seem to be depressed or scared.

"Your clothes are in the dryer," Tony said. He went the few steps to the utility room and pulled them out of that machine. He handed them to Shahla.

"Thank you." She laid them on a chair, then took the bikini bottom, stepped into the leg holes, and pulled it up. She did the same with the shorts.

There was something intimate about watching a woman get dressed. "How do you feel?" he asked.

"I'll be all right. My thigh hurts, my hands hurt, and a few other places hurt, but I'll be fine."

"Would you like some toast? I've got strawberry jam."

"That would be wonderful. I'm starving."

Tony poured orange juice for her to go with the toast. Realizing how hungry she was, he also made eggs and bacon. She ate everything.

After she had satisfied her appetite, her mood improved dramatically. She kidded Tony about his cooking skills, saying that he could get a job as a short-order cook.

Tony was glad to see a spark of the old Shahla. He said, "What do you think about going to school? I could drive you to your house to get some clothes and books."

"The kidnapper probably knows what school I go to. He knew where I lived." She hesitated. "I'm not up to school today. And won't the kids have found out about me?"

Tony smacked his head with his hand. "We haven't looked at the news." He started toward the living room and then said, "Oh, I forgot, I don't have a television set anymore. But I have a radio."

The combination radio-CD player was in the living room. Tony turned on the radio and found a news station. Within a couple of minutes, one of the news anchors said, "Last night, a girl showed pluck and daring by escaping a would-be kidnapper in Bonita Beach." He told the story, which must have been transmitted to the reporters by Lieutenant Stone. He didn't say anything specific about where Shahla lived or where she was staying. Tony was referred to only as a friend. His name wasn't mentioned.

"Good." Tony was pleased. "Lieutenant Stone is protecting your privacy. We can take advantage of that. I have to call my office. Go ahead and finish getting dressed, and then we'll put our heads together and try to create a plan of action. We certainly have more information than we had before."

The telephone rang. The downstairs extension was in the kitchen, next to the family room.

"I'll get it," Shahla called. She was headed back toward the family room to pick up the rest of her clothes.

"Let me get it," Tony said, following her as fast as he could. Maybe it was Mona, his boss. She often called him early in the morning with things for him to do. But by the time he got to the opening into the kitchen, Shahla had already answered it.

He heard her say, "Hello. Hello." She looked at the phone with a puzzled expression. "Hang up. Just like we get at the Hotline."

"Hang up?" Tony didn't normally get hang ups. "Maybe whoever it was hung up because a girl answered," he said as a small joke. Wishful thinking.

"Maybe it's your girlfriend," Shahla said. "The one who likes to put me down."

"Carol? She's my ex-girlfriend at this point. Very ex. And the likelihood of her calling me at this hour of the morning—or any hour—is about the same as the probability that we'll get hit by a meteor today." Unless she had had a falling-out with her boyfriend—Horace, or whatever is name was. More wishful thinking.

"I could hear something in the background that sounded like traffic noise. Whoever it was must have been calling from a cell phone."

"That's annoying. Makes it hard to hear. Like that caller I was reading about in the Green Book yesterday morning when I was trying to figure out what happened to you. It said he always played a television set in the background during his calls. Maybe he did it to help disguise his voice."

"Who was that?"

"Someone called the Cackling Crucifier."

"I remember him. He never gave the same name twice. He talked about religion and Jesus. You're right; he always had a television playing. And he had a weird laugh. Why were you reading about him?"

"I'm not sure. I was going through the inactive pages and for some reason he sounded familiar."

"He was worried about my immortal soul. He asked me if I was a Christian. He said he'd like to take me to church. He got pretty insistent. I was a little afraid of him."

"Did he ever tell you where he lived?"

"No, he was very evasive. And then he stopped calling. I was relieved."

Tony was trying to put some pieces together. "What if that call just now was actually from him? What if he's trying to find out whether you're here?"

"Huh?" Shahla looked at Tony as though she thought he had flipped. "I never gave him any personal information. Besides, he doesn't even know you. How could he know where you live?"

"Stay with me. What if the reason he stopped calling was because he signed up to be a listener on the Hotline?"

"A listener? But who...?"

"How about Nathan? Didn't he attend the training class that started soon after the Crucifier stopped calling? He certainly fits the religious profile."

"Nathan? Nathan has some strange ideas, but I think he's basically harmless. At least, that's what I've been telling myself."

"I've heard Nathan laugh. It could be described as a cackle."

"I've never heard Nathan laugh that I can remember. And I've worked shifts with him. I'd certainly remember if he had a laugh like the Crucifier."

"Here's my hypothesis. He always had to be very careful around you and the others he had talked to on the phone before. And he probably altered his voice somewhat when he was on the phone, like the Chameleon."

"The Crucifier had a fairly high-pitched voice on the phone. Nathan's voice is lower."

"I saw a plastic device at the Chameleon's apartment that is probably what he uses for voice alteration. I did a little research on the Internet and found similar devices that will make you sound younger—that is, they raise the pitch of your voice. Remember the night that Nathan and you and I were working, and I got a call from a guy who said he was a former listener and was badmouthing the other listeners? Talking about orgies and stuff? Nathan seemed to identify with him a little too well. As if he were in his shoes, perhaps as both a caller and a listener. Or is that theory all wet?"

Shahla thought for a moment. Then she said, "Maybe not. I heard you get up, but I couldn't drag myself out of bed. I kept going over and over what happened last night. The more I thought about it, the more I was sure I noticed something familiar about the guy."

"Do you think you've seen him before?"

"I didn't really see his face, and I couldn't see his hair. But his size and the way he moved. It's funny that we've been talking about Nathan."

"He reminded you of Nathan?"

"I couldn't come up with a name before, but maybe it is Nathan. You know how Nathan walks, kind of jerky, like a puppet being controlled by strings? This guy had the same awkward movement when he was trying to stop me from getting to the beach. He wasn't graceful, like an athlete. If he had been better coordinated, he might have been able to do it. He was certainly big enough."

Shahla paused. "But it wasn't Nathan's car, was it? I seem to remember that he drives a Jeep or something."

"That's my memory too," Tony said. "But sometime after we attended that church service, it occurred to me that Nathan's alibi didn't hold water. He said he was at a service until eleven the night of the murder, but the way people came and went during the service we were at, he could have snuck out and never been missed."

"He might even have returned before eleven."

"Right. Let's assume for a minute that it was Nathan who tried to kidnap you and that he called here just now. He could have gotten my phone number off the Hotline roster. He might have been calling to see if you're still here. And of course your address is on the roster, too."

"So he's going to try again?" Shahla looked out the living room window at the swimming pool and shuddered.

"Don't worry; it's not going to happen." Tony chastised himself for scaring her. "Go upstairs and get dressed. I'm going to call my boss and tell her I won't be at work today. Then we'll get on the computer. I found a website for the Church of the Risen Lord back when you and I attended the service. The first thing we'll do is to check and see whether there's any new information there."

***

"Here it comes," Tony said.

He was sitting in the swivel chair in front of his computer. Shahla was leaning over his shoulder, intently watching the screen. The home page of the Church of the Risen Lord appeared; it showed people being carried upward in an endless stream, presumably into heaven, where they acquired wings and started flitting about.

"It's wonderful what can be done with graphics these days," Tony said, hoping he didn't sound too sarcastic. There were a number of hyperlinks on the page. Tony clicked on the one marked, "Day of Judgment." A new page appeared on the screen. It was printed in large, bold text. Tony and Shahla read it together.

"To the Faithful: Hallelujah! The time we have been waiting for has arrived. Gather at the appointed place at sunset on Monday, September 30. Our Ascension will take place at midnight. You already have a copy of the bus schedules showing you how to get there by public transportation. Be sure to bring all your money in cash. Get a maximum cash advance on your credit cards. You must have divested all your worldly goods. Remember that it is easier for a camel to pass through the eye of a needle than for a rich man to get into heaven. As we wait, we will conduct a prayer vigil and sing the praises of our Lord. Do not be late. Anybody who does not show up will be cast into the fiery pits and burned to ashes. You do not want to be among that number." At the bottom, "Reverend Luther Hodgkins" was printed in larger, bolder letters.

"That's tonight," Shahla said.

"Time is running out," Tony said. It was coming together. "That's why Nathan isn't driving his own car. He's probably sold it and is driving a loaner or a rental. But if he wants to take another girl to heaven with him, he has to work fast."

"Another? You mean Joy…?"

"Maybe it works something like the Muslim suicide bombers. They get seventy-seven virgins in heaven, give or take a few. Maybe Nathan has to collect his own."

"You mean, if he kills them, he gets to have them in heaven? Tony, that's horrible."

"I know. We have to keep him away from you until tonight."

"What happens at midnight when…nothing happens?"

"Hopefully, that will expose the Reverend Hodgkins as a fraud. But it would also help if Nathan has already been arrested. I wish we knew where this place was. But the good reverend is too clever to put it on the Internet. I suppose that the only ones who know it are those who have been faithfully attending the church services and giving willingly of their material possessions."

"Should we tell Detective Croyden what we know?"

"Unfortunately, it's mostly speculation. But we need to tell him something." Tony tried to think. "We don't have any reason to believe that Nathan has a gun or even knows how to use one. But if he did, he could shoot through my windows unless we kept the drapes closed all day. And we don't want to feel like animals in a zoo. I suspect we're better off somewhere else."

Shahla looked out the window again at the pool she had run around to evade the kidnapper and said. "Let's get out of here."

"Okay. We'll first go to the Hotline office and find out Nathan's address. I'm sure that Croyden already has it, but I want it for myself."

CHAPTER 35

Tony had Shahla wait in the fenced-in patio behind his townhouse while he went through the wooden gate to the carport and carefully scanned it for anybody who shouldn't be there. In fact, he saw nobody at all, although it was possible that someone might be hiding behind one of the other cars.

He quickly opened the passenger-side door of the Boxter and signaled Shahla to come out. She came, somewhat apprehensively, and once she had done her own look around, she scooted to the car, climbed in, and slammed the door.

Tony got into the driver's seat and started the engine. He was thankful for the purr that promised power, waiting to be called upon, that hopefully would keep them out of trouble today.

He compulsively checked out the other cars through his windows and mirrors during the short trip to the Hotline. He noticed that Shahla also kept swiveling her head. The usual mix of large and small vehicles filled Pacific Coast Highway, which was a grand name for a street like any other street, with traffic lights and congestion. Nobody looked suspicious, however; nobody seemed to have any particular interest in them.

Tony pulled into the parking lot of the shopping center where the Hotline building was located. He drove around to the back of the line of shops. The overflow parking spaces were located here. Here was where Joy had been snatched, and the park just behind the lot was where she had been murdered. Few cars were parked here at this time of the morning. Most were parked in front.

"We can keep an eye on the car from the window of the Hotline office," Tony said. The window in the listening room overlooked the back parking area. Since Nathan had worked night shifts with Tony, he knew what kind of car Tony drove.

It would be easy to spot somebody loitering, since there were few cars and fewer people in sight. They went through the back door of the Hotline building. Shahla went toward the elevator, but Tony started up the stairs.

"If you're a cross-country runner, you should be able to handle a couple of flights of stairs," he said.

He started taking them two at a time. A shot of pain through his knee reminded him that he shouldn't be doing anything this strenuous. Shahla flashed past him before he came to the first landing, and by the time he reached the third floor, she was standing there with her hands on her hips, not even breathing hard.

"Where have you been?" she asked.

At least she didn't say it derisively. And because Tony had been forced to slow down to one step at a time, he wasn't panting as they walked to the Hotline office. The door was unlocked. As they passed through the doorway into the first room, Tony could see Patty, the administrative assistant, working at a computer in the administration area. He rarely saw her since he worked on the phones at night, when she was going to school.

There was a girl in the listening room on the phone. Tony looked a question at Shahla.

"That's Tina Rodriguez," Shahla said. "She was in my training class. She's in college."

Shahla found a copy of the roster of listeners. Tony copied down Nathan's address, his home telephone number, and his cell phone number. He had a Los Angeles address, which could be just about anywhere, but from the zip code, Tony figured that it wasn't too far from the Church of the Risen Lord. His years of driving in Southern California on business had given him a good feel for the area.

Tony and Shahla walked into the office where Patty was working. She looked up and did a double take. "Shahla," she exclaimed. "Are you all right? Detective Croyden called me at home yesterday and said that you were missing and did I know where you were. I was worried sick about you. Then this morning I read in the paper that you had escaped from a kidnapper." She got up and gave Shahla a big hug.

"I'm fine," Shahla said. "And Tony's my bodyguard."

In her relief, Patty gave Tony a hug, too. He had no objection.

"We have reason to believe that Nathan may be mixed up in this," Tony said. "I'm going to call Detective Croyden."

"Nathan?" Patty looked surprised. "I don't know him very well because he usually works nights. But he always seemed kind of quiet and shy. I guess you never know about people."

Tony knew the number at the Bonita Beach Police Station by heart. When he was connected to the desk officer, he asked for Detective Croyden. The officer informed him that Detective Croyden would not be in today.

"All day?" Tony asked in disbelief. He couldn't imagine Croyden not working.

"He will be back tomorrow. Can anybody else help you?"

"How about Lieutenant Stone?"

"She will be in at three."

"I'll call back." He hung up. "Damn. There's no point in trying to tell the story to somebody who doesn't know what's going on."

"There may be another person working on the case," Shahla pointed out.

"Yeah, but I don't know that person, and they don't know me. Why should they believe anything I have to say?"

Tony stomped out of that room and into the listening room where Tina was writing a call report. When she saw Shahla, who had followed him in, she reacted much the same way that Patty had.

"Shahla." Tina stood up and gave Shahla a hug. "I'm glad you're okay."

"Don't I get one too?" Tony asked.

Tina gave him a who-is-this-guy look.

Shahla laughed. "Tina, this is Tony. Tony, this is Tina."

Tina was a cute brunette, dressed in jeans and a Stanford sweatshirt with red lettering on a white background. At first glance she looked something like Shahla.

Tina offered her hand saying, "I've heard about you."

Tony took it and said, "Nothing good, I hope."

Tina shook her head. "Nothing." She turned to Shahla. "Look at all the hang ups I've gotten this morning." She pointed to the board where hang ups were recorded. "I can understand the masturbators hanging up on guys, but why are they hanging up on me? I've got a sexy, feminine voice."

The girls weren't supposed to like getting those calls. Tony asked, "Did you hear anything in the background before the hang ups?"

Tina shook her head. "Maybe a little breathing. Then a click." She looked at her watch. "Ten o'clock. I've got to get to class." She picked up a book she had been reading, said goodbye to them, and walked out the door.

But, presumably, her class wasn't at Stanford University, almost 400 miles away. She probably attended a local community college and hoped to transfer to Stanford.

Tony went over to the desk by the window and looked out at the parking lot. He saw his car sitting undisturbed. He loved that car. He could stand and gaze at it for hours. Shahla joined him at the window.

"What do we do now?" she asked.

"Maybe I should go pay Nathan a call."

"We. Whither thou goest I will go. You're my bodyguard, remember?"

Tina had just come out of the back door of the building and was headed toward her car, which was parked not too far from Tony's. Another car came cruising down one of the aisles toward her.

Shahla caught her breath and said, "That looks like the kidnapper's car."

It was a silver compact. A Chevy, Tony could see from the logo—the bloated parallelogram of Chevrolet. Probably a Cavalier. The door opened when it came alongside Tina and a man jumped out and grabbed her. Exactly how Shahla had described her ordeal.

Tony didn't wait to see any more. He ran out of the listening room. He paused at the door to the administrative office and yelled at Patty, "Call 911. A man is trying to kidnap Tina. Silver Chevy Cavalier."

Before she could say anything, he ran past the closing outer door into the hall. Shahla had preceded him and was already at the top of the stairs.

"Wait for me," he yelled. But she didn't wait. By the time he had reached the top of the stairs, she was already out of sight, going down the second level between the floors. Tony couldn't go as fast as Shahla—that had already been proven—and he had to be careful of his knee. He prayed she wouldn't get herself into trouble. But he also prayed that Tina could fight off the attacker.

He finally reached the first floor after a one-step-at-a-time descent that felt like a slow-motion football replay. He ran to the back door of the building, still favoring his knee. He hoped it would hold up. When he burst through the doorway to the outside world, a quick scan revealed Shahla with her hands to her face, and the silver car disappearing around the end of the last shop in the center. He didn't see Tina.

Tony trotted toward his car while trying to pull the key out of his pocket. When he had it in his hand he clicked the remote, unlocking his door. He opened it and tumbled into the driver's seat, not very gracefully. His motions became more fluid as he started the engine and rammed it into first gear. He roared forward and made a quick ninety-degree right turn toward the end of the building.

Shahla ran in front of the car, waving her arms. Her face looked strange. He jammed on the brakes and stopped. Damn it, she was holding him up. She came forward and felt her way around the car, almost like a blind person. She couldn't seem to open the passenger-side door. Tony was tempted to drive off without her, but she would never forgive him for leaving her behind. And there wasn't time to argue. He reached over and opened the door for her. She stumbled into the car. He started fast and the acceleration slammed the door shut.

As he swerved around the corner of the building, he saw people in front of him, walking to their cars. Double damn. He slowed down—he didn't want to kill anybody—and weaved his way among them, fast enough to draw stares.

He drove clear of the pedestrians and saw the silver car make a right turn onto the public street and accelerate rapidly. A few seconds later, he made the turn with the Porsche in second gear and roared after the other car without shifting, as the tachometer needle climbed toward the red line.

The traffic light at an intersection ahead turned yellow. Tony backed off on the gas pedal and said, "He's got to stop."

The silver car slowed slightly and swerved into the left-turn lane, but instead of stopping, it entered the intersection well after the light had become red. A car starting up from the left barely braked in time as the Chevy fishtailed through the turn and disappeared in the direction of Pacific Coast Highway.

Tony was first in line at the light, but that was small consolation for losing the kidnapper's car. He swore silently, thinking that if Shahla hadn't held him up, he would have caught the other car and at least been able to get the license plate number.

"Seat belts," he commanded.

Shahla fumbled a few seconds before she got hers fastened. She was coughing for some reason. And sneezing.

Tony concentrated on the light. "He'll turn north on PCH." He handed his cell phone to Shahla, saying, "Call the police station and tell the desk officer that. You can use redial."

"I can't see."

Tony looked at her. Her eyes were full of tears. Was this a reaction to Tina's kidnapping? He hoped she would hold up. He took the phone back and placed the call. Then he handed it back to her.

She was still sneezing. She was barely able to talk on the phone for a few seconds. Then her sneezing stopped and her voice became clearer.

While she talked, Tony turned on his emergency flashers, edged forward, and revved the engine. He also hand-signaled the cars coming the other way. There was no left-turn arrow at this intersection, and he hoped that if he showed enough urgency, the oncoming cars would let him make the turn in front of them.

When the light turned green, he started forward, ready to stop fast if it didn't work. However, the cars at the front of the two lanes of traffic heading in his direction hesitated just long enough for him to complete the turn He upshifted and headed toward PCH as Shahla spoke excitedly into the phone. "We're trying to follow the kidnapper's car. We think he's going to turn north on Pacific Coast Highway…It's a silver compact. A…" She hesitated.

"Chevy Cavalier," Tony said, crossing to the wrong side of the street to pass the car ahead of him that was slowing to pull into a parking space.

"Chevy Cavalier." She said to Tony, "He's going to keep us on the line, in case we spot the car again."

When Tony arrived at PCH, the light was red against him, and he had to wait ten seconds before it was safe to make a right turn. More time lost. He despaired of ever seeing the silver car again. He headed north, changing lanes to pass cars, trying to make up time, and wondering whether Nathan—he pictured the kidnapper as being Nathan—would stay on this main street, where it might be easier for the police to spot him, or transfer to a side street.

Actually, his most likely route involved getting on the 405 freeway at some point, perhaps at the Artesia or Rosecrans entrance. If he did that, it would be practically impossible to find him. He might get away with this. Tony's heart sank.

"Did you see how he got Tina into the car?" he asked Shahla as he accelerated past an eighteen-wheeler.

"She was already in the backseat by the time I got outside. He was getting in the front. I ran to the car and tried to open the back door. He squirted something out the window at me and took off."

"It must have been mace or pepper spray. You took an awful chance. He might have tried to put you in the car too."

"I figured if he did you would be there in time to save me."

Would he? "Don't rub your eyes. It'll make it worse. It's a good thing he didn't do that to you yesterday."

"He's getting desperate. Oh, Tony, this is my fault. He took Tina because he couldn't get me."

Her fault? Now wasn't the time for her to feel guilty. And now wasn't the time for him to use listening techniques on her, such as, "Why do you think it's your fault?" He said, roughly, "This is not your fault. And if we're going to help Tina, we've got to stay focused."

Shahla remained quiet until she received a query over the phone. She gave their position and said they hadn't spotted the kidnapper. As Tony approached Artesia Boulevard, he wondered whether he should turn right toward the 405. If he were the kidnapper and he wanted to get to a place north of the airport, that's what he would do.

A police car came racing up behind him with its red lights blinking but no siren. Tony pulled into the right lane to let it pass. The black and white crossed Artesia Boulevard and stayed on PCH, which mysteriously changes its name to Sepulveda Boulevard at that point. Tony turned right on Artesia and headed toward the freeway. Let the cop take Sepulveda.

"What are you doing?" Shahla asked.

"Getting on the freeway." But just then he crossed Aviation Boulevard and realized that if Nathan had been planning all along to take the freeway, he would have probably turned right on Aviation a few blocks back, where it started at PCH, which would have been like taking the hypotenuse of a right triangle. Tony had taken the sides of the triangle. More time lost.

Not only that, he had to wait a significant amount of time for a red light at Hawthorne Boulevard. He felt that the chase was hopeless when he finally accelerated up the onramp onto the 405 and merged with the traffic. The continuous, heavy traffic, which made spotting a single silver car as difficult as spotting a specific silver fish among the thousands in the schools he had seen on his last snorkeling trip.

"We're never going to find the car here," Shahla said, echoing Tony's feelings. She made one more report to the police and then disconnected, promising to call back if they spotted the car.

"We've lost it. I'm going to get off." Tony exited at La Cienega Boulevard, which continued straight north while the 405 headed in a more westerly direction. He drove on that street until curbside parking was available and then pulled into an open space.

"What are we going to do now?" Shahla asked. She looked despondent.

Tony opened the glove compartment and pulled out the *Thomas Guide* he kept there, a book with detailed maps of the Los Angeles area. It was invaluable to him when he made his marketing calls. Then he stuck his hand into his front pants pocket and pulled out the sheet of paper on which he had written Nathan's address and phone numbers. Fortunately, he had done that before they had gone into panic mode.

"We aren't far from where Nathan lives," Tony said. "Let's go to his place."

"Do you think that he might take Tina there? That is, if he's the kidnapper?"

"No more ifs. As far as we're concerned, Nathan is the kidnapper. If we think any other way, we lose all hope. And hope is the only thing we've got right now."

CHAPTER 36

Nathan lived on a quiet street lined with apartment houses that resembled in some respects the one where Fred, the Chameleon, lived, only it was more upscale. Now that Tony had his own house, all apartment houses designed for single people looked pretty much alike to him. The apartments were too small, too seedy, even when well cared for. He was glad that he no longer lived in one. But he became depressed when he thought that if he couldn't keep up the payments on his townhouse, because of the loss of income from Josh, he might have to return to that life.

Tony parked the Porsche on the street, several buildings short of the one where Nathan lived. He turned to Shahla, but before he could say anything, she started talking, rapid-fire.

"I'm going with you. We know that Nathan doesn't have a gun. You're still not at full speed, and I can run faster than you can, in case it becomes necessary to go for help. And it will be easier for two of us to overpower him. Besides, it's not safe for me to stay in the car alone."

Tony had opened his mouth to speak when she started her speech, and then closed it. Finally, he opened it again and said, "That's just what I was going to say."

Shahla said, "Let's go get him, partner," and gave him a high five.

The entrance to the apartment building was through a gate made of vertical iron bars, which Tony discovered was locked. He wondered how they could get through the gate. A young man approached it from the inside and opened it. Shahla smiled at him as he walked past her and grabbed the handle before the gate closed behind him. The man kept walking.

"After you," she said to Tony, sweeping her hand toward the opening in invitation.

They walked through a passage into an interior courtyard, with the apartments forming a rectangle around it, on two levels. The doors to the apartments opened off the open courtyard and the balcony above it. The main feature of the courtyard was, of course, a swimming pool. Maximum sun, maximum fun. The quintessential California experience. Except that nobody was using the pool.

They quickly ascertained that Nathan's apartment was on the ground floor. Tony's first thought was that Nathan was certainly not going to bring Tina here. There would be no way to sneak her into his apartment with all this openness. His second thought was that maybe he had taken her somewhere else to kill her. No, no, no. Don't think like that.

The drapes were drawn over the windows of Nathan's apartment. Tony hesitated. Another effect of the sunny courtyard was to wipe out his feelings that this might be in any way dangerous. He knocked on the door. There were no sounds from within. He knocked again, too soon, like in the movies where they assumed that five seconds was enough time for someone to answer.

"The window's open," Shahla said.

As Tony waited for nobody to answer, Shahla was removing the screen from in front of the window. He looked apprehensively around to see if anybody was watching. He couldn't see into the other apartments, of course, but the shadow cast by the balcony directly above them did partially mask her efforts.

"Cover me," Shahla said.

She had removed the screen and opened the window wider. She meant for Tony to literally cover her—place his body in between her and the courtyard.

"Let *me* go," he said. Nathan might still be inside.

"You have to watch your knee."

Shahla put her leg up on the windowsill. Tony got directly behind her and gave her a boost as she went through the open window and landed on the floor inside. He quickly replaced the screen, hoping that nobody had seen anything and called the police. Shahla opened the door and let him in.

"The place is deserted," she said.

Tony went into the apartment and looked around. All the furniture was gone. The carpet was dirty and there was some trash on the floor. Nathan hadn't attempted to clean the place. This was apparently the living room. A divider doubling as a counter was at the other end of the room, with a small kitchen behind it. Dirty dishes filled the sink. Tony's nose detected the stench of rotten food. The odor came from a metal garbage container, which hadn't been emptied.

A short hallway led in one direction to the bathroom and in the other direction to a bedroom. They went into the bedroom. There was no bed, but there was a built-in closet. Tony opened the wooden folding doors. Some clothes were hanging up in the closet. Pants and shirts. Old clothes. On one side of the closet were built-in drawers. Tony opened each of the drawers and quickly went through the contents: a sweater, a sweatshirt, some underwear, and socks.

In the bottom drawer, underneath some T-shirts, he felt something with a different texture. Smooth and satiny. He pulled it out.

"Shahla."

Shahla turned from where she was investigating some sheets and blankets that had been thrown into a corner. Tony held up a pair of barely-there panties. She raced over and grabbed the lingerie.

"Those belong to Joy. I'm sure they do. They look like something Joy would wear."

Tears were streaming down her face. Tony felt something else. He pulled out a bra. Shahla took it and looked at the label.

"It's a 34B. I'm sure that's right for Joy."

"We've got our man," Tony said, grimly. "Now all we have to do is find him. Put them back in the drawer."

"Put them back?" Shahla looked perplexed.

"I'm going to tip off the police. But we've got to leave the evidence here, where they can find it. If we take it to them it may be tainted, somehow."

Shahla reluctantly put the items back in the drawer, but on top of the T-shirts so that there would be no question about the police finding them. Tony returned to the other room. There was a telephone sitting on the counter between the living room and the kitchen. He picked up the receiver and listened. He heard a dial tone.

"It works." He punched in the number of the Bonita Beach Police. He gave his name to the desk officer, who recognized it in connection with the chase. He asked whether the kidnapper's car had been spotted. Negative. He said he had more information on Joy's murder and Tina's kidnapping. He gave Nathan's full name and address and said he had reason to believe that Nathan was the kidnapper. He said he thought the police would find evidence in Nathan's apartment. He didn't say that Nathan expected to ascend into heaven tonight. He figured that would require too long an explanation.

"We'll have to get a search warrant," the officer said.

"Nathan has moved out so I suspect all you need is the manager's permission," Tony said. He had a thought. "Give me five minutes, and I'll get you the manager's phone number."

He hung up and said to Shahla, "The manager is in the first apartment on the right as we came into the courtyard." They went to the front door. "Wait. Let's see if anybody is about." They peeked through the drapes and saw no sign of life. They went out the door and shut it behind them.

As they walked to the manager's apartment, Shahla said, "If the manager is a woman you do the talking. If he's a man, let me talk."

"Who died and left you boss?" Tony asked. When Shahla looked ready to retort, he raised his arms and said, "Just kidding. We'll go with that."

They knocked on the manager's door. A small, elderly woman opened it. She was bent over, which made her look even shorter than she was. Tony had the nod.

"Good morning, ma'am," he said. "My name is Tony and this is my sister, Sally. "We are friends of Nathan Watson."

The woman looked at them without speaking for a moment. Then she said, "Friends of Nathan? Then why did you break into his apartment?"

"Break in?" Her drapes were open. She had seen them through the window. "Er...we were trying to find Nathan."

"Nathan is gone. He moved out two days ago. So I'm sure you didn't get anything. But I've called the police, anyway, in case you caused some damage."

"*You* called the police?" This was a reversal. Tony couldn't think straight. "What police?"

"LAPD, of course. They'll be here shortly."

Shahla was tugging on Tony's arm. "Let's go."

"Do you know what Nathan is going to do?" he asked.

The woman stared at him coldly, without speaking. Considering her small stature, she looked formidable.

Shahla tugged harder. "Let's go," she said again.

Tony went with her. They moved swiftly through the outside gate and along the street to his car. He looked back when they reached the car. She wasn't watching them. He suspected she had stayed within the safety of her apartment. They got into the car.

"Drive," Shahla said. "If we get detained by the police, we'll never find Nathan."

Tony drove. He wound through the largely residential streets for a mile or so and then, figuring they were safe, he parked again.

"It's a good thing they didn't respond faster," he said, "or we would have been trapped like a fox in the henhouse. I'd better call Bonita Beach and give them an update." He got out his cell phone.

"Don't tell them we broke into the apartment."

"I won't." He told the desk officer that LAPD was going to the apartment building and suggested that this was a good time to coordinate with them to search Nathan's apartment.

"How do you know this?" the officer asked.

Tony disconnected.

"I hope it doesn't get screwed up and the evidence lost," Shahla said.

"We can't worry about that," Tony said. "We've got to find Nathan." His shoulders slumped. "But how do we find him?"

"Give me his cell phone number," Shahla said.

"Why?"

"I'm going to call him."

"You're what?"

"I'm going to call him. What else can we do? We have to keep Nathan from killing Tina."

***

Shahla took the cell phone and the piece of paper with Nathan's address and telephone numbers on it from Tony. Her mind was moving faster than his. And it was going to take speed if they were going to save Tina. But before she tried to call Nathan, she had to call the Bonita Beach Police one more time.

She called, using redial. The desk officer answered after two rings and said, "Bonita Beach Police."

"This is Shahla."

"Where are you?"

She wasn't falling into that trap. "I'm only going to say this once, so listen carefully. We believe that Nathan Watson has kidnapped Tina. He belongs to the Church of the Risen Lord. The church is on..." she looked at Tony and he said, "Brora Street." She repeated, "Brora Street, in LA. The minister is Luther Hodgkins. The members think that they are going to ascend into heaven tonight at midnight. We don't know the location where they are gathering, but it's probably a local hilltop. We know it's somewhere near a bus line. We are hoping that Nathan is going to take Tina there so that she will ascend with them."

"Spell the name of the minister."

Shahla spelled it. "Have you got that?"

"Where are you now?"

"Have you got all the information?"

"I want you two to come to the station and stop playing detective. You're going to mess this whole thing up. Or get yourselves killed."

Shahla disconnected and said, "He wants us to come to the station."

"You did that better than I could have," Tony said.

Shahla was pleased with Tony's compliment. But the hardest part was yet to come. She punched in Nathan's cell phone number. As it rang, she wondered if he still had the phone with him. Or whether the number was disconnected. She should at least get some kind of a message. Finally, voice mail came on. It was Nathan's voice. Shahla felt some relief.

"Nathan, this is Shahla," she said after the beep. "I-I have changed my mind. I feel in my heart now that you are correct. The website of the church says that the ascent into heaven is going to be tonight. I want to go with you, Nathan. Please. Give me a call." She recited Tony's cell phone number.

"Did I put enough passion into my voice?" she asked after she disconnected.

"That will get him if anything can. What should we do while we wait for him to call back?"

"I saw a McDonald's a couple of blocks from here. Let's get something to eat."

***

Shahla ate her Big Mac with gusto and popped each ketchup-drenched French fry into her mouth, separately, in order to fully savor it. Since her brush with hunger, yesterday, food had risen in her scale of importance. She hoped that this newfound appetite wouldn't make her fat. Tony was eating a more sensible fish sandwich.

They were sitting in the car, parked outside the McDonald's. A Porsche wasn't the most comfortable place to eat lunch, but at least it was temporarily shaded from the September sun by the fronds at the top of a tall palm tree, and the top was down so they benefited from a wisp of a breeze.

Other people, young and old alike, continuously streamed in and out of the restaurant, like bees at a hive. The young ones looked like high school students. Apparently this was a lunch hangout for a local school. Shahla remembered that she should be in school. She felt a pang of conscience. She hated to miss even one day.

When the cell phone rang, it startled her, even though she was hoping it would ring. She had the Big Mac in one hand and a couple of fries in the other. "Let me answer it," she said, desperately trying to free her hands without spilling food all over herself and the car. She gave a quick swipe to her greasy fingers with a paper napkin and pressed the talk button on the phone.

"Hello, this is Sa...Shahla." She had almost given her Hotline name of Sally.

"Are you alone?"

Shahla felt a chill as she recognized the voice of the Cackling Crucifier. Or was it Nathan? It was both of them. Tony was right; the Crucifier and Nathan were the same person. She had never heard Nathan's voice on the phone before.

"Yes," she lied." She looked at Tony and put her finger to her lips.

"I hear noises in the background."

"I'm in the parking lot of a restaurant." Stay as close to the truth as possible.

"Where is your maniac boyfriend?"

"He...had to go to work."

"You're using his phone."

"He...he lent it to me. I left mine at home."

"You said you wanted to be part of the Ascension."

"Yes." She clamped her mouth shut so she wouldn't be tempted to say anything more. She had to find out how much information Nathan would give her before she started asking questions and made him suspicious.

"You haven't given up your worldly possessions."

"Can't I...that is, can't you take me as your...guest?" She couldn't bring herself to use a stronger word, such as concubine.

"Is that what you want?"

No. "Yes."

"How can I trust you?"

That question was unanswerable and might lead to her babbling. She remained silent, with an effort.

"Will you still feel the same way tonight?"

"Yes."

"We'll see."

Shahla was afraid that Nathan would hang up. She said, "There is one thing."

"What's that?"

"If you take me, you have to let Tina go."

Silence. Had he already killed Tina? Was this in vain? Shahla could hardly breathe. Beside her, Tony had cocked his ear and was staring at her, as if he wanted to snatch the phone. She put up her free hand to forestall him.

"That might be arranged."

Shahla exhaled. "Let me speak to Tina."

More silence. She wanted to yell into the phone. Only her Hotline training prevented her from doing that.

"Shahla?"

It was Tina's voice, soft but unmistakable. "Tina, are you all right?"

"My hands and feet are taped. He says if I scream, he'll tape my mouth too. He…he's got a knife."

She was crying. Shahla had heard Hotline listeners cry on the phone, and she knew the sounds well. At least Tina was still alive. "Are you in the car?"

"Yes."

"Answer yes or no. Do you know where you are?"

"No."

"Did you travel on the 405 to get where you are?"

"Uh…yes."

"Do you see any hills close to you?"

There was some confusion on the other end of the line. Then Nathan's voice said, "So you know she's all right. I'll call you later to make sure you're still interested."

"Nathan, wait."

There was a click and the silence that signaled a hang up. Shahla turned to Tony. "You may be right. They may not be far from here." She filled him in on the rest of the call.

"You did a good job."

"That isn't going to save Tina."

"It helps." He patted her shoulder. "Let's do some exploring." He started looking at the *Thomas Guide*.

Shahla was glad Tony was with her. He would keep his cool. He would prevent her from going off like a rocket ship.

CHAPTER 37

One of the reasons that Tony was driving around was to show activity. He hoped that they—especially Shahla—would see activity as progress. In any case, it was better than sitting in one place and waiting for Nathan to call again.

Tony and Shahla explored the open areas adjoining La Cienega Boulevard. Tony hadn't realized how many grasshoppers pumping oil still existed in the middle of Los Angeles. They sat on various levels of the hillsides, bobbing their heads up and down with a regular beat, oblivious to the city that had grown up around them.

But the most logical place from which to ascend into heaven seemed to be the Kenneth Hahn State Recreation Area. Tony remembered that there had been a Los Angeles county supervisor named Kenneth Hahn, one of the five powerful people who governed one of the most populated counties in the nation.

The spacious park had amenities to suit various tastes. Some people fished in the lake and others picnicked on the grass of the urban oasis, sheltered from the traffic and noise. But what caught the eyes of Tony and Shahla was the hillside. It was steep, and it had a ridge that extended for some distance along the north side of the park. But the first trails they saw that led to the ridge appeared to go straight up.

"If they have to climb one of these," Tony said, "only the fittest and healthiest are going to get into heaven."

They looked around some more and found an official trail that snaked up the west side of the hill and then went along the crest, according to a map they found at the trailhead. It did not ascend as steeply as the others they had seen. They decided to climb it and did so, slowly, to allow for Tony's knee.

The dirt path was wide enough for a four-wheel-drive vehicle to navigate. They walked east along the ridge and found several roofed shelters where hikers could receive a temporary respite from the unforgiving sun that baked the brushy hillside, parched from a summer without rain. They could see a substantial sweep of the Los Angeles basin. It was like looking over a calm sea—but the sea in this case was composed of houses.

"I'll bet this is beautiful at night," Tony said, "with all the city lights. You can picture millions of people peacefully going about their business."

"Or in some cases, not so peacefully," Shahla said. "Maybe we should have told the police that we talked to Nathan and that Tina is with him."

"If we told them that we talked to him by cell phone they might try to call him. If they did, don't you think he would suspect that we'd tipped them off?"

"That *I* had tipped them off. You're not with me, remember? But you're right. Of course, they may try to call him anyway."

"That's the chance we have to take. But we can be sure they're working on it from the church angle. Maybe they've found the good reverend."

"And maybe not. Los Angeles is so big. How are we going to find Nathan if he doesn't call back?"

"If he comes here, we'll find him. And this looks like a logical place."

Tony tried to exude confidence. Shahla looked vulnerable. He placed a consoling hand on her arm. They held each other for a while. Tony pictured a battery charger connected to a cell phone to recharge it. In this case, both of them were the chargers and both of them were the cell phones. They were trying to recharge each other—with courage and hope.

***

It was 5:30 when the cell phone rang again. Shahla and Tony had eaten more fast food a while ago. Shahla had lost her appetite, but Tony said they needed to eat to maintain their energy levels. She forced herself to swallow, but this time the food was tasteless, and she realized that if Tina was killed, the whole world might be tasteless for a long time to come.

They were sitting at a picnic table in the Kenneth Hahn park, surrounded by the green grass. The grass must be regularly watered or it would look like the brown brush on the hillside. Tony was making notes. He said he was writing a plan of action, in case Nathan didn't call again. Shahla suspected he was doing it primarily to try to keep his spirits up.

Shahla was holding the phone when it rang. She activated it and said hello. Nobody answered and at first she thought it might be a hang up. But there were noises in the background. The line was still open.

"Nathan? Is that you?" There were times when it was just too difficult to stay silent.

"Are you alone?"

She wanted to snap, "Of course I'm alone; let's get on with it," but she forced herself to modulate her voice and said evenly, "Yes."

"Are you still…interested?"

"Yes. Where should I meet you?"

Silence. Had she pushed too hard? But acting passively hadn't gotten her very far.

"Have you got a car?"

"Yes. I can meet you anywhere."

"You'll have to give it up."

"The car? If I'm going to heaven, I won't need it anymore." It was difficult for her to speak those words. She watched Tony's reaction out of the corner of her eye. He was showing signs of impatience again.

Nathan named the two streets of an intersection and said, "Meet me there in an hour. Make sure you're alone."

Shahla repeated them out loud so that Tony would hear them. "Is that where the Ascension is going to be?"

"I'll drive you from there."

"What about Tina?"

There was a pause. Then Nathan said, "I will release Tina at that time. Unless she wants to be part of the Ascension."

"Let me talk to her."

She heard a click.

"Tony, he didn't guarantee he'd release Tina."

"He'd better release Tina," Tony said grimly.

***

"The intersection he named is not far from here," Tony said, checking a page of the map book. Let's reconnoiter the area." He got up and started walking back to the car.

Shahla followed him. "He may already be there. He'll recognize your car."

"Well, maybe we can park a few blocks away and walk to it."

"If he's there, he'll see us. It's still daylight."

True. But Tony was running out of ideas.

"Can we rent a car?" Shahla asked.

"There isn't time. By the time we drove to a rental agency, did the paperwork, drove back…"

"Okay, what *are* we going to do? Call the cops?"

"The question is, what does Nathan do when he spots a police car? Stab Tina, figuring he's going to be taken up to heaven even if he isn't at the exact right spot at midnight?"

"Yeah, too risky. He's unpredictable. What else can we do?"

What, indeed? He certainly wasn't going to let Shahla meet Nathan alone. They exited from the park and started driving in the direction of the rendezvous, still discussing the issue. Soon they were going slowly through a residential neighborhood. A couple of hundred feet ahead of them a man came out of his house and walked toward a pickup truck parked in the driveway.

"Change cars with that man," Shahla said suddenly.

"You're kidding."

"I'm not. Stop, Tony."

"He's…." Tony hesitated.

"He's what? Black? African-American. So what? You're white and I'm mixed and we get along. It's all one world, remember?"

He couldn't do it. He drove past the driveway. Then he slammed on his brakes. He shoved the gearshift into reverse and backed up, stopping in front of the driveway. He saw the man, poised to climb into his truck, looking at him curiously. Probably thought he needed directions.

Tony got out of the car and walked around the front of it. How did one start? "Hi," he said to the man. That was inadequate. "Uh, I was wondering if you'd like to change cars for a few hours."

The man looked past him to the Porsche. If it had been an old VW beetle, the answer would have been obvious. But he looked interested.

"What's the deal; is it hot?" he asked.

"No, no. I've got the registration inside. I'll show you."

"That's okay," the man said, as Tony took a step back toward his car. "But I mean, are you on the level?"

"Yeah." He owed the man a fuller explanation. "We're trying to find a guy, but if he sees my car, he'll bolt."

"I see." The man smiled. "I've always wanted to drive a Porsche. I'm leaving for work. I won't be back until morning. And I generally sleep until noon."

"That's okay. We can change back tomorrow afternoon. Do you know how to drive a stick?"

"This is a stick." The man indicated the truck. "If you want to do it, I'm okay with it."

Shahla was getting out of the Porsche. "Bring the phone and the map book," Tony told her. "And our sweatshirts." He walked up to the man and said, "I'm Tony."

"Richard."

They shook hands. Shahla came up the driveway.

"This is Shahla, my, uh…friend."

They exchanged pleasantries. Tony and the man exchanged keys. And phone numbers. The man reached into the truck and pulled out a metal box.

"Tools," he said.

He glanced at the bed of the pickup. It contained a coiled

rope, a white tarpaulin and some other things.

"Nothing there I can't live without for one night," he said. "Okay. It's all yours."

He strode down the driveway and got into the Porsche. Tony watched apprehensively as he started it and drove away, waving as he went. He accelerated slowly, shifted smoothly, and seemed to be a good driver. Tony and Shahla climbed into the truck. It was somewhat messy inside, but appeared to be drivable. It was quite new. It had a remote for locking and unlocking the doors.

"You need to find a better way to introduce me," Shahla said as he backed down the driveway. "'My, uh…friend' doesn't cut it."

"Sorry. I was going to introduce you as my sister, but then I thought there was no reason to lie."

"Just 'friend' is fine. It's the hesitation that hurts. We are friends, aren't we? We'll still be friends when this is all over, won't we?"

"Of course." Of course. Tony concentrated on getting to the intersection Nathan had named. Shahla watched the map and gave him directions. They approached from the south. Nathan had said the southeast corner. Tony stopped the truck a hundred yards from the corner. Nathan's car wasn't there. They were on a residential street with some vacant lots. The corner lot was vacant. Traffic was light. Nobody was outside.

Tony said, "I know you haven't driven a stick-shift before, but you're going to have to drive this from here to the corner. You can do it in first gear. I'll talk you through it."

"Where are you going to be?"

"On the floor in front of your seat. In fact, let's trade places right now."

They managed the switch with some jostling.

"We need a plan that protects your safety," Tony said. He was getting more and more apprehensive as the meeting time approached. "I will hide when Nathan comes into view. When he parks, drive up until you're behind him, but not too close. We want to be able to pull out fast if we have to. Leave the engine running and the door open when you get out. I hope to hell we're right in thinking that he doesn't have a gun."

"Tina only mentioned a knife."

"All right, but stay behind his car. Under no circumstances are you to get in the car. Do you understand that? If he starts to get out of the car, you immediately get back in the truck."

"But we've got to get Tina out."

"Tell him that Tina has to get out before you get in. But as soon as Tina is out, you yell for me, and I'll get out of the truck. Then both of you hightail it to the truck."

"What if he comes at you with his knife?"

Tony had been rummaging in the glove compartment of the truck. He pulled out a box cutter. "I'll use this. It's what the terrorists used on 9/11."

"It won't do any good against a knife."

"Let's see what else we've got." There were some items behind the seats. Tony found a large flashlight and a crowbar, among other things. "I'll use the crowbar as a weapon. Maybe I should get out of the truck when you do."

"But seeing you will be like seeing the police for him. He might kill Tina before you can do anything."

There was no safe way to do this. The discussion continued. Tony showed Shahla how to use the clutch to shift into first gear and neutral. That's all she would have to be able to do, like the terrorists who had to be able to fly a plane but not land it. They were talking, and when the car came up behind them, Tony almost didn't hear it, even though the truck windows were wide open.

Shahla glanced in the rearview mirror and said, "It's him."

Tony ducked, hopefully before Nathan could see him through the rear window of the truck, and hunched down on the floor in front of the passenger seat. The position was painful to his knee. He heard the car drive slowly past them.

"Tina is in the front seat," Shahla said, sounding relieved, but without moving her lips. "She looks okay. I think Nathan saw me. He's stopping. Now he's parked at the corner."

"All right, drive up behind him." Tony's heart was hammering. He wished he could play a more active part in this. He was afraid for both Shahla and Tina.

Shahla started the engine all right, but when she shifted into first gear and released the clutch the truck stalled.

"A little more gas, and then release the clutch very slowly."

She tried again. This time the engine roared as the truck crept forward. Then suddenly it lurched ahead.

"Foot off the gas," Tony yelled over the noise of the engine. "Depress the clutch and coast."

Shahla got the truck under control and coasted slowly to a stop. She put it in neutral and set the parking brake. She made a move to open the door.

"Wait," Tony said, softly. "What's he doing?"

"Nothing," Shahla whispered, speaking like a ventriloquist. Just sitting in the car."

"Open the door, but don't get out yet."

Shahla did that. After a few seconds, she carefully stepped down to the pavement, moved around the open door, and was out of Tony's sight. He gripped the crowbar hard with one hand and put his other hand on the handle of the passenger door, ready to open it and jump out of the truck. He strained his ears, trying to hear over the idling of the truck engine.

Tony heard engine noise from the other car. It was starting up. Did Nathan have Shahla? In a panic, he raised his head and looked through the windshield. No, Shahla was standing right in front of the truck. Something had spooked Nathan, and he had taken off.

Tony scrambled over to the driver's seat and sat down. Shahla ran around to the passenger side and jumped in. Tony slammed the gearshift into first gear and took off after the silver car. It had immediately turned the corner and was heading back toward La Cienega.

"Call the Bonita Beach Police," Tony said. "They can coordinate the chase. We've got to try to keep him in sight and give the police an opportunity to stop him."

"What about Tina?"

"We'll have to take the chance. As long as he's driving, he won't hurt her—unless he cracks up. And we won't get too close to him"

Shahla got the Bonita Beach station on the line. She gave reports on Nathan, which were passed on to other units. "He's heading north on La Cienega…he's turned left…he's turned left again…he's disappeared."

Nathan had lost them again, through a series of risky but clever left turns. When he was sure Nathan was long gone, Tony parked the truck, despondent. He and Shahla sat slumped in their seats, not speaking. A police car rolled by a few minutes later, but aimlessly, without direction.

CHAPTER 38

"He knows you're with me," Shahla finally said. "I'm sure he won't speak to me again."

"It's time for the faithful to gather," Tony said. The sun had set. "Let's go back to the park. That's where we'll find Nathan." He said it with more confidence than he felt. Even if that was the gathering place, had they scared Nathan so much that he wouldn't show up?

"It's all we can do." Shahla was really in the dumps.

They took the exit from La Cienega that led to the park. As they drove toward the entrance, they saw a police car parked across the road, completely blocking it. Two uniformed officers, one male and one female, were leaning against the car, shining flashlights at Tony's truck to make sure he stopped. He did.

"Don't get out," Tony said to Shahla. He didn't want them making any moves that might look suspicious to the police.

The female officer came to Tony's window and said, "The park is closed."

Tony said, "I'm Tony and this is Shahla. We're the ones who spotted the kidnapper a little while ago. He's with the group that believes they're going to ascend into heaven tonight. We think they might come here."

"That's why we're here," the officer said. "We cleared everybody out at sunset. That's when it closes, anyway. There's nobody in the park. If anybody shows up, they have to go through us."

"When we were here this afternoon, we found a couple of gates leading from the ridge into residential areas. Somebody must have keys to those gates."

"We have units stationed at all the gates." The officer spoke with finality.

"Have you found this Reverend Hodgkins? He's the leader of the church group."

"We know who he is. We're on the lookout for him."

The fact that they hadn't found him wasn't comforting. In fact, Tony felt uncomfortable about the whole situation, but he had run out of possibilities. If the parishioners couldn't come here, where would they go? And more important, what would Nathan do with Tina?

After more conversation, during which the officer tried to convince Tony and Shahla that the police had the situation completely under control and there was nothing the pair could do to help, Tony turned the truck around and headed back toward La Cienega.

"Their uniforms look different than those of the Bonita Beach Police," Shahla said.

And LAPD, which Tony had initially assumed they were. The uniforms were tan, not blue. "They must be sheriff's deputies," Tony said. "Which means that the park isn't within the city limits of Los Angeles."

"Police are police. If there is a way to screw it up, they'll do it."

"We won't stop looking. If we can spot some of the church people, we might be able to find out what they're going to do. And they may lead us to Nathan."

It was unsatisfactory, but it was their only hope. Tony followed a route that went around the large park. Occasionally, a patrol car went by them. He didn't spend much time in the residential area north of the park because he felt that was fruitless. They did investigate some open spaces on the other sides. Sometimes they had to get out of the truck and walk over the mostly bare ground, which was populated with the ubiquitous grasshoppers pumping oil. This took valuable time and didn't produce any results.

Periodically, they called the Bonita Beach Police Station and asked whether Nathan had been spotted. The answer was always negative. They asked the officer on duty to call them with any new developments. By 11:00 they were sitting in the parked truck, waiting for the phone to ring, having run out of ideas. The gloom inside the cab of the truck was so thick that Tony was sure he could spread it on bread.

Then Tony's cell phone did ring. Shahla grabbed it before Tony could move and said hello. She handed it to Tony. "It's Detective Croyden. He wants to speak to you."

Croyden? He had the day off. "Hello."

"Schmidt, this is Croyden."

"I didn't think you were working today."

"I was fishing, but I had to come in because of this mess. I got the word that you spotted Nathan earlier. We've had cars crisscrossing the area, but we haven't seen him. We've got all entrances to the Hahn Recreation Area covered. Maybe he's flown. What are you doing now?"

"Looking for the spot where this Ascension into heaven is supposed to take place. Have you found Hodgkins or any of his flock?"

"We've got units working on that too. LAPD and the sheriff's office have been working together, but they haven't been able to find this guy, Hodgkins. If you're right about him, maybe he's already taken off with the loot."

"Except that the website said to bring cash tonight. But if there's nothing happening tonight, maybe he's gone."

"And by the time he gets to Phoenix, the folks who trusted him will be crying. Anyway, we're drawing a blank. Don't do anything stupid, but if you find anything, call me immediately on this number."

Tony wrote the number down and promised they would call Croyden if they spotted the believers. At least Croyden was asking for his help. Then he had a thought. He said, "Shahla and I would like permission to go into the park."

"Why? There's nobody in there."

"Just a hunch. If nobody is there, we'll come right back out."

"It could be dangerous."

"How could it be dangerous if nobody's there? I don't think we'll be attacked by rabbits."

Croyden was silent for a few seconds, apparently digesting this logic. Then he said, "All right, I'll clear it with the officers at the entrance. But be careful. I don't want to get my ass in a sling because you fell off a cliff."

***

There was certainly nobody in the lower part of the park. The area was relatively flat and open, except for an occasional tree. A group of people would be easy to spot, even in the dark, because they would need some sort of light.

"If all the entrances are being watched, how could anybody get in?" Shahla asked.

Tony had been wondering the same thing to try to justify what they were doing. He said, "In a park as large as this one, there are probably ways to get in other than the official ones. Maybe Hodgkins found one."

"If he did find an alternate way in, it probably leads to the ridge, near where those houses are."

"Okay, we'll go up the road to the east side of the ridge. It's paved."

Tony drove up this road. A locked gate blocked an additional loop of paved road that doubled as the ridge trail at that point. There was a gap between the gate and a tree that stood at the edge of a large grassy area, which Tony remembered as being shown on the trail map as Janice's Green Valley. He squeezed the truck between the gate and the tree, utilizing the four-wheel-drive feature to navigate the rough terrain, and then climbed back onto the road and drove to the other end of the loop.

He shut off the engine, and they opened their windows. The night air was chilly, but not cold. They had put on sweatshirts earlier. Shahla was wearing one of his old sweatshirts that had shrunk with repeated washings. They could see city lights in the distance, blinking like stars. The lights were below them instead of above them, since the real stars weren't visible. Clouds hid them. It was an upside-down universe. It was also a peaceful scene, as Tony had thought it would be when he had seen it that afternoon—too peaceful for the thought of murder.

"This is as far as we can drive," Tony said. "But we can take the flashlight and walk along the ridge trail."

They also carried the crowbar and box cutter as they started to walk west along the dirt path. It had some ups and downs but was fairly easy to follow, even in the dark. They had gone about a hundred yards when Shahla, who was in the lead with the flashlight, stopped. Tony stopped beside her.

"Listen," Shahla said.

Tony listened. He could hear something other than the distant muffled noises of the city. "It sounds like singing."

"It is singing. Remember, the church website said that they would sing until the Ascension. Tony, it's them."

Tony felt himself getting excited. "It sounds far away." He looked at his watch. "We don't have much time before midnight. I don't know if we can get there."

"Remember where the trail goes up to the other end of the ridge? Can the truck make it up that trail? If so, we can probably drive right to them."

The western end of the trail was dirt, but it was wide enough for the truck. And the truck had four-wheel-drive. "Okay, let's do it."

They turned and walked rapidly back toward the truck, being careful not to fall on the rough trail. Once there, Tony drove the truck back around the locked gate and then accelerated down the hill.

"Should we call the police?" Shahla asked.

"There isn't time for them to get here before midnight," Tony said. "And the car they have at the entrance can't climb the hill. Wait until we see what the situation is. And I'm going to need your eyes to help me drive up that trail."

They arrived at the bottom of the trail shortly thereafter. Tony slowed way down as he started uphill, making sure to keep the truck in the center of the path. The trail became fairly steep, but with its four-wheel-drive, the truck didn't have a problem with traction. He breathed a sigh of relief when it leveled off at the top of the ridge.

Tony stopped the truck and turned off the engine. Through the open windows they could hear the singing, much louder than before. But because of the hilly terrain, they still couldn't see anybody.

"We're close," Shahla said. "I hope the sound of our engine didn't scare them."

"Apparently it didn't, or they would have stopped singing." Tony looked at his watch again. "Twelve minutes to midnight. I'm going to drive another fifty yards and then stop again. We've got to find out exactly where they are."

They drove a short distance and stopped. The singing was still ahead of them. Tony repeated the maneuver.

Shahla, whose seat in the truck was on the south side of the ridge trail, said, "The singing is right below us."

They both got out of the truck, leaving the doors open so as not to make excessive noise. They walked to the edge of the hill and looked down. The singing grew louder and they could see lights—candles. The people were lighting candles, apparently in anticipation of imminent Ascension.

Tony's first thought was that open flames were prohibited in Southern California, where the fire danger in September was extreme, especially in this brushy area. But if you were about to ascend into heaven, you didn't care about earthly worries like brushfires. The sound of religious music in this setting was eerie. And when Tony thought about what the singers expected to do, he felt something crawling up his neck.

The people were sixty or seventy feet below them, on a level area. A plateau that stuck out of the hillside. Hodgkins must have spent some time looking for that particular spot. It was inaccessible by motor vehicle. The only way to get to it was to walk down a steep path from where Tony and Shahla were standing. Tony could barely make out the path in the dark.

He had been right about one thing. The faithful had found a way into the park, probably through the fence that bordered the north side, not far from them. If they had cut a hole in the fence, nobody would have noticed because of the inaccessibility of the area, caused by the brush and the steepness of the hill. Then they could clear a path from there to the ridge, through the ice plant and the brush. And avoid the police.

There might be a hundred people, but it was impossible to pick out individuals. Impossible to tell whether Nathan and Tina were in the crowd.

"I'm going down there," Shahla said. "It's too steep for you, with your knee." She looked at her watch. "Ten minutes to zero hour. Come back to the truck. I've got an idea."

Tony wanted to argue, but what she said was correct. He couldn't go down the steep hill with any speed. Especially in the dark. And in ten minutes, when they expected to ascend into heaven, what would happen? Would Nathan kill Tina and then himself if the miracle didn't occur immediately? There was no way to tell. He had killed Joy. He was capable of anything.

Shahla was pulling the white tarpaulin out of the back of the truck. "Help me," she said.

"What's this for?"

"I'll tell you when we get it to the edge."

CHAPTER 39

Tony hoped that Shahla was clear of the path that went from him to the plateau. He had watched her start down it, with trepidation, but she had almost immediately melted into the dark.

He couldn't wait any longer. He turned on the flashlight and propped it up on a small rock, right at the edge of the cliff, so that the light shone upward at a steep angle. Then he picked up part of the tarp and wrapped it around his body. Fortunately, he didn't have to pick up the whole thing, just enough to give the appearance that he was wearing a white robe. In the dark, nobody would see him that clearly, anyway.

When he had the tarp positioned around him, he looked at his watch. At one minute to twelve he stepped in the path of the beam of light and raised his arms. He was impersonating Jesus. Jesus, who was bidding the faithful welcome to heaven. At first, nobody below seemed to see him. And then somebody shouted.

The singing stopped. Now they saw him. They must be looking up at him. Good. This was the distraction Shahla needed so that she could free Tina. If she could find her. She had taken the box cutter to cut any tape holding Tina. But even though he had urged her to take the crowbar, she had refused.

As Tony watched, the lights started moving—toward him. The people were climbing the path because he was going to lead them to heaven. He hadn't figured on this. And they were chanting. What were they saying? As the sound became louder, he understood. They were chanting the name "Jesus" over and over. The path was narrow, and they had to climb slowly, in single file, but still he started to panic. What would happen when they reached him and found out that he wasn't Jesus?

He had to hold his position as long as he could, to give Shahla a chance. Sweat poured down his face, in spite of the night chill. The faithful would be plenty mad when they found out the truth. Fortunately, it was taking them some time to ascend the steep hill. Now he could begin to see their faces, by the light of the candles. Could they make his out? Did he look enough like Jesus?

He couldn't stay here any longer. He dropped the tarp, picked up the flashlight and ran a few feet away from the edge, out of sight. Then he stopped. What should he do? He pondered his options. He couldn't drive away in the truck because he couldn't leave Shahla and Tina here, with Nathan on the loose. It would be impossible to turn it around in the dark, anyway, without driving off the cliff. But he also couldn't face the angry multitude. If they did him bodily harm, he wouldn't be able to help anybody. He closed and locked the doors of the truck and then went a few feet down the other side of the ridge and hid behind some brush.

Tony positioned himself so that he would be able to see the people as they reached the top of the ridge, especially if they still had their candles, but they wouldn't be able to see him in the dark. He waited, not daring to move. The chanting grew louder.

He thought he heard a scream from below, but the sound was muffled by the chanting, and he couldn't tell for sure. And it sounded far away. Maybe he had imagined it. Could he ignore it? He heard it again. No. He had to check. He came out of his hiding place, went to the edge of the cliff and carefully looked down, not showing himself. The leaders were almost to the top. He could follow the movement of the line of people, slowly climbing the hill. But he couldn't see anything else.

Tony retreated to his hiding place and secreted himself again. Just in time. The leader rose out of the earth. A head came first, followed by a body. A second person materialized. Three, four, eight—now there were a dozen. And the number grew steadily as more and more people appeared.

They ignored the tarpaulin that he had left in a heap. They also ignored the truck. Those who were fit assisted the ones who were lame. It was a peaceful group—peaceful, but expectant. They kept chanting the name of their Lord. They thought this was it—that the Ascension was really taking place. And Tony had helped to fool them into believing it.

A few of the faithful had managed to hang onto their candles, even while climbing the steep hill. He might be able to recognize Nathan with the help of their light. But as more and more people appeared, the ones already there blocked his view of those just arriving. This was frustrating. It occurred to Tony that he might be able to mingle with them and find Nathan that way. He was no longer Jesus and they hadn't been able to see him very well when he was. And they were all wearing regular clothes, as he was. No angelic robes.

Tony carefully eased himself out of his hiding place and joined the group. Would they spot him as an outsider? He didn't have a candle and he avoided the light of the candles held by others. But they were looking upward, to heaven, not at him.

He carefully mingled with the parishioners, looking for Nathan, looking for Tina, even looking for Shahla. By the time the last of the flock arrived at the top of the ridge, he was sure that none of these people was among them.

He feared for the safety of the girls, especially Shahla. Should he have let her go down by herself? What choice did he have? Did his ruse work with Nathan? If so, where was Nathan? No acceptable answer came to Tony. He had to go down to the plateau.

The trail was clear of people. Moving slowly, he started down it and immediately disappeared from the view of those on top. Good. But he had to be careful because it was harder going downhill than uphill, especially in the dark. He looked down at the plateau, but didn't see any light or movement there.

It was safe to use the flashlight to guide him, so he turned it on. He made his way carefully downward, spotting where to place his feet before he took each step. He also used his hands to steady himself. He wanted to go faster, but he knew that if he did, he might not make it at all. Shahla had been brave to climb down without a flashlight.

After half an eternity, he arrived at the plateau. He quickly shone his flashlight around the flat area, where the low brush had been trampled underfoot. There was clearly nobody here.

Where were the girls? He listened for some sound, some clue. All he heard was the faint chanting from above. And then he heard motor vehicles. His cell phone rang. He had shoved it into his pants pocket just after he had called Croyden and just before he had played Jesus. He had told Croyden the Ascension was occurring inside the park.

He answered it. It was Croyden asking where he was. "On the side of the hill, but everybody else has gone up to the top. Except Nathan and Tina. I don't know where they are. Or Shahla, either."

"We're coming in with four-wheel-drives and people who know the layout of the area. We'll secure the top of the hill."

That wasn't going to help Shahla and Tina. "When you get there, send some officers down the path to the plateau. I need help finding the girls."

***

Shahla quickly discovered that she couldn't just walk down the trail. It was too steep. She couldn't ski down it on her feet because it was too bumpy. And she couldn't see well enough to avoid the ruts. So she half walked and half slid. She spent a lot of time on her butt, sometimes falling on it, sometimes sliding on it for a few feet. Her hands, already sore from her adventures last night, were getting cut up even more since she used them to break her frequent butt landings.

At least the parishioners were singing and not paying any attention to her. Even if they saw her, they might think she was one of them. Her hand hit something sharp, probably a rock. She suppressed a shout that would have been heard over the singing. She had to sit down for a few seconds, until her hand stopped stinging.

She wished she could have brought the flashlight, but Tony needed it, and it would have attracted the attention of the singers to her before she reached the plateau. He had wanted her to bring the crowbar, but she couldn't take the chance that somebody would spot it and think it odd that she would bring a crowbar to the Ascension.

She had to work on the premise that if Nathan attacked her, the others would intervene.

Two nights ago she had been afraid to go out in the dark. But then the enemy didn't have a face. She was still afraid, but at least Nathan had a face. And there were other people around. In addition, she owed it to Tina.

Shahla was almost close enough so that she could identify people by the light of the candles they held. Except that they stood facing away from her, toward someone who was leading the singing. She arrived at the level area and looked them over. She wanted to spot Nathan before he spotted her. She strolled carefully among the singers. A few glanced at her, but even though she was wearing shorts, they didn't seem to think she was out of place. The others were dressed in clothes suitable for walking.

She spotted Nathan because he was separated from the rest of the crowd. And he was taller than most and whiter than most, although in the dark that wasn't much of a distinguishing characteristic. Shahla edged closer to him, from behind. She didn't see Tina. Had he...?

There was a movement at his feet. It was Tina, sitting on the ground. Still alive. Shahla found herself saying a silent prayer of thanks. Tina was one of the few who weren't standing. And she wasn't singing, either. Was she still taped? Shahla couldn't tell. She looked at her watch. It was time for the party to begin.

She looked up the hill and saw a light come on at the top. Then, as she watched, Tony appeared in the light, dressed in white, and raised his arms. The vision was faint enough and ghostly enough to make it look authentic. He made a good Jesus. But nobody saw him. The singers weren't looking up the hill.

Shahla moved a few feet to one side so that several people were between her and Nathan. She put her hand over her mouth to disguise her voice and yelled, "Look up there," over the sound of the singing.

Everybody looked up. The singing abruptly stopped, and there was a collective gasp from the crowd. The faithful stood transfixed for several seconds. Then, as if on command, they started moving up the path toward Tony. They had to walk slowly, in single file, but the ones in back waited patiently for those in front to clear the way. Some required help, but they would all make it, given enough time.

A murmur started somewhere in the crowd and grew louder as others picked it up. After a few seconds, Shahla could make it out. The people chanted the word, "Jesus," in time to their steps, as if they were mesmerized.

Shahla waited impatiently, hoping that Nathan would get caught up and follow the crowd. As the people in front of her moved forward, she could see the spot where he had been standing. He wasn't there. She spotted him marching up the hill with the others. But Tina was still sitting there. How long would it be before he remembered her?

This was Shahla's opportunity, but she had to act fast. She made her way swiftly to Tina's side and said, in a stage whisper, "Tina, it's Shahla."

Tina turned her head and looked at Shahla, startled. Her hands were behind her back

"Are your hands and feet taped?" Shahla asked, kneeling beside her.

"Just my hands."

"I'm going to free you." Shahla pulled the box cutter out of her pocket and slid the blade clear of the handle. She grabbed one of Tina's arms and felt carefully for the tape. She didn't want to cut Tina. The duct tape was wound around her wrists several times. Shahla sliced through it with the box cutter. That instrument was sharp, which made the job easier.

"Ouch," Tina exclaimed.

Shahla had cut into her wrist a little. "Shh," she said. "Sorry." The tape severed and Tina moved her arms.

"I can't feel my hands," she said plaintively.

"We've got to get away," Shahla said. They couldn't go up the hill toward Tony and the truck. That way was blocked by the throng and, besides, it wouldn't be smart to follow Nathan. She ran the short distance to the edge of the plateau and looked down the hill. A trail descended from where she was standing to the picnic area. It was dimly lit by the city lights, shining down below. That was their escape route.

Tina was still sitting down when Shahla ran back to her. Shahla took hold of her arm and said urgently, "Tina, there's a trail going down. Run down the trail and get away. I'll be right behind you."

Tina continued to sit. She must be in shock. Shahla placed her hands under Tina's armpits and tried to hoist her up. It took a lot of effort, until Tina started to bear some of her own weight. Finally, she stood shakily on her feet. Shahla grew impatient.

"Come with me," she said. She led Tina to the start of the trail. "Run, Tina," she said. "Run as fast as you can. I'll follow you."

Tina seemed to wake up. She looked down the trail. She looked at Shahla. "It's too steep."

"Slide down it then. Get down it any way you can."

Still Tina hesitated.

"Go," Shahla said. "Go, go, go." She gave Tina a push that almost knocked her down the hill.

Tina went, stumbling, down the trail. Shahla went after her, half sliding, half running. The bumping was painful, but she ignored the pain. They made good progress. Just as she thought they were going to get away, she heard sounds behind her. Sounds that were getting closer. She looked over her shoulder. It was Nathan, all right, silhouetted against the night sky, swooping down on them like an avenging demon. Well, not as graceful as a demon, but just as determined. She thought she saw something in his right hand, probably a knife.

Shahla had to make a quick decision. She couldn't speed up or she would overtake Tina, who was having trouble with the steep descent in the dark. She had to protect Tina. If she went off the trail, would Nathan follow her, or would he stay on the trail and go after Tina?

Shahla stepped off the trail to the left, in the direction away from Nathan's knife hand. She stood in the low brush and watched Nathan approach. His out-of-control rush threatened to send him sprawling, but, unfortunately, that didn't happen. Shahla placed the box cutter in her left hand. If Nathan stayed on the trail, she would attack him as he went by.

He slowed down. He wanted her. As he came abreast of her, Nathan tried to slide to a stop. He managed to grab Shahla's right arm with his left hand, but his momentum carried them both down the hill. Shahla felt the pain of a thousand needles in her back as she fell against the stiff branches of the brush. Nathan fell partially on top of her and then bounced off.

Shahla twisted her body and tried to stand up, but she didn't have a solid footing and fell forward into the brush. More pain. Nathan was beside her, also struggling to right himself.

She heard him say, "You're coming with me," as he raised the knife. "Even if I have to cut you up."

Shahla was still off-balance, but she was able to shove him in the chest with both hands. As she did this, she lost her grip on the box cutter. It disappeared into the brush. His knife cut across her left shoulder. Then he fell backwards, and so did she. She received more damage from the sharp wooden spines. Now she and Nathan were separated by a few feet. She tried to stand and make a run for it, but the brush was too thick to allow easy movement.

She turned to face him. He was uphill from her. He stood up and towered over her, with the knife raised high, a fearsome apparition. Shahla felt naked without the box cutter. She wondered whether she was going to die. Even in the dark, she could make out a manic expression on his face. He was crazy.

Although they were only a few feet apart, the thickness of the brush kept him from coming straight toward her. He stood, motionless, and seemed to ponder the problem. She started edging away from him, slowly, working her way through the brush. It scratched her bare legs, but she hardly noticed. She had put a few more feet between them when Nathan came to life. He yelled something unintelligible and stumbled forward, surprising her.

With his initial rush, he covered most of the distance between them, but his legs became caught in the unyielding branches, and he lost his balance. Shahla tried to duck away from the upraised knife as he fell. His body hit her, but she managed to twist clear of him so he didn't land on top of her.

Her face went into the brush, and she felt a branch stab her close to her eye. Now she was mad. She pushed herself up. Nathan was sprawled face down beside her. She jumped on his back and shoved his head into the brush. Hard. He screamed. She saw the knife, still in his hand. She lunged and grabbed his hand, twisting it so that the knife fell into the bushes.

He started to get up. Shahla climbed back on top of him and shoved his head into the brush again. He screamed again.

"Don't move," she hissed.

She felt his muscles tense for another try. She pushed his head down. He grunted, and his muscles relaxed. This might work. He was lying in the brush, facing downhill at a steep angle. It must be very painful for him to move in this awkward position. As long as Shahla stayed on top of him and could keep him from moving, she had the advantage. She wondered how long she could maintain it.

CHAPTER 40

Tony found the trail that went downhill from the plateau to the picnic area. He couldn't wait for the police to get their act together and send officers to help him. He started down the trail by himself. He went slowly, being careful of his knee, shining his flashlight to the right and to the left, searching among the bushes and the shadows for signs of life.

If he hadn't been afraid of what had happened to Shahla, he would be enjoying himself, hiking in the cool of the evening with the lights below, knowing that even though he could see the city where millions of people lived, here he was alone.

He had gone some distance when he heard a cry for help, somewhere below him. He shone his flashlight down the hill. At first he couldn't see anything except dirt and brush. He moved the light in an arc, covering both sides of the trail. Then he saw somebody, off to the left of the trail.

"Down here," shouted the urgent voice.

It was Shahla. "I'm coming," Tony called. She appeared to be sitting in the brush. "Are you all right?" he asked, as he came closer to her.

"I've got Nathan," she said. "But I don't know how long I can hold him."

Tony picked out Nathan with the help of the flashlight. Shahla was astride his back, with her hands on his head. He was face downwards, with his feet higher than his head, and he looked about as helpless as a man could be.

"Where is the knife?" Tony asked, working his way through the brush toward them.

"In the bushes."

Tony climbed onto Nathan's back, behind Shahla. Nathan groaned as the additional weight pressed him further into the spines.

"Am I happy to see you," Shahla said. She shifted her position and sighed. "That's better. You came along just in time. Branches were sticking into my legs, but I was afraid to move."

Tony saw a mess on her shoulder and said, "You're bleeding,"

"I am? Just another scratch. I think he got me with his knife. Even though he wanted me unmarked." She raised her voice. "Is that why you strangled Joy instead of stabbing her? So she would be beautiful for you?" She shoved Nathan's head into the brush and received a groan in response.

Tony pulled a handkerchief out of his pocket and pressed it against Shahla's wound to try and stop the flow of blood. He said, "I think wearing my sweatshirt helped you. It's loose enough so that the knife didn't penetrate it very well. But it's torn."

"It gave its life to save me."

"We'll have it framed. By the way, the police should be down here shortly."

"Oh yes, the police. They missed all the fun."

***

Tony didn't like hospitals. He didn't watch emergency room shows on television. The last time he had been admitted to a hospital was when he had suffered a ruptured appendix, at the age of eleven. He didn't visit other people in hospitals if he could avoid it.

However, he wasn't going home without making sure that Shahla was all right. He hadn't realized she had other wounds besides the one on her shoulder until the police arrived and released them from their positions on top of Nathan. Then he saw that she had scratches all over her body, the most dangerous one being close to her eye. A policeman had driven her to a hospital in Culver City, and he was going there now.

Tony had been up all night, and he felt exhausted, now that the adrenaline was wearing off. He had wanted to go to the hospital with Shahla, but she had told him to stay and help in the search for Tina. She had been adamant about it.

So he assisted the police as they combed the level part of the park. He was reminded of the story of the man who searched for his wallet underneath a streetlight, even though he thought he had lost it in a dark alley. However, Tony had to agree that it didn't make any sense for Tina to go back up the hill after she made it down. And she wasn't on the trail. So why not search in the easiest place?

There was a small fishing lake near the picnic ground. Tony walked to the lake, with the help of his flashlight. He didn't spot anybody around the lake, but he did see restrooms. Where would a girl logically hide from a man?

He knocked on the door of the women's room. He didn't hear anything so he opened the door. It was dark inside. He shone his flashlight around and called, "Tina. It's Tony. We got Nathan. You can come out."

One of the stalls was locked. By standing on his toes he could look over the door. He shone the flashlight around the stall. Huddled in a corner beside the toilet, looking scared, sat Tina.

It took him a couple of minutes to coax her to come out of the stall. Then he escorted her to the picnic ground. When Tina saw the police and realized she was safe, a torrent of words came out of her mouth. She said, among other things, that she and Nathan had entered the park while it was still open, through an entrance from a residential area. This was before officers had been stationed at the entrances.

The two had scurried through the gate in broad daylight when a nanny tending a baby had opened it with a key she had. They had hidden in the brush when officers and employees searched the park, after it closed. Nathan had taped Tina's mouth during this period. They had joined the others on the plateau only a few minutes before the action started.

Throughout, Nathan had controlled Tina with the threat of his knife and by keeping a strong grip on her arm. She had been too scared to scream or to ask anybody for help. In spite of her name, she didn't speak Spanish, and so she didn't try to communicate with the nanny in that language. And she thought the members of the congregation were somehow working with Nathan. It sounded as if she had convinced Nathan she believed in the Ascension so that he wouldn't kill her.

Tony went to a local police station with a mixed group of officers, including police from Bonita Beach and LAPD, and Los Angeles County sheriff's deputies. Detective Croyden was there. After he told them about borrowing the truck, they found the owner, who was still at work, and effected an exchange of the vehicles. Tony suspected they did this because they thought he had stolen the truck.

As he told his story, he learned that they had found the bra and panties at Nathan's apartment. They appeared to have no doubt that Nathan had murdered Joy. The testimony of Tony and Shahla would be vital to the prosecution. That was nice to hear. Nobody criticized him for not working more closely with the police, now that the case was solved.

As for the faithful who had not been carried up to heaven on schedule, Detective Croyden said they told him that they had entered the park from the backyard of one of the parishioners, much as Tony had envisioned. Luther Hodgkins had stationed himself at the entrance, which was through a hole in the fence, acting as ticket taker, meaning that he took all their cash. But then he disappeared. Nobody remembered seeing him on the plateau. The police had put out an APB for him.

In spite of this, the parishioners still believed in the Ascension. Some believed they had seen Jesus. They tended to blame the police for screwing it up. However, it would still happen. But, as Croyden wryly remarked, their faith wasn't going to help them survive without food and shelter until they got the timing right.

Now, as Tony walked out of the morning sunlight and through the doorway into the hospital, the first thing he saw was a shop selling flowers and balloons. Women liked flowers. He went into the shop and purchased a bouquet in a vase. He learned Shahla's room number from an attendant at the information desk and took an elevator to the third floor.

He walked along the corridor, past the nurses' station, trying not to look into the rooms, until he came to the correct one. As he went through the doorway, the first thing he saw was Shahla, asleep in a hospital bed, complete with its fancy gadgets for raising and lowering the whole mattress or sections thereof.

Shahla's body looked like a disaster area. Her left shoulder was bandaged, and she had a patch over one eye. Scratches covered her face, arms, and legs, which were bare. However, she seemed to be sleeping peacefully. Her dark hair was spread out on the pillow. She had an IV going into her wrist. She was wearing a hospital gown, and a sheet covered the trunk of her body, to give her what little modesty could be had in a hospital.

Tony noticed Rasa, who was sitting beside the bed. For some reason, he hadn't pictured her being here. When she saw him, she smiled and stood up. She took the flowers and placed them on a table beside the bed. Then she gave him a big hug.

"Thank you for helping Shahla," she said softly.

Helping Shahla? He had almost gotten her killed.

"Shahla told me everything," she continued. "How you rescued her from man who tried to kidnap her and how you looked for Nathan and Tina."

That was definitely the abridged version. Tony asked anxiously, "Will she be all right?"

"She will be fine."

"Her shoulder and her eye?"

"Her eye is not hurt, for which we are thankful. The cut on her shoulder is not serious. She can go home this afternoon."

Rasa was a nurse so she should know. They didn't keep patients in hospitals very long these days, but it was probably just as well. From his own experience, he knew that a hospital wasn't a good place to rest. As if to prove his point, a young lady bustled into the room and said that she had to take Shahla's "vitals."

Of course this woke Shahla up. As soon as she saw Tony, she held out her arms for a hug. She gave him a surprisingly strong hug, considering what she had just been through. The nurse's aide told her to calm down or it would affect her blood pressure and heart rate.

Shahla tried to stay still until the nurse's aide was through with her, but as soon as the woman left, she pointed to a television set attached to the wall and said, "We saw on the news that they found Tina, but I want to hear your side of the story."

"*You* are most of the story," Tony said. "After all, you stopped Nathan."

"Shahla is hero," Rasa said proudly.

"She certainly is," Tony said. "But don't you need your sleep now?"

"I can sleep this afternoon at home. Besides, I feel fine. I'm going to school tomorrow. So tell me what happened after I left."

Tony told the story, answering Shahla's questions. When Shahla had heard it all, Tony said, "I have a question. You know and I know that Nathan is no poet. So who wrote the poem about spaghetti straps?"

Shahla was silent for a few seconds. Then she said, "I did."

"But…why?"

"Because I wanted to make sure you stayed involved in the case. I needed your help to solve it. And I wasn't about to leave it to the police. I placed the poem by the door when you were taking a call, so it would look as though somebody had slid it underneath."

"Without getting any fingerprints on it."

"Yeah. Wasn't that clever? I held it with a napkin. I didn't even get prints on the paper when I printed it with my computer."

"So our trip to Las Vegas was for nothing."

"Nothing?" Shahla's face fell. " Didn't you enjoy it? At least until you hurt your knee? I am sorry about that."

Rasa looked from one of them to the other and said, "Did Shahla trick you?"

Tony said, "I take full responsibility for my actions. And yes, I did enjoy the trip to Las Vegas."

"I have a question," Shahla said. "We have been to Las Vegas together, we have eaten many meals together, I have even slept in your…house." Tony was sure she had been about to say "bed." "But it's always been business. We've never had a real date. When are we going to have a real date?"

"Uh." Think, Tony. "When you're eighteen."

"I'll be eighteen on December twelfth. Okay, good, I'll put it on my calendar."

"I'd better get going so I can catch up on my sleep. I suspect Mona will really be pissed if I don't show up for work tomorrow."

"Give me a hug."

But instead of hugging him, Shahla pulled his lips down on hers and kissed him hard. When she finally released him, he gave a head-fake of embarrassment and looked at Rasa. She was shaking her head—but she was smiling. Dating Shahla wasn't going to be the worst thing that had ever happened to him. And it definitely wouldn't be boring.

About the Author

After spending more than a quarter of a century as a pioneer in the computer industry, Alan Cook is well into his second career as a writer.

His Lillian Morgan mysteries, *Catch a Falling Knife* and *Thirteen Diamonds*, explore the secrets of retirement communities. They feature Lillian, a retired mathematics professor from North Carolina, who is smart, opinionated, and skeptical of authority. She loves to solve puzzles, even when they involve murder. Alan's short story, "Hot Days, Cold Nights," appears in the Mystery Writers of America anthology, *A Hot and Sultry Night for Crime*, edited by Jeffery Deaver.

Alan splits his time between writing and walking, another passion. His inspirational book, *Walking the World: Memories and Adventures*, has information and adventure in equal parts. It has been named one of the "Top 10 Walking Memoirs and Tales of Long Walks" by the walking website, walking.about.com. He is also the author of *Walking to Denver*, a light-hearted fictional account of a walk he did.

Freedom's Light: Quotations from History's Champions of Freedom, contains quotations from some of our favorite historical figures about personal freedom. And *The Saga of Bill the Hermit* is a narrative poem about a hermit who decides that the single life isn't all it's cracked up to be.

Alan lives with his wife, Bonny, on a hill in Southern California. His website is alancook.50megs.com.

Printed in the United States
28949LVS00004B/43-51